Attic of the Mind

Hemmie Martin

This publication is a work of fiction. Names, characters, places, and incidents either are products of the author's imagination or are used fictitiously. This work is protected in full by all applicable copyright laws, as well as by misappropriation, trade secret, unfair competition, and other applicable laws. No part of this book may be reproduced or transmitted in any manner without written permission from Winter Goose Publishing, except in the case of brief quotations embodied in critical articles or reviews. All rights reserved.

Winter Goose Publishing
2701 Del Paso Road, 130-92
Sacramento, CA 95835

www.wintergoosepublishing.com
Contact Information: info@wintergoosepublishing.com

Attic of the Mind

COPYRIGHT © 2013 by Hemmie Martin

First Edition, February 2013

Hardback ISBN: 978-0-9881845-1-0
Paperback ISBN: 978-0-9889049-2-7

Cover Art by Winter Goose Publishing
Typeset by Michelle Lovi

Published in the United States of America

To Peter, Jessica, and Rosie
for letting me dream
Happy sixteenth birthday, Rosie!

To Vicky

Best wishes

Chapter One
1985

Rivulets of sweat ran down the patient's face as he lay on the cold tiled floor.

Charge Nurse Walker's voice resonated around the stark room, as did the sound of the dripping water in the sinks. He bent down and hoisted the patient up by one arm until his feet were dangling off the floor. The giant frame of Walker dominated the slight figure of the patient who was only clothed in the top half of his pyjamas. As the patient looked at Walker, he caught sight of his flaring nostrils, and his hot breath brushed across his face.

"Now go and change your bed."

Walker flung the patient in the direction of the men's ward where the sodden bed lay; he then scanned the dormitory for signs of any other troublemakers. Patients pretended to be asleep as they recoiled under their bedding.

He watched the patient climb back into his clean bed then strode up to him and cuffed him around the head.

"Make sure you keep your bloody bed clean," he said, spraying droplets of phlegm as he spoke.

The patient cowered beneath his starched sheet and itchy blanket, holding his breath until Walker had left his bedside. The sound of receding footsteps allowed the patient to drift off into a fitful sleep.

At seven in the morning the day staff arrived for their shift. They sauntered in, bleary eyed and apathetic.

"Peaceful night?" asked Nurse Clements as she poured herself a mug of strong black coffee.

"Nothing to report," replied Walker as he gathered the patients' files ready for hand-over.

With his low monotone voice he read through the fifteen female and fifteen male patient names assigned to Poplar Ward; he then told the staff what jobs he wanted completed during the day.

They all sat in the nurses' station that had windows on three sides. One window overlooked the male dormitory, another overlooked the female dormitory, and the last one faced the day room where both sexes mixed and undertook activities run by the occupational therapist.

All of a sudden, a breathless young man with mousey brown hair arrived at the door, eyes darting around the room.

"You're late, Doctor," said Walker without looking up.

"Yes, sorry. I got lost."

"Well, now you know where we are, I don't expect you to be late again."

The junior doctor entered the room and took the seat closest to the door, his white coat folded across his lap. A nurse glanced across at him as he squirmed and shifted about on his chair; her hand barely concealed the smirk on her face.

As Walker rose to leave, he stood over the doctor, casting a vast shadow over the slender young man.

"You'd better acquaint yourself with the patients and try not to get hurt in the process. I don't like filling in incident forms."

The doctor watched Walker stride off the ward swinging his arms back and forth. He'd already heard of Walker's fearsome rule over the junior doctors on rotation and the nurses. His reputation preceded him.

"So, Doctor, do you have a name?" asked a nurse. She couldn't help noticing his hazel eyes and the smattering of freckles across the bridge of his nose.

"Nathan Rine. And you are?"

"Judy Clements," she replied as she beckoned him to his feet. "Come on, I'll show you around."

As he followed her down to the male dormitory, he noticed the insipid veal-coloured walls and the rancid stench of sweaty feet and bad breath. He wrinkled up his nose at the puerile smell of urine-soaked bed clothes and sheets.

"Come on, rise and shine," she ordered as she yanked the bedcovers off the still sleeping men.

They arrived at Robert Cormack's bed where he was lying on his side. "Come on, Cormack, you know better, he's been in here long enough," she said, addressing Nathan.

As Cormack heaved himself up on his elbows and turned to the other side, Nathan noticed the red swelling on his left cheek bone and eye.

"What happened here?" Nathan asked as he nodded towards Cormack.

"God knows. They're always getting into scuffles with one another."

Judy kept moving down the ward whilst Nathan hovered over Cormack to assess his wounds. Cormack averted his eyes as he levered himself out of bed in his semi-naked state and shuffled towards the toilets.

Mid-morning, the day room appeared dimly lit considering the tall windows that flanked either side of the long room. Nathan watched as lofty poplar trees swayed in the breeze outside the windows blocking out the much needed light. The trees looked like a second row of bars at the windows, prohibiting the mentally challenged people from integrating with the mainstream world.

Nathan spent most of the morning trying to remember the patients' names and their diagnoses. Most were in a catatonic state thanks to their drug regimen. He was pleased when his shift was over, if only to breath in sanitary air once more.

"How was your first shift?" asked Hugh, his housemate.

"A bloody nightmare, I can't stand insane people."

"That's not very charitable. There for the grace of God, blah-dee-blah . . ."

"For pity's sake Hugh, grow up," said Nathan as he opened a can of baked beans and ate them straight from the tin.

"All I'm saying is . . ." he saw Nathan wasn't listening. *Oh never mind.*

That night the rain ripped out of the sky and the security lights outside Poplar Ward cast sinister shadows on the walls. The wind whistled through some of the windows that no longer closed properly.

In the female dormitory, a recently admitted nineteen-year-old sat up in her bed with her knees tucked under her chin and her arms firmly clasped around her legs. She hadn't acclimated to the shadows and noises on the ward at night. Unfamiliar stifled screams and shouts penetrated the darkness, causing her emotional state to fluctuate wildly.

She heard footsteps approaching her, but she was so dislocated from life that she didn't flinch from her position even when Walker was by her bedside.

"What have we here?" he said, bending down until they were almost face to face.

The girl remained mute and still, as though her actions acted as some form of invisibility cloak.

"I said," he repeated as he took her slender chin in his shovel-like hand and directed her face up towards him, "what have we here; a reluctant sleeper?"

The girl gazed above his head as she stoically avoided eye contact.

"I know what'll relax you," he hissed, with a steel glint in his eyes.

The girl closed her eyes and took her mind away to a safe place.

"Now go to sleep, you little bitch," he said after a while, before walking back to the nurses' station.

As the morning shift arrived, the stillness was broken by a piercing howl and the sound of a metal bed frame smashing against the wall. Walker sprinted in the direction of the noise, followed closely by the other staff.

In the far corner of the male dormitory, they saw a male patient straddled across the patient in the adjacent bed. He was rocking the bed as his fists pounded his victim around the head. The victim was weakening with the weight of his assailant on his chest. A fist caught the victim on the mouth, rattling his teeth together and causing blood to spurt through his lips.

Walker grinned at the spectacle when he suddenly saw the flash of a white coat out of the corner of his eye.

"Help me, someone," ordered Nathan as he tried to intervene, but alone his efforts were ineffectual. Nurse Clements went to his aid, but in the ensuing battle she was hit in the eye by the assailant's elbow.

"Shit," she cried, as her eye instantly began to sting. Undeterred by the swelling eye, she fought on until she and Nathan had separated the pair of brawling men.

For a brief second, as fleeting as a kingfisher darting across a river, Nathan saw the glint of pleasure in Walker's eyes, as he watched from his spectator's position.

Nathan realised at that very moment he was going to hate the placement, hate the staff, and hate the patients. He had little time for the mentally unstable as they weren't easy and straightforward to treat. He had already decided a few years earlier that he was going to work in a private clinic, treating the insanely rich for their fashionable illnesses that could be treated with some trendy and expensive medication. He made a mental note to keep his head low and do the minimum work required to pass the rotation. And to pass it, he also needed the approval of Charge Nurse Walker.

The patients were sedated so the staff could continue with their duties. Absentmindedly, Nathan noticed how slim Judy's ankles were as he followed her into the treatment room to tend to her eye.

"I can manage, thank you, Doctor."

Surprised by her rejection, he deflected her disinterest by changing topic.

"He's a strange one, that charge nurse, isn't he?"

"Who? Oh Walker, yeah he is. He lives with his older sister," she replied as she applied a cold compress to her puffy eye. "I imagine he rules that household, too," she added, raising the only eyebrow that would move.

Nathan went for a walk around the day room. One patient that caught his eye was a nineteen-year-old girl with a vacant aura. She had long, straggly, strawberry-blonde hair and muted grey eyes. She was slight of build and barely spoke. He looked at her chart; clinical depression, self-harmer, and anorexia nervosa. *How dull*, he thought to himself.

He was vaguely aware of her staring at him intently and, had he been a man who cared, he may have read the message behind those beseeching eyes. He shrugged off her gaze by walking away and trying to find a patient with a more interesting diagnosis.

The day passed with only occasional psychotic episodes to break the monotony. Nathan couldn't wait to leave the patients with their tawdry lives. He had a life to live, not like them, they had no hope of a future like he had in mind for himself, he reflected.

Later that evening, as he watched banal drivel on the television with Hugh, he remembered he'd left his stethoscope on the ward.

"Bugger, I'd better go and retrieve it before some thieving bastard nicks it."

Hugh raised his glass of beer as Nathan trudged out into the dark, inhospitable night.

The security lights guided him through the maze of buildings until he reached Poplar. The silence felt oppressive as he entered the building, a building that rightfully should have been upgraded to legitimately house the mentally unwell. *But who cares enough for these unlucky souls*, thought Nathan to himself as he mounted the stone stairs.

On entering the ward he expected to be greeted by Walker to check he wasn't an intruder. But he didn't come.

Nathan crept to the nurses' station, and as he passed the female dormitory he saw Walker standing over a patient's bed. He was about to get his attention, when Walker turned his head and saw him standing there. With a swift movement, he shoved the patient back onto the mattress, said something to her in a low voice, then turned to face Nathan.

Nathan ran through those brief actions and began to realise what he'd seen. A lump formed in his throat and his mind began scrambling a million messages, none of which reached his mouth.

As Walker approached him, he could see his face was rippled with anger.

"What are you doing here; I didn't page you."

"I left my stethoscope."

"That could have waited until morning."

Nathan could feel the adrenalin coursing through his body. He knew his choice of action was going to be flight. He avoided eye contact and felt the silence muffle his hearing.

"I don't know what you think you saw, Doctor, but I'm warning you now, many have tried to cross me and their careers have ended in tatters; nurses and junior doctors alike." He rolled his shoulders and breathed forcefully through his nostrils. "You've such a pretty face, dear Doctor; it'd be a shame to ruin your career as well as your looks."

Nathan wanted to speak but his mouth was dry and his jaw was clamped shut. He tried to see past Walker's broad shoulders to see if the patient was all right, but his movement was just too obvious.

"I had a junior doctor just like you once before. He was struck off for lewd behaviour that I alone witnessed on this ward. Catch my drift?"

Nathan's resolve to do the right thing melted and not even the desperate plea from the patient's subdued gaze could ignite his withered tenacity. He slunk back to the house, with his stethoscope gripped firmly in his hand, feeling like his soul had been sullied and crushed.

A blinding headache raged through his skull and, as he had no desire for company, he took himself off to bed. The muted grey eyes of the patient bore into his head every time he closed his eyes.

The next morning, Nathan dragged himself through the process of eating breakfast and walking to the ward. The tall poplar trees appeared to mock him as they bent back and forth, rocking with laughter.

He was the last one to arrive. As he entered, his eyes met with Walker's, confirming that something had happened that night. Walker's words echoed in Nathan mind and he knew he didn't have the inner strength to confront him. A subtle sneer on Walker's lips corroborated that fact. And with his eyes portraying the terror that would descend on him should he dare speak out, Nathan felt trapped by fear.

Suddenly, all the bruises, marks, and dead stares of the patients he'd witnessed, all directed themselves to Walker. And now Nathan was privy to the disgusting and distressing knowledge. All he could hear was his heartbeat pounding in his ears.

He forced himself to visit the female patient, Maria Langer, whom he had seen with Walker the night before. Her grey eyes looked blank and lifeless, as though any hope and life she had before had been dragged out of her. She had the faint signs of bruising around her mouth; the same mouth that food had barely passed through and the same mouth that uttered no words.

She stared not only at him, but almost through him. He felt she could see his weakness, his cowardly soul and his inertia. She was right and he felt damned.

Nathan wanted to protect her, but he also wanted to pass the placement and move on up the career path. Was this woman worth saving? Was it his place to intervene against such a strong figure? He had no proof, so what could he do, he thought to himself.

He had a subtle word with Judy, and she confirmed that allegations had been made against Walker in the past, but they were unsubstantiated and no patients were willing to testify against him. As for herself, she had never witnessed anything untoward and hence had nothing to offer.

"If you're thinking of going against him I'd be careful, he's a strong character and has some unsavoury comrades, if you know what I mean."

He understood, but he wasn't happy about the situation. But being young, he had a flippant attitude towards life. The knowledge was hurting him, but he figured that as time passed, he'd forget about the despicable character and the tainted feelings he was accumulating from working there.

Nathan kept the episode quiet, even from his housemate and best friend, Hugh Carlton. And as time passed, the pain dulled and the memories faded. Doctor Nathan Rine had a life once more.

Chapter Two
2010

Lily found the clinic easily, positioned as it was in the town square surrounding a public garden. She smoothed her hands over her chestnut bob and checked that her skirt was perfectly aligned before ringing the door bell.

"Hello," said a voice via the intercom.

"Er, hello, it's Lilith Fields for the interview."

"Yes. Push the door."

She pushed on the door and found herself in the reception area that was in complete disarray.

"Doctor Carlton," said the doctor as he greeted her with an outstretched hand, whilst he ran the other hand through his blond hair.

He noted her flaccid handshake which betrayed her cool and controlled exterior, and she noticed his clear blue eyes.

"You'll have to excuse the chaos. We open to the public next week. Still loads to do."

"So I can see," she said politely.

"Well, you've come for the receptionist post. You will need to be a medical secretary, too, and . . ."

"An all-round good egg with dark edges," she interrupted.

"Sorry?"

"I'd also have to deal with difficult patients, too, I'd imagine."

"Oh yes," he replied, "they'll be plenty of those."

Doctor Carlton glanced down at his shiny brown brogues, before continuing.

"Let's walk and talk," he said as he opened the door marked "private" and ushered her through.

He cursed his partner for letting him deal with the interviews alone and he feared his ineptitude was poorly masked by the *walk and talk* technique.

"You have excellent references, Lilith. May I call you Lilith?"

"I prefer to be called Lily, if you don't mind?"

He blushed and began drumming his fingers on his desk.

"Well, all seems in order; the position's yours if you want it."

Lily raised a perfectly groomed eyebrow but said nothing. She looked around the room with a slight air of distain.

"Just the one doctor, is it? I thought the advert said it was a two doctor clinic."

"Yes, I'm sorry. My partner couldn't make it, emergency call."

"I see. Don't you have other candidate's to see?"

"You're the last one, which is why I can offer you the job."

Lily rose from the chair in a single, graceful movement.

"Do I start tomorrow?"

"God, please yes. I mean, that would be great. We're in such a mess."

Although Lily thought the set-up was rather disorganised, she accepted the offer and breathed a deep sigh as she left the building.

"Where the hell have you been?"

"Hello to you, too, Hugh. We don't open until next week."

"I'm aware of that fact. I've been interviewing all bloody morning."

"Any suitable candidates?"

"I've offered the job to . . ." Hugh shuffled his papers around, "ah yes, to a Lily Fields."

"Stunningly beautiful, I hope."

"Stunningly efficient, actually. And in case you've forgotten, I'm married."

"Sorry," replied Nathan with a soupcon of sarcasm.

"You've got to smarten up before next week," Hugh said as he placed a mug of coffee on the table. "You look unkempt and dishevelled."

"Well, unlike some, I don't have a wife to keep me presentable."

"You did, but you couldn't keep her."

Ever since meeting at medical school, the pair had bickered but remained friends no matter what else happened in their lives. It was joked about on campus that they were like a married couple, and perhaps they were more so now since opening the clinic together.

Hugh's referral to Nathan's inability to keep a relationship going for longer than three years was rather a sore point.

"Fancy a celebratory drink tonight?" asked Nathan.

"No thanks. And I think you should give your liver a rest for the evening, too. Why don't you come round for dinner instead? Faith won't mind."

Nathan shook his head as he knew Faith would mind. She wasn't even happy about her precious husband starting a clinic with him.

"Thanks, but no, I have other plans."

Hugh knew that would not be true, but he didn't like to pressure his friend. He knew that Nathan often saw thoughtfulness as blatant pity, which he abhorred. As they were leaving, Hugh turned to Nathan.

"She does have illuminating green eyes."

Nathan took a few seconds to understand what his friend had just said, and he was relieved to see that he could still take in the beauty of women, even though he was a married man.

Later that evening, Nathan tucked himself away in a secluded corner of The Spread Eagle pub, where the atmosphere was less salubrious than The Crown, Hugh's favourite haunt. Nathan preferred the dark and Machiavellian atmosphere of his pub, which offered gloomy corners and dirty floors.

He watched the cluster of scantily clad women with their pierced navels and over-processed hair as they hovered around the bar. It was not long before one of them spotted him and sashayed over to his table.

"Why the long face? Lonely?" she said as she bent over so he could see her shrivelled breasts and the blue stain of a tattoo just above her bra.

"Nope, and you're blocking my view."

"Charming," she said as she flounced off to rejoin her mates who were surrounding another poor friendless soul.

Nathan brooded quietly and immersed his soul in beer. The divorce had hit his pride hard, and he'd lost the few friends he had to his ex-wife, except for Hugh. He hoped that the move to the town would offer him the opportunity of a new life.

Hallbury was a walled town, with a smattering of tea houses, coffee shops, and pubs. Shops selling riding accoutrement, flowers, and clothes were tucked away in little side streets.

The walled town mirrored Nathan, in that they were both impenetrable. Secretly, he envied the mundane, habitual lifestyle that Hugh had carved out for himself. Conversely, when he was married, he found it terminally tedious and soon shed the shackles of matrimony.

Suddenly, a more alluring model of the last woman approached his table, and the outcome was indefinably different. As they walked to his home together, the woman linked her arm through his and rested her head on his shoulder. He felt her head loll around and he knew she was intoxicated, but that made no difference to him.

A few hours later, the woman pulled up her skinny jeans, almost falling over in the process, and stuffed her feet into her cowboy boots. She turned to face Nathan, who was still lying in bed.

"Fancy doing this again, sometime?"

"Not really. Here's money for a taxi," he said as he flung a note in her direction.

"You're not much of a conversationalist, are you?" she said as she crumpled the note in her hand.

"Keep the change," he replied before rolling over and shutting his eyes.

He heard her boots stomping down the stairs, and the slamming of his front door signalled her departure. At last, he could fall into an alcoholic, post-coital sleep; numbing him to his perverted actions in the distant past.

The telephone stirred Nathan from his sleep. He reached out from under the quilt and grabbed it.

"I need to do something for Faith this morning. I can't get to the clinic and that new woman's going to be—"

"God, Hugh, I'm not sure I'm up to much. Can't she manage?"

"Nathan, she'll be there in half an hour and she hasn't got a key."

Nathan sighed and levered himself up onto his elbow. Silence swayed between them before Nathan heard Faith badgering Hugh in the background.

"I'll be there," Nathan said finally, before replacing the receiver.

He heaved himself out of bed and meandered to the shower. Heavy droplets of hot water thudded on his head. He turned his face upwards to allow the water to run down the contours of his face so the globules were akin to the tears he could never cry.

He grabbed a piece of cremated toast and took a swig of black coffee before heading to the clinic. Along his walk, he peered through the bay windows that allowed him to observe other people's lives. He saw couples entwined by their souls, and families cobbled together by fate, for better or for worse. Whatever their situation, he thought how comfortable their lives looked. But as a doctor, he was aware that appearances could deceive. He wondered how many of them were toying with the notion of committing suicide. Although he was not a religious man, he was a believer that suicide was only a solution because people were just too lazy to work through complex issues. He thought to himself how life was a mere collection of emotions and moments.

Attic of the Mind

Chapter Three

Nathan was walking with his head bowed when he bumped into a stationary person outside the clinic. Before he had time to look up, the person spoke.

"Doctor Rine, I presume."

"Sorry?"

"I'm Lily Fields, didn't Doctor Carlton tell you about me?"

"Yes, he did, sorry. How do you do?" he said with an outstretched hand.

Lily noted that his handshake was as lifeless as her own, which pleased her.

Once inside with the preliminary introductions executed, Lily went to the kitchen to make a pot of coffee.

"I shall need to order stationary supplies," she said to Nathan as he stared out of the window.

"Whatever," he replied with a wave of his hand.

She shrugged her shoulders and poured the coffee.

"Black, I presume," she said as she handed him the mug.

"Good guess."

The morning dragged by, not helped by the lack of communication between the pair, with only the delivery men's voices to slice into the silent mood. Lily tried to instigate conversation with banal pleasantries which only fell wasted around her.

"No point in us staying any longer, the deliveries for today have arrived so you might as well go home," he finally said.

"Are you going to stay on?"

"No. I'll see you tomorrow, or Hugh will."

"Hugh?"

"Doctor Carlton. God, didn't he even tell you his name? I thought

I was the misanthrope around here." He shrugged his shoulders and turned his back on her.

Lily gathered her belongings together and glided out of the door with a lighter heart than earlier in the day.

Nathan watched her through the window as she walked through the garden and stopped to look at the tulips. *Typical woman*, he thought to himself, *she probably likes fluffy lambs, too.*

His sarcastic comments whirred around his head, disturbing the peace in the clinic. He despised his acrid attitude at times, but he'd honed it for so many years that he was beginning to forget how he used to be, he was sure he used to be a more amenable man once upon a time. He pondered on his future at the clinic and came to the conclusion that Hugh was a reliable partner and Lily seemed organised and personable. He felt that the pair could pull him through his current malaise.

As he wandered around his room and ran his hand over the green leather chair behind his desk, he realised that everything he touched was tainted and that he struggled to find joy in anything. His past and his divorce had left indelible marks on his very essence of being.

"Off to the pub I go," he muttered to himself as he shut the clinic door.

Chapter Four

Lily was busy registering the new patients who'd arrived at the clinic whilst discreetly covering her nose and mouth every time someone coughed or sneezed over her.

Periodically, one of the doctors would appear from his respective room and call in the next patient. Hugh would offer Nathan a reassuring nod if they happened to coincide. Lily noticed how comfortable Hugh looked in his role, whereas Nathan looked defeated and haunted, surprisingly ill at ease, she reflected.

At the close of surgery a welcomed hush descended over the building and Nathan felt the scotch bottle whispering his name.

"Right, you two, I hope you've both remembered we're dining out tonight to mark the opening," said Hugh as he stood in the reception rubbing his hands together.

"Damn, I forgot, another time maybe."

"No, Nathan, this is important. We're going with Faith. Don't let me down." Hugh didn't give Nathan the chance to reply as he returned to his room to gather his brief case.

"I'm really not fond of socialising," whispered Lily. "I feel rather awkward about going."

Nathan nodded and gave her a self-conscious smile.

"Well, let's just leave; I'll square it with him tomorrow. He can have a romantic meal with his wife. I'm sure she'd prefer that anyway."

Before Lily knew what was happening, Nathan had ushered her out of the door. They both marched quickly through the public garden before separating down different streets. Lily felt bad for Hugh, but she couldn't face a meal with just him and his wife.

Hugh returned to the reception area to find that he was all alone. A rush of anger flooded his mind. He called his wife to tell her he would be late before heading off to The Spread Eagle.

His footsteps echoed like thunder as he pounded down the cobbled street. He pushed through the smokers standing outside the pub and made his way inside. His eyes had to adjust to the dimly lit interior, but it wasn't long before he spotted Nathan sitting in a dark corner.

"I thought I'd find you here. What's going on?"

"I don't really want to talk right now. I'm conversing with my Scotch"

Hugh pulled a stool up to the table. "I'm not going until you're honest with me."

Nathan had no intention of offloading his past misdemeanours as he didn't need his best friend hating him, too.

"Stop feeling so bloody sorry for yourself. We've got our clinic, we've made it," said Hugh leaning forward to grab Nathan's attention.

"This isn't 'made it' for me," Nathan hissed. "This is being kept down where I belong."

"Charming."

Nathan didn't really want to hurt his friend, so he pushed a local newspaper towards him. Hugh cast his eyes over the page, then shrugged his shoulders and looked blankly at his friend.

"I believe that this local candidate is the same charge nurse that was on the psychiatric ward I worked on and . . ."

"And what?" encouraged Hugh.

"He wasn't a great guy to know and I think he'd make an appalling Member of Parliament."

"I don't really see your problem; he could have changed for the better in twenty-five years."

Nathan drank another shot of scotch. "Look, it's great for you; you and Faith can now see your life and even your retirement emblazoned in the future. I see nothing but a dark tunnel through which I move snail-like towards death."

"What's happened to you over the years, Nathan? In our student days you were interesting and fun to be around. After qualifying, you disappeared from my radar then up you popped again. And here we are today."

"You wouldn't be happy if you were me. Honestly, Hugh, just go and have a pleasant evening with your wife."

Hugh ran his hand over his chin and gazed at his friend. "One last thing, though," he said as he stood to leave. "Don't overdo the scotch, you've got patients to see tomorrow."

Nathan raised his glass as he watched his debonair friend weave his way through the sleazy crowd.

That evening Nathan returned home alone and opened the bag of chips he'd bought along the way. He sat at the kitchen table with the newspaper folded at his side.

Later that night, the nightmare returned and roused him from sleep. He was doused in sweat which had him reaching out for the glass by his bed. He took a large slug of scotch and turned on the TV so he could fall asleep to the droning voices on the shopping channel. He lay there staring wide-eyed at the ceiling waiting for sleep to take pity on him.

In their plush home, Hugh and Faith had been asleep for hours with their stomachs full of steak au poivre and profiteroles. They never mentioned Nathan, because Hugh knew what Faith thought of him anyway. Lily was pardoned for her role in the whole sorry event, as she was new and was probably persuaded to leave by Nathan.

As for Lily's evening, she had taken a long scented bath before eating her salmon and salad. She retired to bed with a book and fell asleep as always, with the book still clutched in her delicate hands.

The next morning, an awkward atmosphere filled the surgery. Hugh wasn't harsh with Lily as he knew she was shy and had been misguided by Nathan. Besides, she'd apologised first thing to Hugh as soon as they saw one another. And Nathan hadn't. Both doctors managed to remain distant until lunchtime.

"You two are suited together, not that I'd wish that on her," said Hugh as he poured himself a coffee, and took a biscuit from the tin.

"Who do you mean?" replied Nathan, only half interested.

"You and Lily."

"What on earth makes you think that?"

"You're both social misfits, although Lily is easier to be around than you."

"I'm not a bloody misfit. If anything, you've become an arsehole since marrying your prissy wife."

They were about to launch into a bitter row when Lily walked into the kitchen to get her salad from the fridge.

"It's so lovely out there that I thought I'd eat my lunch in the garden," she said. She felt a frisson run up her spine as she sensed the atmosphere in the kitchen. She hovered for a few seconds, clutching her salad box tightly.

"Good idea, enjoy," said Hugh as his eyes never moved from Nathan.

Outside, she picked at her salad, preferring to people-watch instead. It was a change to watch people being happy in the sun instead of watching the two doctors fight. She felt sorry for Hugh as she thought he was too kind a man to suffer the destructive behaviour meted out by Nathan.

"Look, I'm sorry about last night," said Nathan as he put his mug down.

"I'll forgive you if you tell me what's wrong."

"I'll need a drink to do that, Hugh."

"Okay, The Crown after work."

Nathan gave a half smile as he reluctantly agreed.

Lily was pleased, on her return to work, to find a more convivial atmosphere, although Nathan still looked pallid and preoccupied.

The two men walked to The Crown in silence. Hugh was reflecting on his day at work and Nathan was ruminating over his past. As he looked down, he noticed how polished Hugh's brogues were compared to his aged loafers. He did need to make more of an effort. Hugh was right, as always, he thought to himself.

Hugh had a pint of beer and Nathan had the same with a Scotch chaser.

"I'm listening," said Hugh as he sat back on the nutmeg-brown leather Chesterfield sofa.

"It's not easy to talk about. I've bottled it up for the past twenty-five years, so much so that I'd kind of forgotten that era."

"Why is it bothering you so much now?"

"We're both fifty this year. You have much to show for it, some of which is to do with your amiable personality. People like you, and like to be around you."

Nathan stopped to moisten his mouth with beer. Hugh remained silent and engaged, hanging on every word.

"Remember when I worked in that psychiatric ward when you had the children's ward?"

Hugh nodded.

"Well, things happened there that I should have reported."

Hugh sat up straight. "Like what?"

As Nathan told him about that night on the ward, the fear in the patients' faces, the bruises and the charge nurse, Hugh had an incredulous look in his eyes.

"You mean to tell me that you reported nothing to the authorities."

"I'm ashamed to say I didn't. His threats were real and he frightened me. I just wanted to keep my head down and pass. I became focused on beer and socialising after that, if you remember."

"There was more to you than that, or else we wouldn't have been friends."

Both men hid their faces behind their beer glasses.

"You've shocked me. Why didn't you tell me back then? I would have made you speak out."

"I think that's why I didn't tell you . . ."

"You can speak out now."

"That won't work, the hospital was demolished, I don't know where any of the victims are, and I have no proof. Besides, I'm still scared of him." Nathan's face reddened and he averted his eyes from his friend's periwinkle-blue eyes.

Attic of the Mind **21**

"Bloody hell, Nathan, I can't believe what you're telling me. You let patients continue to be abused by that bastard and did nothing? This can't be left alone. You do know that, don't you? I'm disgusted by your admission," Hugh said as he got up, leaving most of his beer untouched.

Nathan watched him, knowing that what he had just said may have changed the best friendship he had ever had. His life was on a collision course with his past, and he felt powerless to control it.

He trudged home with Hugh's words slicing into his mind. His stomach felt like it was going to expel the alcohol he'd drunk.

That night, he knew that those eyes would haunt him again. And he believed he deserved every piercing look.

Chapter Five

When Nathan awoke the next morning, he contemplated phoning in sick, but he knew that would make things even worse with Hugh.

The shower did not wash away the dirt he felt encrusted in every pore, the same dirt that had suffocated the only ounce of compassion he ever had. He was under no illusion; he had never been an affable person like Hugh. But he did have some redeeming features that were now erased by the black deed of the past. He thought about his ex, Carol, and how perhaps the invisible wall he had built between them was due to his own perceived weakness and crime.

Hugh was right; they would not have been friends if he were the man he was today. The insidious negative thoughts over the past twenty-five years had eroded his genial side, and had left him as the self-centred, egotistical, misanthropic man he now despised so much.

He could not bear to lose his best friend, his only friend, because of his atrocious omission in the past. He wondered how Hugh would be that morning at work. Would the solid, reliable Hugh still be there for him?

"You're quiet this morning," said Faith as she passed Hugh the toast over their large kitchen table.

"A lot on my mind, darling."

"Nothing wrong at work, I hope."

Hugh knew she meant nothing wrong with Nathan.

"No, love, everything's fine, I'm just tired."

Hugh so wanted to tell Faith the grimy news imparted by Nathan, but he knew she would be apoplectic. His friendship with Nathan ran deep, but Faith was one to bear grudges. Nathan would be banished from their home forever if she found out.

Nathan was not surprised to see that he was the last to arrive at the clinic. As he entered, the smell of freshly brewed coffee pervaded the air.

"Good morning, Doctor Rine," said Lily as she switched on her computer at the reception desk.

"Morning, is Hugh in?"

"Yes, I'm here," said Hugh as he appeared from the kitchen with two mugs of coffee, one for him and one for her. "There's coffee in the kitchen," he said without giving any eye contact.

"Thanks. Could I see you for a minute?" asked Nathan.

"No time now, I'm afraid," and with that, Hugh disappeared into his room and shut the door.

Lily was not oblivious to their interaction but she decided not to interfere. It wasn't her place.

Lunchtime could not come soon enough for Nathan, as he wanted to clear the air with Hugh. With the last patient dispatched clutching a prescription, Nathan ambled into the kitchen to wait for his friend.

With the newspaper under his arm, he felt dirty from even touching the picture of Finlay Walker. The paper trembled so much that he had to put it down.

"I need a drink," murmured Nathan as Hugh walked in.

"Not during working hours, you don't."

Nathan held his head in his hands and squeezed his eyes firmly shut. Beads of sweat formed along his brow and his head felt like exploding.

"If that's him you have a duty to speak out," said Hugh as he stood over Nathan, noticing the paper on the table.

"What proof do I have? It would only look like a smear campaign in the political climate. Besides, as I've said before, I don't know where any of the victims are, and a big part of me is still frightened of him. It's hopeless." Nathan's shoulders hunched over so his head was only inches from the table.

"Well, perhaps you should confront him, so you are no longer afraid of him. There is power in knowledge and it may prick his conscience just to see you again, after all this time."

"He's a wilier man than me; I would make no impact on him at all. Furthermore, I feel partly responsible for his actions."

"Complicit, I would say."

Nathan shot Hugh an angry look. He clenched his fists so tightly that his nails dug into his palms, leaving tiny crescent moon shapes in the plump flesh.

"I need to think things through. I can't go on with the clinic this afternoon." As he stood to leave, Hugh blocked his way.

"You're not letting me down. I didn't listen to Faith because I trusted you. You're staying here and finishing the working day."

He held Nathan by the shoulders and his legs were braced for any potential action, his blond fringe flopping over his eyes. Nathan looked defiant but that soon melted into a deflated disposition. Hugh felt a subtle wave of sorrow for his friend, but it didn't last.

"Could I get to the fridge please?" asked Lily as she crept up behind Hugh.

The men stood aside for her to move in silently. She was gone just as quickly, and just as silently.

Lily sat on a bench in the flimsy sunshine and wondered what was going on with the doctors. It was spoiling her work environment and she resented that. She wondered about telling them off like naughty school boys, but she didn't want to intervene. It wasn't her place.

The steady flow of patients in the afternoon did nothing to distract Nathan from the unsettling discovery. He wanted, no, *needed* some scotch, and the patients were standing in his way.

Finally, all the patients had gone and Nathan moved swiftly to the kitchen to grab the newspaper. He yelled "bye" to the others and darted out of the building. He hurried along the pavement, passing groups of meandering people, until he reached his usual pub where sat at his usual secluded table. He drank a shot of scotch before touching his pint and before opening the newspaper.

Walker's face leered up at him from the paper, and the smug look on his face sickened him. All he could read from Walker's eyes was that he got away with his crimes. And that was indeed true; Nathan knew that it was he who had helped keep them hidden. The feeling of guilt compressed his chest until he felt as though his lungs were restricted to the size of un-inflated balloons.

He read Walker's interview, and his ideas appeared to be subtly homophobic and borderline racist. *So even his ideals stink,* thought Nathan to himself. Walker was standing as a candidate for The English Party, who proclaimed not to be racist, but wanted to put England first. Their whole policy and ethos made Nathan's flesh crawl.

As he read on, he saw a public meeting was scheduled for the following evening at six o'clock in the local community hall, for the candidates to introduce themselves. Nathan wiped his sweaty palms on his trousers as he contemplated attending the meeting. He knew he should go to see if it was indeed the same man; after all, the grainy picture could be deceiving him. The atheist in him prayed it wasn't.

Some woman approached his table and hovered over him. He felt compelled to look up.

"Hi, lover," said the woman with overly painted lips.

He could not remember her name, but he recognised her from a previous alcohol-fuelled caper. It would have suited him any other night, but not that night.

"Not interested," he said before returning to the newspaper.

"Suit yourself." And with that she was gone.

Normally, Nathan would have had the so-called "Friday feeling" on the last working day, but not that Friday. He was going to attend a meeting later that evening, where he could come face to face with his nemesis. The outcome could change his life forever and he wasn't sure he was ready for that. His admission to Hugh had changed their friendship, without a doubt. Although Hugh tried to disguise it, the unavoidable change was tangible.

What if the whole world knew of his failings and his weaknesses? What if everyone could see his cowardly soul? He would be doomed to pitying stares and whispers behind his back. Perhaps patients would refuse to see him. He couldn't see his way clear.

"Are you going this evening, then?" said Hugh breaking Nathan's trance as he put his dirty mug in the sink.

"I'm envisaging the pros and cons."

"You'd regret it if you didn't go. You'd be left wondering whether it really was the same Walker fellow."

"I know, but it may turn out to be a bigger regret if I do."

Hugh shook his head slightly. "It has surreptitiously eaten away at you for all these years, isn't it time you dealt with it head on, whatever the outcome for you?"

Nathan rubbed the back of his neck.

"You're obviously ashamed of your lack of action; otherwise you'd have told me about this a long time ago."

"I wish I had."

Hugh headed for the door then turned back. "Word of advice, don't get drunk before you go, as only madness lies that way."

Nathan cast a wry smile then locked his desk drawer.

The two men left together before parting in different directions. Nathan could just make out Lily ahead of him. He knew she lived locally, but he wasn't sure where.

Nathan found himself sitting in The Spread Eagle with Hugh's words ringing in his ears. Thankful of his friend's advice, he bought only a pint of beer. He quaffed his drink and headed out, clenching his jaw as he pushed through the gathering outside on the pavement.

As he approached the community hall his footsteps slackened and he dawdled on the pavement to scrutinize everyone who entered the building. His mouth felt dry and he repeatedly wiped his sweaty palms on his tweed jacket.

No one looked familiar and no one seemed to recognize or even notice him. He closed his eyes briefly then with a deep breath he followed an elderly couple into the building.

The room was far more intimate that he'd anticipated. There was barely any space between the candidates' seats, positioned on a platform, and the first row of the audience. Nathan side-stepped along the back row and sat in the corner.

To his chagrin there was a poor turn out, so only a smattering of people sat dotted around the room. He wasn't as hidden or as protected at the back as he'd hoped.

He was just considering leaving when a door opened and in filed the candidates. The first person was an auburn-haired and ruddy-cheeked woman, followed by two men of non-descriptive value, and the last one was Finlay Walker.

The chill that ran up Nathan's spine confirmed that it was the very same man he knew years ago. His stature hadn't diminished, although his shoulders were slightly hunched and his stomach hung over his belt. He still looked at his entourage with the same arrogant manner, and the slight smirk that rested continually upon his lips gave him the facial grimace of a sinister ventriloquist's doll. Nathan slunk down in his seat and pushed himself further into the corner.

Each candidate stated their designated party, their principals, and their values. When it came to Walker, Nathan was hardly surprised by what he heard.

"I represent The English Party, and we value what is English and what makes us a proud race to represent." A few cheers arose in the room, and Walker looked fiercely conceited about his statement and position. His eyes swept across the room before he finished with, "I'm British and I'm proud."

The only thing missing was the Nazi salute, thought Nathan to himself.

A few people in the room began muttering their agreement and Walker smiled at the undercurrent of obvious support.

The elderly man from the couple that sat in front of Nathan raised his hand to ask a question. His action drew everyone's attention to the back of the room.

Just as Nathan was about to close his eyes he was met with a forceful stare from Walker. There was recognition in his eyes and a flame of fury blazed a hole into Nathan's soul. He felt riveted to his seat as though Walker had some supernatural force over him.

The proceedings drew to a close and people were offered coffee and a chance to chat with the candidates on a more personal level. A woman on the back row with numerous carrier bags was slow to move which blocked Nathan in. His heart was pounding so hard that he could hear every beat in his ears. He needed to get out, and fast.

He stood next to the woman and coughed. She turned to him and offered an apology but she didn't pick up her pace. By the time she had levered herself out of her chair and gathered her belongings, Nathan came face to face with Walker.

"Well, well, small world, Doctor Nathan Rine."

Nathan's neck flushed red. "Yes," he slurred as his lips stuck to his teeth.

"Interested in politics are you?"

"Just interested in the local candidates."

"I wonder where your loyalties are placed, doctor," he said as he placed his huge hand on Nathan's arm.

Nathan wasn't blind to the loaded words, or to the feel of his grasp. "I must be going," he said, with his eyes looking towards the door.

"Well, just remember, doctor, what hurts one, hurts the other," he growled in a low voice as he gave Nathan's arm a pinch.

Walker then released him physically but not mentally. As Nathan left the room he could feel Walker's eyes boring holes into his back. He felt branded by Walker, as though he had the tattoo of Satan on his back that only he and Walker could see.

With faltering steps, Nathan headed for The Spread Eagle, anxious to have some alcohol swilling around his system. The nauseating feeling of being followed prickled up his spine.

Chapter Six

Lily cleared away the debris from her meal and then picked up the local paper to read with her cup of tea.

The early evening was her favourite time, as the day was over but it wasn't yet dark. The darkness frightened her, but over the years she had developed an inner strength to cope with her fear; living alone had ensured that.

Browsing through the paper, she caught her breath as a picture of the monster who'd helped create who she'd become stared back at her. Feeling dizzy, she scanned the picture, allowing her eyes to pick out the distressingly familiar aspects of his face.

She continued to punish herself by staring at the picture, evoking the rancid odour of his trousers, and the feeling of his grimy hands gripping onto her hair. Although the feelings were painfully intense, there was also serendipity to it all. The jigsaw was almost complete and it was time for the games to begin; only this time she'd be the master.

She fetched a pair of scissors from the kitchen and cut out the picture and article of Finlay Walker and placed it in the box with some other artefacts. "I mustn't rush," she muttered to herself, as she closed the lid and put the box back in the cupboard.

She couldn't face a bath as she needed the water to run off her body and down the plughole, instead of lying in a tub full of polluted water. She needed to wash his clammy hands off her flesh.

She stood with her face tilted upwards and mouth open wide, so that the shower gushed water straight into it. She let her mouth fill with water and then allowed the overflow to cascade out of it like a waterfall.

Her body was covered in goose bumps as she rubbed herself dry, and it was then that she caught sight of her haunted look in the mirror.

She lifted the toilet seat and vomited up her partially digested meal. Her eyes watered as some of the acrid fluid entered her nostrils. She gripped onto the toilet rim for balance until her knuckles turned a gleaming white.

The mood in the clinic following the weekend was subdued. The patients in the waiting room would have blamed it on the Monday-morning blues, but for the individuals who worked there, the blackness ran much deeper than that.

Lily stood at the reception desk looking pallid and more introspective than usual. Hugh was forcing himself to be his amiable self to the patients. And as for Nathan; he felt sullied by Friday's encounter with Walker. He knew on some emotional level that he was better than Walker, but every fibre in is being screamed that he was just as despicable. He wondered whether his inner turmoil was etched on his face so that everyone he met that morning could see it too.

It was approaching lunchtime when the gigantic figure of Walker entered the clinic. Lily had her head bent over some data sheets so she wasn't aware of his arrival.

Without raising her head, she was initially aware of a familiar reek pervading the atmosphere. As if in slow motion, her eyes travelled up a recognizable figure, still as bulky and tall, until she reached the ragged crevices of his bulldog-like face. She had to control her gagging reflex that wanted to swing into action in his presence.

With unrivalled calmness, she greeted him like any other member of the public.

"Good morning, how may I help?"

"I'd like to see Doctor Rine."

"Do you have an appointment?"

"No, but I'm sure he'll see me."

"Whom may I ask is calling?"

"Mr. Finlay Walker."

Lily's fingers trembled slightly as she dialled Nathan's number.

"A Mr. Finlay Walker is here to see you." All she heard was silence. "Shall I send him in, Doctor?" She could hear Nathan grinding his teeth before he asked for Walker to be shown through.

Lily pointed the way, and once he'd gone through she sat on her chair and screwed her eyes tightly shut.

Walker pushed open the door to Nathan's office, ignoring the sign to knock first before entering.

"What can I do for you? You're not sick I hope."

"On the contrary, good doctor, I've never been better."

"So?"

"I'm just checking that you understood the advice I gave you on Friday. We don't want a misunderstanding now, do we, Doctor?"

"I have no understanding with you."

"Ah, but you see you do. A few well-placed bad words about you stealing drugs from the ward would see you and this clinic ruined before the year is out. How would your good friend Doctor Carlton feel about that?"

"He's got nothing to do with this."

"What do I care, and if I'm not mistaken, I don't imagine you care either. You were always looking out for number one. No one else ever mattered."

Walker grinned as he looked down on Nathan; his yellowing teeth and receding gums barely disguised by his thin lips.

"Just leave," Nathan said, aware of his reddening face.

"If I don't, what will you do? Make me?"

"I haven't decided what I'll do yet. Just go."

"I'm sure we'll keep in touch," he replied as he placed his large hands on the desk and bent over towards Nathan.

Nathan screwed up his nose as Walker's rank breath wafted his way. His composure had all but expired when Walker finally left the room leaving the door open. Nathan watched Lily escort him to the door and then bolt it firmly behind him. As she turned around their eyes connected briefly and then she moved towards the kitchen, where Hugh was making himself a sandwich.

"Did you have a good weekend?" he asked.

"A peaceful one, thanks. And you?"

"Faith's parents came to stay so it was far from tranquil."

Lily smiled even though she had no idea what having in-laws really entailed. Her life had been barren of relationships and the trappings that came with the package deal.

"Where are you from originally, Lily?"

"Dolling village in Buckinghamshire, but I've travelled around a fair bit."

"Do you have any family nearby?"

"No, my mother died three years ago and my father's in a care home. He's got dementia."

Hugh's cheeks reddened slightly. He normally preferred Faith to do the socialising whilst he observed the proceedings, even though he was always perceived to be socially adept. He needed his wife's support more often than not.

"Sorry to hear all that. Do you visit him often?"

"No point, as he doesn't know who I am anymore."

Hugh felt awkward and gauche. Whilst he was a medical student he did consider becoming a surgeon so he wouldn't have to communicate with people as much. His special interest actually turned out to be mental health. As Nathan had pointed out to him once, people liked opening up to him, so the field of mental health was perfect.

"Where's Nathan?" Hugh asked.

"He was talking to a Mr. Walker. He's just left."

"Walker, did you say?"

"Yes. Why, do you know him?"

"I know of him."

Lily smiled and nodded, as knowing Walker and knowing of him were two very different concepts. Hugh excused himself and went in search of Nathan.

"I just wanted to say that I'm proud of you," he said as he stood in the doorway.

"I haven't done anything," Nathan replied with a blank look on his face.

"Well, your presence had obviously worried Walker, otherwise he wouldn't have called here."

"You couldn't be further from the truth. He said that if I expose him, he'll take me and this clinic down with him. Unwittingly, it seems I've involved you too." He moved to the window, hands in his trouser pockets.

"There must be a way to beat him," Hugh uttered.

"Well, fill me in when you figure it out, as I'm stumped."

Hugh stood there for a few seconds looking at his friend, the very friend who could potentially drag him under. *What would Faith have to say about that*, he wondered.

Chapter Seven

Lily walked home quickly that evening in order to increase her heart rate. By the time she arrived, she felt lightheaded and giddy. But rather than capitulate to the hunger pangs she drank some hot lemon water.

Things were moving too fast for her and she began to feel like Walker was taking back control. She was convinced that he didn't recognise her, but that element of doubt twisted her stomach into agonising knots.

For years she'd tortured herself believing that she should have been stronger and that she should have fought him off during those hospital days. It was only over time that she realised she'd had no choice in the matter. This time around she had to be the one in control.

She felt the urge to self-harm once more, an adolescent habit which only resurfaced in times of heightened distress. The thought of the warm, gloopy redness seeping down her arms was tantalisingly delicious and releasing. And once again, the thought of death was beginning to swamp her every waking thought, and suffocating what little joy she had.

Looking out of her kitchen window she could see a goldfinch on the supple branch of a silver birch tree in her garden. The delicate sight of the bird's unyielding trust in nature eclipsed her dim view of the world and the venom that could flow from one human being to another.

She knew she'd have to keep moving towards her goal as failing wasn't an option. She retrieved the tatty box from the kitchen cupboard and began sifting through the items until an idea came to her mind.

She pulled out a pillowcase with "Poplar Ward" stamped on it. She smoothed the creases out with her fingers. The fabric was rough and unforgiving, and smelt of rotting dampness. She pulled out some scissors from a drawer and began to slice around the printed letters. She cut the word Poplar in two and then placed the pieces into two envelopes.

Then, painstakingly, using an alphabet stamp set, she addressed both envelopes and applied a postage stamp to each one with equal care.

Waves of nausea kept washing over her, engaging her stomach in a roller-coaster ride of damning emotions. She bit her bottom lip to remind herself that she was still alive. All the pains of her past had joined together and risked to overwhelm her sanity.

She placed the envelopes on the kitchen table ready for posting in the morning. She knew in the recesses of her cobwebbed mind that the nightmare journey had finally arrived. Life had never been the same for her after her stay in the hospital. But that was a secret only she could know.

That night, the recurring nightmare had crowded Lily's sleep. Only the morning light brought some semblance of relief from the dark shadows.

The sky was overcast with taunting clouds that seemed to deride her sordid mood. The chill in the air mimicked her iceberg soul, and from that moment on, she knew that she'd have to act the lead role in her own movie until the credits rolled and the curtains closed. She would be the one to choose the denouement.

Breakfast consisted of a glass of hot water with a slice of lemon and a sparsely buttered slice of toast. She nibbled the toast around the edges until she felt satiated.

Standing in front of the mirror in the hallway she pulled her cashmere scarf around her neck and picked up the letters to post. Like a soldier on a mission, she strode to the post box and slid them through the slot. *Let the games begin*, she thought to herself.

Lily was surprised to find the clinic door unlocked as she arrived. She didn't see Hugh's car in his allotted space and Nathan had never been known to arrive first.

Gingerly, she pushed the door open and peered around the reception area. Nothing looked amiss and even the door to the kitchen room was still closed. She could feel her heart beating in her mouth as she urged the faltering voice within her to call out.

"Hello. Doctor Rine, Doctor Carlton. Hello."

The sound of her voice clearly disturbed someone, as no sooner had the words left her mouth, than someone in a dark blue duffle coat ran out from the kitchen squealing like an animal in pain. The figure ran towards Lily, who was still blocking the door, flinging their arms in a windmill fashion.

Lily was barged through and landed with a thud on the floor, crashing onto her elbow. The searing pain sent an electric shock down to her fingers and her body convulsed in agony. A silent scream tumbled from her gapping mouth.

She was still on the floor when Nathan arrived, nearly tripping over her.

"Good God! Lily, are you all right?" He stooped next to her so that her nostrils were filled with his aftershave instead of the foul stench left by the intruder.

"I startled a burglar," she said as he helped her up and onto a chair.

"I think I might have seen him running through the garden. A homeless person by the look of him and the smell in the air," he said as he wrinkled up his nose.

Hugh arrived uncharacteristically late to see Nathan kneeling in front of Lily.

"What have we here?"

"Come in Hugh and shut the bloody door. Lily's been hurt."

She recounted her tale to a concerned Hugh whilst Nathan made her a cup of tea.

Hugh scanned the room for clues and to see what was missing. He and Nathan locked eyes and communicated their disconcerted thoughts about the occurrence. Nathan mouthed the word "police" to Hugh, but Lily was quick to catch on.

"Unless you really want to, don't call the police on my behalf. I've got nothing useful to say to them," Lily whispered. She wanted to recoil into the foetal position under her quilt at home.

"You can go home, Lily. I'll get Faith to stand in. You look pretty shook up. One of us will accompany you if you'd like."

"Thanks, but I think I'll cope."

"Let me know if you change your mind. Nathan, a word in my office."

"What are you going to do now?" asked Hugh as he closed the door. "It's already getting out of hand," he said as he ran his hand through his hair.

Nathan threw himself on the chair like a petulant child. "Oh, so this is my fault, is it?"

"It's up to you to sort out this Walker chap. He's a menace and he looks intent on carrying out his threats."

"We've no proof it's him or anything to do with him."

They met stale mate and neither party was willing to compromise or stake a claim in the nasty business. It was bigger than both of them.

"I'm worried for Lily. I believe that under her controlled exterior lies a rather fragile woman," said Hugh as he paced around the room.

"Not sure I believe that to be so. Anyway, what would your wife say about you being so concerned about another woman? She's quite possessive of you."

Hugh's face reddened and he actually felt like punching his friend, but thankfully he was a man of peace.

"Faith would have no problem with me worrying about Lily. Unlike you, I have the ability to feel concerned for another human being without the need to jump into bed with them."

"Touché," said Nathan as he walked out of Hugh's office, being careful not to slam the door.

By the time the clinic closed that evening, everyone was ready to go home with the thoughts of the day weighing heavy on their minds.

Lily had more colour in her cheeks but Hugh remained concerned for her welfare.

"I can drive you home if you wish."

"Thanks, but I enjoy the walk. Please don't worry." She placed a hand on his arm, and then withdrew it sharply, blushing as she did so.

Hugh knew that he would have cared for someone like her in the past, in another world. Perhaps he would have the opportunity in a parallel world, he thought to himself.

Nathan left the clinic feeling vulnerable as he walked along the pavement. He kept looking behind him and clenching his fists if a lone man was near him. He wondered how many enemies were out there ready to harm and destroy him.

Chapter Eight

A finger of sunshine danced on Nathan's face as he valiantly tried to wake up. The alarm clock buzzed for the second time and all he could do was growl at it.

His head felt full of smog thanks to the alcoholic fumes furling around. His mind kept replaying yesterday's appearance of the intruder at the surgery. He opened his eyes and stared at the ceiling wondering what Walker might do next to frighten him.

The shower did very little to stimulate him but he felt obliged to carry on for Hugh's sake if nothing else.

He forced himself to eat some toast, dripping butter onto his chin and leaving a greasy trail. The post arrived as he was about to leave so he picked it up and threw it on the half-moon table in the hall. Nothing looked of immediate interest except for an envelope with printed letters on it; it almost looked like it was sent by a child. He shoved it in his pocket and trundled off to work, plodding the same pavements and observing the same perfect people along the way.

He was the last to arrive at the clinic and he found Hugh and Lily chatting over a coffee in the kitchen. He noticed that Lily looked rather flustered.

"How's everyone this morning?" he asked.

"Fine" they replied in unison.

Lily then excused herself and went to her desk.

"Did you mention the intruder to Faith?" asked Nathan.

"No, I have kept Walker and all recent events a secret. I don't want her worrying more than she already does."

Nathan nodded and put his hands in his jacket pockets. One hand touched the envelope which he duly pulled out and opened.

At first he couldn't make out what the piece of grubby white fabric was and why it came without a letter. He turned the fabric over in his hands and saw the word "Pop" printed on it.

"What's that?" asked Hugh.

"I've no idea. It came this morning and . . ." Nathan's face flushed and he suddenly felt an overwhelming sensation of vertigo, making him stumble.

"Good God, man, sit down," said Hugh, noticing Nathan's distress.

Nathan felt physically sick as he touched the fabric. He also felt frightened and defenceless.

"Bloody hell, it's a piece of bed linen from Poplar Ward."

Hugh whipped it out of Nathan's trembling hand and inspected the fabric closely. He felt that the fabric was rough enough to be hospital bedding.

"Who would pull such a dark joke?"

"It's no joke, it's a warning." Nathan's mouth was so dry his tongue stuck to the roof. "It must be Walker," he continued after a sip of coffee.

He inspected the envelope that had clearly been designed to disguise the identity of the sender. It wouldn't be a helpful clue for the police, not that he could go to the police.

The fact that it was sent to his home address meant the sender knew where he lived. Suddenly he felt very exposed.

"You'll have to see Walker again to show that you're not frightened by his threats."

Nathan cast his eyes down, unable to look Hugh in the eye lest the coward in him be exposed further.

"I need to think what to do next," was all he could reply.

Lily entered the kitchen to announce that the first patients had arrived. She noticed the fabric on the table and walked out again.

Finlay Walker sat in the back of a chauffeur-driven car with his campaign manager, Jim, whilst he opened his post. Walker had weeks to go on the campaign trail and he was feeling confident about his position with the electorate.

He gave a cursory glance at each letter then piled them on top of his manger's lap to sort out.

He was intrigued by the envelope with the printed-out address. He tore it open and pulled out a single piece of fabric. He checked the envelope again to check that it was actually for him.

The fabric felt very familiar to him as he rubbed it between his thick finger and thumb. On the fabric was printed "lar."

"Everything okay? You look rather angry," said Jim as he noticed Walker thumping his thigh with his balled-up fist. His other hand screwed up the fabric and rammed it into his pocket. He didn't reply to Jim.

They were heading for a photo-opportunity meeting at the local museum where local archaeological finds were displayed. Part of his campaign was supporting local places of interest such as the museum and castle. He was trying to fulfil the role of community politician.

Only now he was in a murderous mood. He would have to fake his interest and demeanour even more than usual to enhance the outcome of the appointment with the awaiting staff, press, and public.

"You'll have to cancel tonight's meeting for me, something's come up."

Jim knew better than to contradict or challenge Walker, but he wasn't pleased with the request.

"Could you possibly manage both if I moved around the times?" he ventured.

"No." His raised voice made Jim flinch.

"Find out what time that doc's clinic closes; the one on Viking Street."

"You're not ill are you?"

"No, just do what I ask."

Walker feigned interest as he was shown around the archaeological finds and had numerous photographs taken of him shaking hands and discussing issues with the staff, who were all flushed and camera shy.

Internally, his emotions were rumbling like an awakening volcano preparing to erupt.

Jim could see that Walker was troubled as his deep brown eyes looked almost black and his jaw muscles kept clenching and twitching.

Jim came off the mobile and informed Walker that the clinic shut at six thirty.

"Do you need me to make an appointment?"

"No, he'll see me when I arrive."

Walker hung around the public garden to keep an eye on the clinic. The steady drip of patients leaving stopped at about six fifty. Now Walker had to wait for the staff to leave. He wanted Nathan alone.

He watched as the woman he recognised from the reception left and marched down the street, then he knew just the two doctors remained. Just as he was deciding whether to approach or not, he saw one of the doctors leave, which meant that the one he wanted was alone.

For a man of a bulky frame, Walker could move swiftly. He entered the building and shut the door behind him. He listened for any sounds, and he could hear someone talking in a back room.

He moved silently into the waiting room until the voice could be heard more clearly. He approached Nathan's door to see if he could hear another voice, but it soon became apparent that he was talking on the phone.

Walker waited for him to finish, then silently he turned the door knob. Nathan was busy scribbling something on a note pad with his head bent over and totally unaware of the intrusion.

"You should lock your door in the evening, doctor; you don't know who'll turn up."

Nathan almost bolted out of his chair at the presence of someone in his office. And not just anyone, it was him.

Walker whipped out the piece of fabric from his pocket and slammed it onto the desk, bearing down over Nathan as he did so.

"Your feeble little threats don't bother me," he said as he sprayed Nathan's face with droplets of saliva.

Shaking, Nathan looked at the fabric and realised that it was the other half of the piece he had. He pulled out the piece from his pocket and laid it next to Walker's. It read "Poplar."

"I thought you'd sent me this piece. Look, together they read 'Poplar.'"

"I can read, you fool. Nice try, but I can see right through your pathetic attempt to cover your back, doctor."

Walker leaned further towards Nathan and put one of his huge hands around Nathan's throat.

"You have too much to lose by exposing me, and besides, where's your proof? No one's going to believe a bunch of fucking loonies anyway, even if you could find them."

He squeezed Nathan's throat just enough to make his face redden and his bulging eyes water.

Nathan felt like a rag doll in the hands of a tormenting child. He knew he couldn't match Walker's strength, so he tried to use his brain.

"Hasn't it occurred to you," he rasped, "that one of them may have found us?"

Walker slackened his grip and glared. "What's that supposed to mean?"

"What if one of your victims has sent us a warning? How many victims were there?"

"Intriguing thought, Doctor, but hardly likely twenty odd years later."

"Do you remember their names, or were they just nameless and faceless victims?"

"They weren't victims; they deserved the treatment they got. Most were too thick or too drugged up, thanks to doctors like you. They didn't know what was happening half the time. They enjoyed it, anyway," he said with a smirk on his face.

Nathan physically shuddered and gritted his teeth.

"Don't you bloody laud it over me, you arse wipe. If you knew so much, why did you keep it quiet, or were you up to tricks too? You were with the nurses by all accounts," sneered Walker.

"How dare you come in here and accuse me of behaving in the same degrading manner as you. You're worse than a—"

Nathan was interrupted by Walker's fist slugging him on the jaw, smashing his teeth together and biting his tongue in the process. The force of the punch sent Nathan backwards in his chair and he only stayed upright because his head hit the wall behind him. Stars flashed across his eyes and disorientated him.

Nathan struggled to his feet, only to be pushed back into the chair and to feel Walker's hot, sour breath on his face.

"I'm warning you, you could get hurt and ruined if you cross me again. And don't think I don't mean it, Doctor. Everywhere you go, someone will be watching and listening to you. You are no longer free to roam this glorious town," he said as he walked towards the door. He then swung around and continued. "You will feel my eyes and breath on you wherever you go," and with that he walked out and slammed the door.

Nathan sat back in his chair and clasped one hand on his heaving chest, feeling the dampness through his shirt. His other hand touched the crown of his head where he felt another kind of dampness.

It was only when he looked down at his desk that he realised that Walker had taken both pieces of fabric with him.

Chapter Nine

Hugh began to feel trepidation for his friend who appeared more unnerved as the days went by and who sported a bruise on his lower jaw without any explanation, so after another hectic day, he suggested that they go to The Crown.

They strolled down the narrow cobbled streets, flanked by tall buildings with small leaded windows and uneven roofs.

The hanging sign of The Crown swayed gently in the evening breeze and beckoned their heavy hearts into the cosy atmosphere.

"Usual?" asked Hugh as he walked towards the bar.

"Please."

Nathan found a table by the open fireplace that housed a huge vase of flowers instead of the roaring fire reserved for the winter months. His mind wandered to recent events that he'd purposely kept secret from Hugh, but he guessed would come out over a drink.

Hugh arrived and placed the pints on the table.

"You've been quiet over the past few days, what's troubling you? Or is it still Walker?"

"I thought it was only Walker, but now I fear there's someone else, too."

Hugh raised his eyebrows and waited for Nathan to clarify himself.

"I had a visit from Walker who thought I'd sent him some fabric. Both of our pieces made up the word 'Poplar.'"

That explains the bruise, thought Hugh to himself. He wasn't sure what Nathan was getting at, and his puzzled face gave him away.

"For a doctor, you can be bloody dim at times. Someone sent us both a piece of fabric to alert us that they know what happened on Poplar Ward."

Hugh was beginning to wish he'd listened to Faith and not opened a clinic with Nathan. The sordid events from the past were catching up thick and fast, and there was no way of knowing how or when it would end.

"Who the hell could that be then?"

"I've no idea. Have you spoken to Faith about this yet?"

"No, I haven't. She'd kill me."

Nathan nodded but he thought how she'd kill him first. His whole future seemed muted by the mistake of his past, and his regrets were racking up. He was a fool then and a fool now, he thought to himself.

The pair felt uncomfortable in each other's company, but paradoxically they were compelled to stay together.

"I'm truly sorry, Hugh, for my demeanours. I was too altruistic back then. You would have done the right thing at the right time."

Hugh drank his beer in quiet contemplation. He felt torn between the love for his wife and the loyalty he felt for his friend. They were poles apart and yet so crucial to his everyday life. He couldn't imagine being without either one.

He didn't want to disband the clinic, but he knew that would be Faith's demand should she find out. The quandary was making his head spin.

"What about talking to Walker to see if he has any clues?"

"I'm not becoming friendly with him just to sort this out. It's his bloody mess. I was stupid but he was abusive, not me. Besides, I already broached him about that, and he didn't believe me. He was adamant that I sent it."

"Well, you'll have to think of something."

"I'm going to leave it, see if anything else happens. It may end now. Maybe it was a one-off."

"Ever the optimist," replied Hugh as he finished his pint.

The pub was unusually busy. A group of young men were singing "Happy Birthday" to the man with glowing cheeks standing in the centre of them.

"I must be going. I did say to Faith that I wouldn't be back late."

Hugh stood to leave and noticed how crushed and defeated his friend looked.

"Why don't you come back for dinner, Faith always cooks too much food."

Nathan had the urge to say yes, but his eyes questioned whether Faith would mind.

"I'll square it with Faith so don't worry about that," Hugh said as he smiled an almost pitying smile at Nathan, which Nathan chose to ignore. Nathan downed the remainder of his pint and got up to follow his friend.

They sat in the car in silence. Both men nursing troubled minds.

Hugh and Faith lived in a village just outside Hallbury, as Faith preferred a quieter environment. Hugh would have liked to live in Hallbury as Nathan did, but he allowed Faith to dictate where they lived as she was the one to stay at home all day.

As Hugh pulled onto the gravel drive, he hoped he had done the right thing. *I should have texted Faith to warn her but it's too late now*, he said to himself.

Faith went to greet her husband, having heard his keys in the door. Her delight at having her husband home was soon tempered when she saw Nathan behind him.

"Nathan, what a surprise," she said as she pecked her husband on the cheek and then ushered them both in and into the lounge.

"I've brought him back to have a home-cooked meal for a change."

"Good job, there's plenty of beef casserole to go around. I'll set another place at the table."

Faith disappeared leaving the men to cautiously look at one another.

"Please don't say anything to Faith about you-know-what," whispered Hugh.

"My lips are sealed," replied Nathan as he mimed zipping up his mouth.

Faith returned and beckoned them into the dining room with a silent gesture. Nathan was already feeling uncomfortable.

The meaty smell of the casserole pervaded the air, enticing them all to eat. Faith was an accomplished cook and Nathan missed home-cooked food. It made Nathan regret the atmosphere between him and Faith, but he wasn't sure what he had done wrong.

Fortuitously, Faith had put some classical music on in the background so the silence was filled with melodious strings and harpsichords.

"So Faith," ventured Nathan, "what do you do with yourself during the day?"

Faith finished her mouthful and returned her cutlery to the plate before answering.

"This house and garden take a lot of my time. Then I'm a member of the WI and I have choir practice every Thursday at the Minster."

Nathan had forgotten what a beautiful singing voice she had. Another thing he missed about her.

"Faith also has a kitchen garden so most of our herbs and vegetables are home grown." Hugh smiled at Faith whom he knew had given him a relaxed and stable home life. He felt a lucky man.

"So, Nathan, have you found someone to settle down with or are you the same old philanderer?" said Faith as she stared at him over the top of her wine glass.

Nathan laughed. "The former seems unachievable and the latter may or may not be true; you'd have to ask the women of Hallbury."

"Most of them, no doubt," she whispered under her breath, but loud enough to be heard. She gave a faint smile and proceeded to clear the plates.

"We usually have crackers and cheese at the end of the meal. Would you like some?" Faith hovered over him.

"No thanks, I've taken up enough of your time. I'll get a taxi home." He was very insistent. And so to the private relief of all, Nathan took a taxi home.

It was fairly late, but not too late to walk down to The Spread Eagle to see if anyone took his fancy.

Lily had slowly picked at her salad whilst she gazed through the window at the doves sitting on her garden fence. The cherry tree required pruning as it cast a vast shadow over the garden just like her past that cast a dark shadow over her heart.

The past few nights had seen the return of her reoccurring nightmare. It begins in a white room with no windows. In the centre of the room is a mortuary slab and on that slab lies a body. The body has a white sheet draped over it so only the head is exposed.

As she walks closer to the body, she see's that it's Walker. His head is shaven and etched on his scalp are the names of all his victims. Dried streaks and pools of congealed blood are seen on his scalp and neck. Although he is dead, the etching of the names was done whilst he was alive, and his screams could still be heard reverberating around the room. Underneath the sheet his hands are tied down, and his body and face are contorted with the excruciating pain that was inflicted before his life finally expired.

Lily found that the images of the nightmare stayed with her during the day. She would find herself smelling a certain odour or tasting a salty sensation in her mouth. Everything was repulsive and everything was real. She was glad that at least in her nightmare Walker was dead.

She'd seen the pain on Nathan's face when he was in the kitchen with the fabric on the table, and that was gratifying. However, she didn't know how Walker reacted and she needed to find a way to rectify that. She still had more to do.

All her life since Poplar Ward, she'd plotted her revenge on the parties concerned. And at last she was able to set the wheels in motion.

She took the tatty box from the kitchen and moved to the lounge to put it on the sofa next to her. Opening the lid was like removing her breast and looking straight at her blackened heart that was barely beating. The visible scars were reminders of the suffering caused by those around her. She'd been alienated all her life from the mainstream friendships that others experienced, and although she projected an amiable character to the world, inside her lived a seething rage of hatred and intolerance of others.

She pulled out a leaflet from the box that showed a picture of Ringlands Psychiatric Hospital and its grounds. It looked like a hotel in an Agatha Christie movie. Just seeing the image brought back the coldness and noise of the place.

She wondered if her last action was too subtle to cause a reaction, although Nathan seemed rather shaken. She decided to take the leaflet to work to photocopy before carefully block printing a few more envelopes.

Chapter Ten

Lily found a campaign leaflet from The English Party on her doormat the next morning. On the front was a photo of Walker grimacing in an attempt to smile, surrounded by his supporters. The leaflet had a reply slip attached requesting monitory or voluntary support.

As she sipped her hot lemon water it occurred to her that she could get closer to Walker if she volunteered for the party. It could be dangerous, she thought to herself, but it was worth undertaking to further her plans.

She slipped the two leaflets into her handbag along with the carefully printed envelopes. She knew that revenge wasn't the most charitable option to pursue, but she didn't have the spirit or strength for forgiveness. She stopped in front of the mirror in the hall and smoothed down her hair and then left for work.

Nathan walked out of his home with a woman whose name he'd already forgotten.

"I really enjoyed last night," she said as he locked the front door.

He was too self-absorbed to reply, and it was only when she moved towards him to give him a kiss did he become aware of her presence.

"Don't forget to call me," she said as she put her hand on his chest for one more feel of his defined muscles.

Nathan strode down the road towards the clinic, leaving the woman to stand and watch him, hoping he'd turn around to wave before disappearing out of sight. She was disappointed.

Nathan unlocked the clinic door, a new security measure since the intruder, and found Lily at the photocopier, secreting the copies into her handbag.

"Oh, morning, Doctor Rine, you startled me," she said as she put a hand over her heart.

"Sorry," he mumbled.

He wanted to ask how she was, to interact socially before the clinic opened, but he found he was unable to dredge up any words to say. He moved to his office and shut the door.

With each patient he saw, he found himself wondering whether they were goading him. He endeavoured to dampen his suspicious outlook lest it interfere with his professional conduct. However, by the end of the day he found that his anxiety had heightened to such a state that he longed for some alcohol to numb his weary mind.

The day couldn't end soon enough. But he vowed that all he would take home from The Spread Eagle that evening would be a hangover.

Nathan's soul relaxed as he sat in the pub with his pint and scotch. He sat as close to the wall as possible to hide in the shadows.

Watching the mating rituals between the sexes was better than television for him, as long as he remained a voyeur. Once he participated in the games he never knew when to stop until it was too late.

He noticed a burly-looking man watching him from the bar where he was standing. He wasn't sure how long he'd been watching him, but Nathan was beginning to feel on edge. He tried to remember whether he'd seen the man before. He had a familiar aura about him, but tall, well-built men with shaven heads tended to all look alike.

Nathan decided that he was being paranoid and that more alcohol was required to blur his mind. He walked up to the bar and ordered his usual. There was only one customer between him and the burly man. Nathan's nostrils flared at the pungent body odour emanating from one of the men.

"Hello again," said a female voice that belonged to the fingers which were slowly walking up his spine. "I bet you can't remember my name, can you?"

"I'm not in the mood for guessing games."

"You've been in the mood for a lot of other stuff before now."

He looked at her and saw that she looked the typical type of woman he'd take home; blonde, provocatively dressed, vacuous and eager to please. She had low self-esteem written all over her.

"I'm sorry, my mind's elsewhere," he said as he tried to peer around her to see if he was still being watched. He locked eyes with the burly man but he couldn't sustain the eyeball conflict for long.

"Change of thought, fancy coming back to my place?"

"I thought you'd never ask," she replied as she plunged her cleavage in his direction.

The blonde was eager to please and Nathan was just plain eager not to leave alone. He ushered her out as he followed close behind. As he passed the burly man he noticed him downing his pint whilst maintaining a fixed sight on him.

The blonde pawed at Nathan's arm and giggled in his ear. He strained to listen for footsteps behind them but he couldn't hear with all the whispering in his ear about what she'd do to him when they got back.

As they walked up his street, Nathan was sure they were being followed. As they stood at his front door, he quickly glanced around and saw the man standing further down the street.

Nathan's hand shook as he tried to put the key in the lock.

"Oh sugar, are you feeling desperate?"

He shoved her inside, taking one last look to see if he was mistaken. The man was clearly leaning against a lamp post on the opposite side of the street, smoking a cigarette. Nathan quickly shut the door, locked it and then ran to the lounge to peer out of the bay window. The man was still out there smoking and staring in Nathan's direction.

"So sugar, are you wanting it on the sofa?"

Nathan had momentarily forgotten her presence and the fact that she was expecting sex. With all the stress bouncing around, sex was the last thing on Nathan's mind. However, he didn't want to be alone. His vulnerability seemed to be encouraging her advances as she began to disrobe and shed her clothes around the dimly lit room.

"Why don't we have a drink?" he asked.

"Need courage, sugar? Not like you."

He moved away from the window and tripped over one of her shoes. It was only then that he realised she was half naked and ready for some action.

"I said I need a drink first," he repeated as he moved towards the kitchen to fix himself a large scotch before returning to the lounge.

Dawn, as her name turned out to be, was slumped next to him on the sofa with her hand underneath his shirt. Whilst she rolled his chest hair around her finger, Nathan's mind was preoccupied with the man by the tree, wondering whether he was still there.

Was the burly man the one who sent the fabric? Had he moved onto the next phase in his deadly plan? The questions and the alcohol were making his head whirl.

"Oh God, sorry," he said as he abruptly left the sofa and dashed to the toilet.

Dawn wrinkled up her nose as the noises and the acrid scent travelled to the lounge. Suddenly the atmosphere felt less sexy, so she swiftly got dressed and left the house with her stilettos in her hand.

Nathan's forehead was covered in a dew-like sweat and his throat stung from the acid waterfall. He staggered back to the lounge with excuses in mind only to find that he was alone.

The solitude sobered him up quickly as he realised that he needed to be alert. Every creak of floorboard or rustle of branches outside the window made his heart size decrease to the diminutive size of a walnut. His chest felt tight and he became breathless.

Summoning up his waning courage, he crept to the window to see if the man was still standing there. Nathan saw he'd gone but the relief was short lived as he wondered whether the man had moved closer to his home instead.

He forced himself to go to bed, but all he could do was pull the quilt up under his chin, and stare at the ceiling, watching the shadows of the tree branches spider across his ceiling. He knew that he would have a fitful night's sleep.

Eventually, his eyelids became heavy, and he was no longer able to guard himself. Danger could find him asleep and there was nothing he could do about it.

Nathan descended the stairs after a few hours of disrupted sleep, his head thick and his stomach queasy. "Thank God Friday has arrived," he muttered aloud as he switched on the kettle.

He heard the post thud onto the doormat. Bubbles of anxiety rose up his body like a newly opened bottle of soda. He quickly flicked through the numerous envelopes until he came across a block-printed envelope. He ripped open the envelope and pulled out a blank piece of paper. He turned the paper over and over and checked inside the envelope. *What the hell?*

He opened his front door quickly glancing around to see if he was being watched; but no one nefarious could be seen. He wondered whether Walker had also received some blank paper that morning. If he had, he imagined that one of Walker's cronies would be round to give him a message in the near future.

Chapter Eleven

"Any plans for the weekend?" Hugh asked as he stirred his coffee.

"I think I should do some gardening as it's looking rather neglected," replied Lily as she nursed a mug of black, unsweetened tea.

"I think Faith has similar plans for me. No peace for the wicked."

"If only that were true."

"Pardon?"

Lily shrugged her shoulders and smiled. "I'm just being cynical."

They were interrupted by Nathan, who had arrived with his usual tardiness. He walked straight to the coffee pot.

"Rough night?" asked Hugh.

"Spectacularly so," he replied.

Lily watched Nathan from under her eye lashes to try and gauge his mood. She took her time washing her mug to see if he revealed anything to Hugh, but she was sorely disappointed when he retreated to his room without uttering another word.

"He's a great example of health and *joie de vivre* isn't he?" said Hugh as he passed her on his way to his room.

There was a slow trickle of patients which kept the doctors busy, but Lily wasn't inundated. So she took the opportunity to phone The English Party headquarters. She took the leaflet from her bag and dialled the number.

"TEP headquarters, how may I help?" said a young voice.

"Er, hello. I got one of your leaflets through the door and I'd like to offer my services in my spare time."

"Cool. Why don't you call round later and have a chat with us?"

"I could come around seven if that's any good."

"Yep, just press the buzzer and announce yourself. What's your name?"

"Lilith Fields. See you tonight at seven then."

The woman Lily spoke to sounded young and friendly, which eased her mind although her body was in adrenalin overdrive. She wanted to ask the woman if Walker would be there, but she worried that she might sound too familiar. She'd have to wait and see.

Everyone congregated in the kitchen at lunchtime, each one preoccupied with their own concerns. The atmosphere was made more bearable by banal conversation about the local election and the weather, the latter being showery, hence Lily remained in the clinic with her salad.

"Hope I'm not speaking out of turn Lily, but you look like you've lost some weight. Are you okay? Not still troubled by the intruder are you?" asked Hugh.

"I'm fine, thank you, Doctor Carlton. I hadn't noticed a change in my weight."

Both doctors raised their eyebrows to one another but chose not to comment.

At six thirty, Lily made sure the waiting room was in order and shut down her computer. She didn't want to see the doctors so she called "goodbye" and scurried out of the door, making sure she locked the door behind her.

The English Party headquarters was on the other side of town, so she pulled her coat around her and walked briskly across the cobbled stones, past the upmarket boutiques and tea shops.

She searched the street for the headquarters which she found to be above an estate agent. She took a deep breath before she pressed the buzzer on the intercom and announced herself. Her face was flushed and her lungs felt like two deflated balloons.

She mounted the poorly lit staircase, all the time aware that her heart beat so loudly in her ears that it rendered her partially deaf.

On reaching the top, she came across a glass-panelled door through which she could see a flurry of activity taking place in a room. The walls were covered in campaign posters and George Cross flags. She couldn't see Walker but it was too late to turn back as a young woman was beckoning her in. She quickly wiped her clammy palms down her skirt.

"Lilith Fields?"

"Call me Lily."

"Hi, I'm Rachel. We spoke on the phone."

Lily smiled and moved towards the desk where Rachel was sorting leaflets into piles.

"You can help me do this so they're ready for tomorrow."

Lily stood next to the girl, who looked no more than nineteen, and copied her actions. It was a painfully laborious task, made more so for Lily by the words printed on the leaflet. She detested their views and more so the photo of Walker on the front of the glossy paper.

"What work do you do?" asked Rachel.

"I'm a medical secretary and receptionist in a clinic."

"Cool."

"And you?"

"I'm studying social sciences at college; that's what got me into this. Finlay is so inspirational."

"Finlay?"

"Yeah, Finlay Walker, our candidate." Rachel looked wide eyed at Lily.

Lily felt stupid as she only knew him as Walker. His first name was of no consequence to her.

"Will he be here tonight?"

"Not sure, as he's got a meeting with some local shop owners."

Lily bowed her head to hide the disappointment, yet relief oozed from her eyes. She then listened as Rachel talked about the manifesto of the Party and the work she could do.

It was close to eight thirty and there had been no sign of Walker, so she decided to go home. She donned her jacket and picked up her handbag when the man himself strode into the room.

He had a dynamic effect on the room as everyone stopped talking and turned towards him. Lily felt rooted to the spot as she always did in his presence.

Certain people spoke with him as he circled the room in his long brown coat. Some girls blushed and averted their eyes as he walked past them. As he walked towards Lily and Rachel, he stopped.

"Don't I know you from somewhere?" he said to Lily.

"I work at a doctor's clinic you visited recently," she replied as her heart pounded in her chest.

He studied her face for a while longer.

"What does Doctor Rine think about you being here?"

"He doesn't know. I can do what I like in my own time."

"Indeed."

He paused for a few seconds longer before moving towards a man who looked like a nightclub bouncer. Lily considered that he may be one of Walker's body guards.

She watched him as closely as she possibly could without looking too obvious or suspicious. She saw he would be hard to get close to because of his loyal entourage.

"I think I might go now," she said to Rachel.

"Okay then. Any chance you could help out tomorrow leafleting?"

"Sure, what time?"

"We're meeting here in the morning at ten."

"At ten it is then," she said as she headed for the door. As she turned to close it, her eyes briefly met with Walker's. He didn't smile; instead, he stared coldly into her soul.

She walked down the stairs biting her bottom lip. On reaching the pavement she felt that she could breathe fresh air once more, as the air in the TEP office felt soiled and poisonous.

Chapter Twelve

Nathan had a poor night's sleep, so he was pleased it was the weekend, when he didn't have to face any patients.

The Saturday post usually arrived later than during the week so he had longer to wait. That allowed plenty of time for his anxiety to notch up to an unbearable level.

Waiting for the post had become a torturous affair, along with answering the door and the phone. Of late, Nathan had begun to feel like a fly trapped on a web waiting for the spider to inevitably devour him. Thoughts lay heavy on his heart and mind and the only thing to alleviate such woes was alcohol. *It's too early to venture down that road*, he thought to himself.

Sporadically, he peered out of his front windows to see if anyone was watching him. Anyone strolling past the house was scrutinised as a potential suspect.

His mind rummaged through the debris of his past. He didn't have much to be proud of apart from becoming a doctor, and even that had been tainted by Walker's behaviour, and his own.

The thud of letters on the doormat alerted Nathan of their arrival. He bent down to collect them and began scanning through the envelopes straight away. And there it was, like a weed in a bouquet of flowers, the dreaded block-printed envelope.

Anxiety coursed through his body as he held the envelope in his shaking hands. He noticed the continued precision used by the sender to address the envelope and to place the postage stamp with care.

He slit the envelope with a knife and then pulled out the contents. This time it was another piece of fabric, a faded yellow paisley-patterned piece.

He was puzzled at first until he remembered that the women wore nightgowns made of that fabric. He threw it on the floor and felt repulsed by touching it. Sweat gathered on his top lip and a wave of nausea edged its way across his stomach.

He paced around the room looking at the fabric and rubbing the back of his neck. He was trying to figure out who could be doing this.

Twenty-five years was a long time for him to try and remember all the staff there. Perhaps a staff member knew what was going on and had now decided to blackmail both him and Walker.

He still, however, hadn't ruled out Walker's involvement in it all. It didn't matter that he had denied all knowledge and was outraged by receiving the bed linen in the first instance; all that could be a rouse to hide his guilt from Nathan.

Sod it, he thought to himself, *it's only ten in the morning but I need a scotch.* He took the bottle from his writing desk, picked up a tumbler and sat in his battered leather armchair. He poured himself a drink and stared at the fabric that was now lying on the wooden floorboards near his feet.

He reached over for the phone and dialled a number.

"Hello, it's Nathan. I need to see you."

"Bit difficult, I'm afraid, Faith's got DIY jobs galore for me."

"I got another piece of troubling post today and I feel close to cracking up."

"What the hell now? I'm also close to the edge with all of this, Nathan. I was a damn fool to have faith in you," he hissed. "If you don't sort this out bloody quickly, I'll turn you and Walker in to the police myself. I've got to protect the clinic for my sake."

Nathan's silence spoke a thousand words.

"Faith's calling me, I've got to go."

Nathan was still holding the receiver when Hugh hung up on him. He felt abandoned and scared. The scotch, his only friend, was calling him again.

Lily arrived just before ten o'clock at the headquarters of the TEP and found there were more people than the previous night. She moved silently amongst them. Her presence hardly made a ripple of recognition until Rachel saw her and waved her over. Rachel was in charge of giving each person a white canvas messenger bag with the TEP logo on it, filled with the party leaflets.

A surly man then put everyone into groups of four and assigned them an area to cover. Instructions were that they were to knock on doors, talk about the TEP manifesto, and hand out the leaflets. If no one was in, they were to post the leaflet through the door.

Lily only half listened to the orders as she searched the room for Walker, but he was nowhere to be seen. Her disappointment made her want to rush home to avoid the odious task that lay before her. She was glad she was a least with Rachel, if nothing else she quite liked her even if she didn't share her views. She believed she was just a misguided youth who would soon see the error of her ways.

"Be prepared to have a few doors slammed in your face. Not everyone appreciates us," said Rachel as she hoisted her bag over her shoulder.

Lily resisted the urge to say *is there any wonder*, but chose instead just to nod her head. The canvas messenger bag was heavy for someone with a slight frame but she decided it would be pointless complaining. She followed the two menacing looking men who were in her group. They looked in their fifties, with gleaming bald heads and broad shoulders. With Rachel by her side, they clattered down the stairs behind the men.

After fourteen house calls, Lily had seen a variety of outcomes from the polite and interested to the rude and potentially volatile. She found the task trying and embarrassing. As they progressed along their route, she suddenly realised that they were approaching Nathan's street. She was mortified. *What would he think of me?*

"Shall we start this side and let the men go over there?" Lily suggested to Rachel.

Perhaps because it was the most she had spoken that morning, Rachel took up her idea. The men crossed the road begrudgingly and as they approached to being opposite Nathan's house, Lily kept a low profile.

Nathan was still sitting in his leather chair in the lounge when he saw two heavily built men walk past his window and then up to his front door. He sat rigidly in his chair as he heard them thump on the door a couple of times. He gripped onto the arms of the chair and held his breath. After a few minutes of silence he heard the letterbox flap and then he watched them retreat, heavily in conversation.

He downed the last drop of scotch from his glass, heaved himself out of the chair, and headed to the hallway. On his doormat he saw a photo of Walker staring up at him on a TEP leaflet. He picked it up with his sweaty hand and searched the leaflet for a sign or message from Walker, but he found nothing out of the ordinary. Nathan could tell they were Walker's men and he wondered which of the two was spying on him the other night. He kept away from the window in case they were still watching his house and getting ready to pounce on him if he opened his front door.

Lily watched the two men approach Nathan's house and she was relieved to see that he didn't answer his door. She couldn't relax totally until the humiliating morning was over and she was as far away as possible from Nathan's home.

After walking several more streets with Rachel, she suddenly felt a large hand on her shoulder. She flinched at the touch and turned around to see Walker standing there.

"You're here again, you must be committed."

Lily tried to control the fear in her eyes by focusing just above his head as she used to do years ago.

"Once I've made my mind up to do something, I do it well and see it through to the end."

"I like that in a person, it shows a fighting spirit. Perhaps we should meet up after this to discuss your ideals."

Lily swallowed hard but agreed all the same. She wanted to get closer to him and now she was being given the chance, although it was sooner than she expected. She needed to remain in control, so she inhaled deeply as Walker crossed the road to talk to the two men from the group.

"Wow, you must have caught his eye," whispered Rachel. "He never meets up with new ones."

"I've no idea why he wants to, but I do feel rather intimidated by him."

"I hear his bark is worse than his bite, by all accounts."

Lily raised her eyebrows and pushed her last leaflet through a letter-box, relieved at the lightness of her bag. The group walked back towards the headquarters. Walker had already gone and the two men continued talking without acknowledging the women at all.

Lily's palms felt sweaty and her mouth was parched. She didn't feel quite prepared for her tête-à-tête with Walker so she decided to play it cool and see what his agenda was.

She wondered whether he'd recognised her in some way but she felt it was highly unlikely after twenty-five years. She concealed her identity well with her name change, with dying her strawberry-blonde hair chestnut brown and by wearing green coloured contact lenses to disguise her soft grey eyes.

She mounted the stairs behind Rachel who was busy making social arrangements with a friend on her mobile. Lily was beginning to feel protective of her, much like a mother-daughter relationship. An experience she knew she'd never have.

As they walked into the headquarters, she could see Walker standing by the window, also on his mobile. He saw her and waved her over even though he appeared to be deep in conversation.

"Keep tabs, still. You don't have to be overly discreet, fear works wonders." He ended his call abruptly and turned his attention to Lily.

"So, what attracted you to TEP?" he asked, shoving his mobile in his pocket.

"I'm worried that we're getting so multi-cultural that we're forgetting our own roots. I'm fond of our country and I wanted to see what your party had to offer."

"D'you think people are ready to vote for us or are we too extreme?"

"I think the voters are ready for a change, and I don't just mean from one standard party to another, but a complete change."

Walker nodded at her response and his shoulders loosened up slightly. His face looked softer as he relaxed the frown lines between his still, black eyebrows.

"It's good to have a fresh face to talk to and to trust. I always have to be vigilant in my position."

"Understandable."

Lily couldn't believe how he swallowed all the phrases she'd previously rehearsed. It was easier that she imagined.

"So . . ." he floundered for her name.

"Lily."

"Right, Lily. Perhaps we should have dinner tonight and you can talk through your ideas to promote the party."

A voice inside her head screamed "no" but she felt she didn't have a choice.

"Okay," she replied, monitoring the tremor in her voice.

"Tonight at seven in The Queen's Head. Keep this between us, right?"

"Of course."

He signalled for her to leave him as he dialled a number on his phone. She was more than happy to be released from his company. Her flesh crawled as she walked away and she believed that not even a shower would rid her of the sensation. She could taste him in her mouth, making her gag as she stumbled down the stairs.

She hurried through the strolling Saturday shoppers, sometimes accidently catching people's bags or elbows along the way. She was irritated by the throng. She saw each person as an enemy who'd ignored her when she needed to be heard, not just when she was on Poplar Ward, but in the days leading up to her admission. She had no time for anyone, and the swear words and insults rang out in her head. She wanted to snarl at strangers, but her self-governing persona stopped her; she needed to save her acrimony for those who deserved it.

Chapter Thirteen

Nathan jumped as the telephone rang. He left it to ring, preferring to let the answering machine pick it up.

"Nathan, I feel bad about earlier . . ."

"Hugh," he said as he intercepted the call. "What's up?"

"As I was saying, I feel bad about earlier and wondered if you fancied going out for a pint tonight."

"You got brownie points from Faith then."

"Don't be sour. How about I come round about six?"

"Not sure how sociable I'll be, but I'll see you at six."

After putting down the receiver Nathan rubbed the back of his neck and contemplated how his life had become stifling. His mind began to sift through recent events.

He wasn't sure if he wanted to go to the pub as things were beginning to add up, leading him to feel threatened like never before. The smell of the man in the pub reminded him of the smell in the clinic after the intruder left. Who was that man? Was he one of Walker's cronies, or did he belong to the days of Poplar Ward? The man knew where he lived, worked, and socialised. *Shit.*

And the worse thing was, he hadn't been totally honest with Hugh.

A few nights ago when he arrived home, he found a hangman's noose dangling from a tree in his back garden. His spine still tingled with an ice-cold frisson every time he thought about it. It sent him a powerful message, in that only death could save him.

His leaden limbs were bogged down in a quagmire of regrets and anxiety. He grasped his head in his hands and rocked back and forth in an effort to regulate his erratic heartbeat. *Maybe Hugh could bail me out,* he thought to himself.

On the other side of town, Lily was in the shower, exfoliating her body until she began to feel sore. She washed her hair three times and allowed the soapy water to cascade into her mouth.

She deliberated several scenarios that could take place with Walker later. Ultimately, she wanted to make him pay and she wanted to make him suffer. To be able to carry out her revenge, she was going to need to get close to him, even though she knew she'd feel ill in the process.

She couldn't decide what to wear, but she wanted to look as though she had not tried too hard. She rifled through her wardrobe until she found a pretty floral dress that she wore to her final appointment with the consultant psychiatrist. She'd gone for the carefree, hippy chick look that went some way in masking her inner darkness. She worked hard to hide it from the consultant as she wanted to break free from the shackles he'd put her in.

The fluid fabric of the dress skimmed over her body, and although she had no curves to speak of, it gave her the air of gentile feminine innocence. She put pearl-drop earrings in, and added blusher and pale pink lipstick to give the illusion of a healthy glow.

She'd bought some perfume on the way home from work the day before, hoping that the rose scent would mask the foul odour of Walker.

Before leaving the house she smoothed down her hair and checked how she looked in the hall mirror. Her fragile appearance satisfied her. She shut the front door quietly behind her and set off for The Queen's Head.

It was a pleasant evening for a stroll as the birds twittered in the trees lining the street. A splash of sunlight remained in the burnt amber sky. She tried to banish any apprehension about the evening ahead as she knew that if dwelt upon, it would make her run back to the sanctuary of her home. She owed it to herself and to the others that suffered at the hands of Walker. She had to continue with her slow-burn plan.

Just ahead, she saw the pub sign swinging gently to and fro. Her pace slowed as she got closer, and she wondered whether Walker would be waiting for her. A tight band constricted her ability to breath and her sense of isolation and vulnerability suddenly dawned on her, almost winding her.

She checked her watch and it was exactly seven o'clock. It was time for her to enter the fighting arena.

Her eyes took a few seconds to adjust to the dimly lit room as the pub only had a small window facing the street, restricting any natural light. She looked around and saw that Walker was already seated at a small, round table.

"I commend you for your punctuality," he said as she approached the table. "I took the liberty of getting you a white wine."

"Thank you," she replied, even though she preferred red.

"Tell me a bit about yourself, I'm intrigued," said Walker.

"Not much to tell really, I'm not an exciting or interesting person. I'd much rather know more about you."

Walker did not need asking twice, and clearly relished talking about himself. He talked eloquently about his political role and his vision for the future.

"I'm interested in your background and what got you to this point in life. What did you do before politics?"

"You're quite nosy. You're not a journalist are you?"

"No. I'm just curious, that's all."

"I was a charge nurse. I commanded a team and earned respect from all on the ward, including the doctors. A lot of what I do now mirrors my work back then."

Lily bit her bottom lip and shuddered.

"What an interesting life you've had. Do you miss nursing?"

"Not at all, it's changed too much for my liking. Politics is my bag now."

So as not to look pushy or to arouse suspicion, Lily moved onto the topic of Hallbury and the local places of interest. She listened to Walker as reams of rehearsed speech spewed out of his vile mouth.

Lily began to tire of his company. "It's been a long day. I'll head home now if that's okay?"

She wondered whether he would try and stop her.

"We'll have to do this again," was all he said.

It felt like an order rather than a request. She left him nursing his pint as she hurried out of the pub.

Darkness had descended, making the narrow street feeling even more claustrophobic. Her breathing became shallow, making her light-headed. When she finally arrived home, she shoved the key in the lock and then leant back on the door once she was inside.

Tears streamed down her face and disgust filled her stomach. The urge to purge her body of those feelings was overwhelming. She slowly moved to the kitchen to get a sharp knife out of the drawer. Then, with determined footsteps, she walked upstairs to the bathroom and locked the door.

As she perched on the rim of the bath she saw how the stainless steel blade caught the light, flashing like lightening in the sky.

She rolled up her sleeve and caressed her alabaster skin with the side of the blade. The coldness felt both comforting and powerful at once. She then proceeded to run the blade across her arm, until red fluid filled the slices she had made.

As she watched the deep red blood flow, she sensed her anxiety and anger flooding out of her body, leaving a sensation of peace and release. She closed her eyes for a few moments to soak up every nuance of the warmth that was wrapping around her like a feather-filled quilt.

After several more slices, a pool of blood gathered in the bottom of the bath, and she felt high from seeing her achievement.

After several minutes, she carefully bandaged up the wounds and pulled down her sleeve to hide the scars from the world.

Nathan and Hugh had run out of pleasantries to discuss, whilst skirting around the main area of concern, as they sat in The Crown. Nathan felt safer in that pub, for now at least.

"I can't stay for long," said Hugh before taking a mouthful of beer.

"I've received another piece of fabric that looks like a nightgown from Poplar." Nathan held his head in his hands.

Hugh looked aghast. "That's gross. You've got to go to the police.

Who knows what you'll receive next? A death threat?"

Nathan swallowed hard. "Who'd want me dead? I didn't commit the crime."

"You're every bit as guilty as if you'd forced yourself on every one of Walker's victims. You raped them every single time he did when you didn't stop him!"

Nathan looked stunned, as though Hugh had just slapped him across his face. But he knew he deserved it, even though it hurt more coming from his only friend.

"It didn't happen to you. You weren't there. He's a frightening man, for God's sake."

"And how frightened must those patients have been? You violated both the law and your conscience, and I stand to pay for your crimes by losing the clinic. I'm truly pissed at you for this." Hugh was struggling to keep his voice low.

The pub began to fill up with a rowdy bunch of students which rendered the atmosphere inhospitable for quietly spoken conversation.

"Okay Hugh, you win. I'll sort this mess out somehow. Let's go back," he said as he slung his jacket over his shoulder.

Once outside, Hugh stopped on the pavement and turned around to face his friend. "If I'm not being helpful it's because I really don't know what to say or do. This is bigger than the both of us, and I'm afraid for us both."

Nathan knew Hugh was right and he appreciated the honesty of his friend's words. He knew that Hugh was almost pathologically honest, even to his own detriment at times.

Nathan was alone at home once more. He slumped into the leather chair and stared into the fireplace that was blacked by previous fires lit by previous owners. He resolved not to let Walker win this time around, whatever the cost.

Chapter Fourteen

It was a muggy Monday morning, but Lily wore a long sleeved blouse to cover the scars carved from her emotional hell. New bandages replaced the blood-soaked ones.

As she moved around the lounge, she caught sight of a stocky man staring right at her house from across the street. He was a stranger to her, but his stance made her feel uncomfortable and edgy. She moved back from the window and waited a few minutes. Then, with her arms folded across her stomach, she peered out of the window again to see if he was still there. He'd vanished.

She gathered her belongings together and hastily headed to work making sure her house was securely locked before she left.

Lily was the first one to arrive at the clinic. She was in the kitchen when Nathan entered.

"Good morning, Lily. Good weekend?"

"Average. And you?"

"So-so."

He knew he couldn't talk about his worries with her as she may get too scared to continue working there, and they needed her. However, he did think that she'd be a good listener and would probably have some insightful thoughts on what to do, unlike Hugh.

"If you don't mind my saying, Doctor, you look rather pale this morning. Are you all right?"

"I'm grateful for your concern, just feeling rather tired, nothing to concern yourself over."

Lily tilted her head as she looked at him. She knew there was more behind his response. She wanted to hear him talk about the emotional anguish he was suffering, and the torturous nights he was experiencing.

She wanted to hear about his soul stripping nightmares and his inability to eat, even though his stomach screamed for food. His weakening form and dishevelled look increased as the days racked by. She gleaned small pleasures from his downward slide, but his silence disappointed her.

Nathan watched her leave the kitchen and thought that she had the aura of a delicate flower that needed nurturing. He noticed her translucent skin and the way her eyelashes curled like the antennae of a butterfly, and wondered whether she was happy. That passing thought left a trail in his subconscious.

Hugh was the last one to arrive.

"Jeez, you look rather agitated," said Nathan.

Hugh just grunted as he poured himself a coffee.

"Do you want to tell me what's wrong?"

"Faith and I had a huge row last night."

"And?"

"And it was about you, if you must know."

"Me?"

"I would like to socialise with you both a bit more, because when I see you alone, Faith becomes livid. I can't understand why you two don't get on."

Nathan shrugged his shoulders and looked at the floor. He wondered whether it was because alcohol could make him exuberant and tactile, which she perhaps found difficult to handle. He also knew that over the years his attitude had turned maudlin, which could spoil an evening for a socialite such as Faith.

On many an occasion he'd got Hugh roaring drunk which he knew Faith disapproved of and always blamed him for. He was worried about losing his only real friend.

Both doctors retired to their rooms and morning consultations began.

At lunchtime, Nathan contemplated staying in his room to keep out of everyone's way. As he sat in his swivel chair, he looked around the room at his certificates on the wall, all proclaiming his medical expertise and success. He had been a fun-loving medical student and a loyal friend to Hugh, and then it all went wrong for him on Poplar Ward. His life had become empty with a failed marriage, and it was entirely his fault. He had no one else he could blame for his circumstances.

There was a knock at his door and then Hugh's head appeared.

"I've apologised to Faith on your behalf and she's agreed to having you and Lily round for dinner this Saturday."

"Me and Lily?"

"Not as a couple, you burke, but as a way of celebrating the opening of our clinic. Like we were supposed to do, remember?"

"I appreciate that, thanks."

"Just remember to behave."

Nathan laughed as Hugh retreated from the room, already regretting his actions.

Lily, on the other hand, took a bit of persuading to attend. Hugh cajoled her into accepting the invitation which made him feel strangely warm inside.

Lily arrived home that evening to find a message on her ansaphone. She pressed the play button and heard Walker's brusque voice booming out of the speaker.

"Lily, I want to see you tomorrow. Meet me in The Queen's Head at seven."

She was unclear whether it was a business meeting about the party or whether it was a social meeting. He didn't leave his telephone number and he obviously got hers from her TEP application form. She dialled the last number received and got his mobile number. She wrote it down on a piece of paper and then put it in the tatty box in the kitchen. *That could come in handy*, she thought to herself.

She felt, however, that Walker was getting too close too soon. She wanted to take back control. She absentmindedly twirled a strand of hair around her finger until a few hairs became detached from her scalp.

The shower did nothing to alleviate her distress and even her growling stomach did little to help her mood. She slipped into her jogging clothes, and although it was late in the evening, she ignored the darkness and set off along her route.

With each step she ran she imagined her body getting thinner and she visualized Walker's demise.

She couldn't get him out of her head, no matter how fast her pace was. She wanted to reach inside her head and rip out the images of her tormentor.

By the time she got home she needed another shower. She set the water temperature as hot as she could bear so that it lashed onto her porcelain skin leaving red whip-like marks.

In his own home, Nathan also needed a shower but for vastly different reasons. As he lay in his rumpled bed, he watched the bleached blonde get dressed.

"I don't suppose I could have a coffee," she asked.

"At this hour?"

"Well, tea then. I'm thirsty."

Nathan sighed, but got up all the same and donned his threadbare dressing gown. He padded downstairs and switched the kettle on. He mulled over the woman in his bedroom. She was pretty, she flattered him and she gave him what he wanted, but not what he needed.

He wasn't quite sure what he needed, but he knew it wasn't a woman who was so ready to jump into bed on the first night. He was getting to the stage in life where he wanted to find companionship. He wanted to have meaningful conversation over meals, he wanted to watch TV with someone and he wanted to be able to sit in comfortable silence with someone by his side.

Hugh seemed to have all of that and Nathan had to admit that he was envious of his friend.

The bedroom woman appeared in his kitchen and he handed her a mug of tea.

"Maybe next time I could stay over?" she said as she blew on the steaming tea.

He was tired of being harsh with people, but he didn't want to fill his bed or his home with that particular kind of woman.

"Maybe," he replied.

At least she'd come in her own car so he didn't need to pay for a taxi.

"See you soon, lover. Call me," she said as she teetered out of his front door. Nathan appreciated the way she moved, but his interest ended there. *I'm a shallow bugger*, he thought to himself.

The following morning in the clinic, Nathan noticed how distracted Lily was. She disconnected a phone call to him from the hospital and she'd needed him to repeat himself when he was dictating a letter to her.

For his part, another morning with no ghastly mail had meant that his demeanour was more relaxed. In fact, Nathan felt he was the only one that day who was feeling okay as even Hugh appeared to have things on his mind.

"This Saturday thing isn't causing more problems between you and Faith is it?" Nathan asked.

"No, why?"

"You seem to be distracted today, that's all."

"It's nothing. I'm just being an old fool."

Nathan looked at him and gestured for him to continue.

"As I said, I'm being foolish. Faith still looks stunning and I sometimes worry that my long hours mean she has time to meet someone else." He paused to watch a squirrel scamper up a tree through the kitchen window. "Not being able to have children has always been a source of unhappiness for her."

"I'm not quite sure what you're driving at?"

"She's been going out quite a bit during the day and she doesn't always answer her mobile."

Nathan knew that she attended the Women's Institute and the Minster Choir. Faith also had various female friends to lunch with.

"She attends this book group about twice a week, but she's very vague about it when I ask."

"Is that all the circumstantial evidence you have? God, Hugh, there's probably little to say about a book group."

"Okay, I'm a sad old fool."

Lily walked into the kitchen and avoided eye contact with either doctor. Her face was flushed and she appeared more frail than usual.

"Would it be okay if I left five minutes earlier today?" she asked.

Both doctors agreed before she returned to her desk.

"Do you think she's in love? It's just I'm finding her a bit preoccupied and distant today."

"I hadn't noticed," replied Hugh.

"Must just be me then."

Lily had spent most of the afternoon at her desk watching the clock. She was short tempered with patients and she needed to visit the bathroom frequently.

At twenty-five past six, Lily left the safety of the clinic and headed for The Queen's Head with her heart pounding in her chest.

Chapter Fifteen

The town was relatively quiet and the lack of people around made Lily feel defenceless. Her stomach churned and her bottom lip quivered.

On approaching the pub she saw a broad-shouldered man outside the door, smoking a roll-up between his sausage-like fingers. She wondered whether he was waiting for her arrival. As she brushed passed him to get through the door, a tingle traversed her neck and the hairs on her arms stood up on end.

Inside the pub she found only three customers, with Walker being one of them. He was sitting in a poorly lit corner with his pint and a glass of white wine placed ready and waiting on the table.

"Good evening," he said in his gravelly voice as he motioned her to sit.

Lily smiled and nodded as she sat on the low stool opposite him. She had to look up to him due to his height advantage.

"I can't stay late as I've work tomorrow," she said quietly.

"Not a very auspicious start to the evening."

"Sorry. What did you want to meet about?" she asked before taking a large gulp of the dry white wine, which was akin to vinegar in her mouth.

"I didn't know there had to be something specific. As I told you the other evening, I need people I can trust to talk to. I can trust you, can't I, Lily?"

"Of course you can."

"In my position I often find women fawning over me. It's the power that's intoxicating. Women like power," he leant towards her. "Is that what you like about me, Lily, my power?"

She sipped her wine and locked eyes with him over the rim.

"I'll take that as your answer," he said as he sat back and ran his finger round the rim of the glass. "So when are you going to invite me back to your place?"

Lily's heart thudded in her temples as she searched for an answer to his question. "I don't normally have people round. I don't socialise much."

"That's as maybe, but I want to visit you. And what Walker wants, Walker gets," he said as a tiny trickle of saliva seeped out of the edges of his mouth. "I've noticed you looking on edge in my company. Do I scare you?"

"Not at all. I'm generally nervous around new people, and I've almost forgotten how to socialise."

"Believe me, you'll soon remember what to do," he said as he stood up to get some more drinks.

Adrenalin surged through her body and it took all of her strength not to get up and run out of the door. In preparation she leant down and picked up her handbag. As she straightened up, Walker's hand pressed down on her shoulder.

"Not thinking about leaving, are you?" He placed the drink in front of her and his hand lingered on her shoulder, giving it a forceful squeeze before releasing it.

"I can't stay for long as I have to be up for work tomorrow."

"So you keep saying," he replied.

She gripped her handbag tighter with both hands as Walker stared at her. She felt he'd seen every secret in her soul.

"You must come to the party headquarters on Saturday morning as we are going to have a TEP stall in the town square. You can hand out leaflets."

Excuses raced through her brain but not one of them developed into a tangible phrase.

"Anyway, I'll remind you Friday evening when I come round to yours at eight. You can cook me a meal."

Lily forced the sweetest smile from her lips and tilted her head. "What do you like to eat?"

"Nothing poncey, I'm a meat and two veg man."

In a bid to hurry away, she took large gulps of her wine. The alcohol flooded her delicate system and made her head spin.

"Do you know where I live?"

"Of course. You clearly underestimate me."

Lily finished her wine with two more large gulps and proclaimed that she was going. She thanked him for the evening and gingerly made her way out, holding onto the wall as she did so.

Hugh and Faith finished their fish risotto and sat in the conservatory looking out onto the garden. The twinkling lights under trees and shrubs made the view mysterious and romantic.

"We haven't been out for a meal in a while, how about this Friday?" suggested Hugh.

"Maybe."

"It would give you a rest before having everyone round on Saturday."

"We'll see."

Hugh found her dismissive replies tiresome. He wanted his dynamic wife back. He wondered who'd taken her?

"Do you fancy a drink?"

"A cup of tea would be nice."

Hugh had meant an alcoholic beverage, and he suspected she'd guessed that. He reluctantly got up to make her a tea and pour himself a beer. He used a silver tankard bought by Faith for his fortieth birthday. Faith had the words "Happy 40th BD, Darling" engraved on it, but those words now felt hollow when they were once filled with sentimental pride.

"What book are you reading this week?" he asked as he placed the cup of tea on the side table.

"Pardon?"

"I said what book are you reading for the group?"

"Oh that. *The Bell Jar*, by Sylvia Plath."

"That's rather gloomy."

Attic of the Mind **85**

"I'm enjoying it immensely. I find that Plath speaks to me."

Hugh picked up the local paper and browsed the front cover.

"Local election in a couple of weeks. Have we got our voting cards yet?"

"Yes, they're on the mantelpiece."

He flicked through a few more pages whilst Faith continued to stare out at the garden.

"For God's sake, Faith, connect with me."

She jumped at the strength of his voice. "There's nothing wrong with me. Stop hounding me, will you."

"Hounding you," he stood up and paced around. "I just want you to talk to me and to be the tactile person you used to be. I feel you are keeping something from me."

"Oh grow up. I can't fawn around you like your patients. Sometimes I have worries that I need to think about. My life doesn't revolve around you," she replied as she slammed her cup of tea down, sloshing the liquid into the saucer. "I'm going for a bath. And by the way, stop bloody clenching your jaw. It drives me mad."

As she slammed the door, he screwed up the newspaper and threw it at the floor with all the force available to him.

He dropped into his armchair and closed his eyes to see images of his wife in the arms of another man. He felt sick inside, and the beer was doing little to stultify his melancholy.

Lily felt guilty about phoning in sick, and when she stated that she had a migraine, it wasn't far from the truth. Hugh said not to worry, Faith would cover for her. He even offered to bring over some stronger pain relief, but she declined his offer. Her head was pounding and her eyes felt as though they were going to be pushed out of their sockets.

Walker was coming later that evening, and she was struggling to focus on the task in hand. Her body was fatigued and her hands trembled. She was grateful that she'd bought the food and wine on the way home from work the previous day. She'd planned a roast chicken dinner which she thought he would be satisfied with.

The texture of the raw chicken felt like the skin of an old man, and she imagined that's what Walker's skin would feel like. The thought of his flesh made her heave in powerful convulsions.

Her house didn't need much of a tidy as she had few possessions. There were no photos of her parents or of her as a child. She had very little need of such frippery. She'd purchased a bouquet of flowers to put in the crystal vase on the console table in the bay window.

Time flew faster than desired. The last time she remembered looking at the clock it was eleven fifteen and suddenly it was seven thirty.

She dressed in a conservatory manner, with navy blue Capri pants, metallic bronze ballet pumps and a Breton jumper. Her hair was coiffed with its usual finesse and her nails were freshly painted with a French manicure. She liked the way her ribs were beginning to protrude quite prominently through her jumper, and the slimness of her wrists gave her an overall air of fragility.

Lily sat bolt upright at the kitchen table and watched the inevitable time tick away on the oversized clock on the wall. At exactly eight o'clock, the doorbell rang. She stood up, smoothed her jumper down, and then smoothed down her hair before taking the dream-like steps to her front door. *Let the games begin.*

Chapter Sixteen

Walker strutted into Lily's house as though he owned the place. He didn't wait to be shown into the lounge, he just moved around the space like a prowling lion.

Lily was worried her trembling hands would give her away.

"Not what I'd expected. Minimalist and unrevealing," he said.

"Why, were you expecting a replica *Miss Marple* home with pill boxes and bone china on display?"

"Not quite that, but I imagined some clutter, a more homely approach perhaps."

"Appearances can deceive. Would you like a drink?"

"A beer."

Lily blushed as she realised she'd only bought wine, so she asked his preference between white and red.

He raised his coarse eyebrows. "Not bothered which, both taste like gnat piss to me."

Lily opened the red and poured out two large glasses. The aroma of the chicken cooking with garlic and herb wafted around the room, filling the void that was sucking the life out of her.

"There aren't any clues about your past around the place. I'm curious, who lies behind Lilith Fields?"

"No one of interest. I'm an only child. I studied to be a medical secretary. I've never been married, and I dislike pets."

"Succinct."

"I'm more interested in you," said Lily as she allowed her eyes to look directly. "I find you hard to read."

"Do you? I'm an enigma to you, am I? I think you're teasing me and it doesn't suit you."

Lily sensed his hackles rise, but she begged herself to remain calm.

She smiled as she got up to serve the meal. She plated up the food, ensuring that Walker had an adequately vast portion, whilst she just had mere morsels dotted around the plate with the merest sliver of chicken. She covered the gaps on her plate with gravy, a trick she learnt a long time ago.

"You're a good cook," he said between bulging mouthfuls.

"Thank you."

"What plans do you have for your future?" he asked, gravy dribbling down his chin.

As most of Lily's life after Poplar Ward had revolved around finding her perpetrator and bystander to exact her revenge, she'd never given any thought to her future. *What to say?*

"My future is as my life is now. I want nothing more."

"Not even a husband or children, or is it too late already?"

She took umbrage at that last comment but brushed it off. "You can dissolve a marriage but you can't dissolve parenthood. I have never wanted anyone to be that dependent on me."

Walker finished his last forkful then pushed his plate to one side. His trained eye noticed that Lily had a poor appetite, and the little tricks she used to hide her discomfort around food failed to fool him.

"Are there any seconds?"

"Yes, there's plenty." She rose and took away his plate to refill it with a second portion. Her stomach lurched as she poured tepid, gloopy gravy over the mound of food.

She sat opposite him with good grace and sipped her wine whilst she watched him shovel food into his cavernous, black hole.

"I was wondering what this evening was in aide of?"

"Come, come, woman, I'd have thought it was obvious."

Lily shifted around in her chair and her toes scrunched up in her shoes.

"A man like me and a lonely woman like you . . ."

"I'm not lonely," she snapped as she clenched her fists in her lap.

"Really? I don't see postcards from friends on the fridge. You don't go out much, if at all, and you jog alone."

She took a deep breath and wound strands of her hair around her finger as she heard the wealth of information he spouted about her.

"How do you know so much about me?"

"I have a woman checked out before I really get to know her. A man in my position has to."

"I'm no threat, I just admire your party," she replied, pinching her thumb until it was bright red.

"Good to hear. I don't admire women in general, but I like what they can offer me."

She refrained from asking what he meant. "Would you like tea or coffee to go with the cake?"

"Neither. You need to have beer in the house for my next visit. I'm off to the pub now, but I'll see you tomorrow at ten sharp at the headquarters."

As he rose, Lily was reminded of his intimidating colossal frame. She then stood up and smoothed down her hair before moving determinedly, yet calmly, towards the front door.

As they both stood side by side in the hallway, he turned to her and grabbed her by the shoulders. She stood transfixed before him as he planted his rubber-like lips on her mouth. He continued to hold her with his left hand whilst his right hand held the front door firmly closed. His mouth pushed into hers and his tongue darted in and out of her unenthusiastic mouth until she managed to pull away to gasp for breath.

"That took me by surprise. I'm not sure I'm ready for anything like this yet," she said as she looked at him cautiously, still panting for breath.

"I knew you were a tease." He pulled her in harder, covered her mouth with his and then bit her bottom lip until it bled and she couldn't help but wince.

"See you tomorrow," he whispered in her ear, leaving a trace of her blood on her lobe from his mouth.

He opened the door and strode out. She was sure she heard him chuckle in his low, gravelly manner.

Lily shut the door and locked it quickly. The fetid stench of his saliva crawled up her nostrils. She ran upstairs into the bathroom and spewed what little food she'd ingested into the bleached white bowl. Her bony knees hurt with the pressure of kneeling on the vinyl floor, but she was too weak to stand and crouch over. Blood had congealed on her bottom lip and she couldn't extinguish the smell of him on her face; even her vomit smelt of him.

She tore the clothes from her body and stood in a scalding hot shower which stung her scalp. The steaming water mixed with her salty tears. Her mind was numb and her body was repulsed, but she had to keep going. She was getting closer to her destination.

Dressed casually in jeans and a tight-fitting jersey top, Lily made her way to the TEP headquarters. Her mind was like steel and her body moved like a willowy branch of honeysuckle bending in the breeze.

She buzzed to be let into the building and then as she mounted the stairs, she took shallow breaths, anxious about coming face to face with her tormentor once more. On entering the room she saw him. She smiled with her mouth but not with her eyes as she walked over to him.

"What would you like me to do?" she asked.

"I shall be wandering around the square talking to shoppers. You can help run the stall, hand out leaflets, and look pretty."

Her facial muscles twitched but she managed to smile once more. Picking up the canvas bag full of leaflets, she could feel her heart throbbing in her neck and she panicked that she might faint.

As she stood in close proximity to Walker, she noticed his face began to glisten with sweat. He bent down and put his mouth so close to her ear that she could almost hear his heartbeat reverberating in his damp cavity.

"I'm going to have you tonight, no excuses."

She swallowed hard before speaking. "I'm afraid you'll have to wait; I'm going for dinner at a friend's house."

He eyed her suspiciously. "Very convenient. I'll find out if you're lying."

He pulled away and bellowed to the group that they needed to get going.

Lily's head continued to feel light and fuzzy so she steadied herself on the table.

"Are you all right? You look pale," asked Rachel.

"I'm okay. I just skipped breakfast, that's all."

"Here, have an apple, it's better than a coffee, I've got loads to keep us going." Rachel threw the red shiny apple to Lily then bit into one herself.

As Lily opened her mouth to bite into the apple, Walker watched from across the room as her lips moved over the fruit. They locked eyes as she ripped a morsel from the apple and chewed it slowly. She was filled with dread as she watched another coating of sweat cover his obnoxious features.

They all marched out together carrying political paraphernalia. Some men had left earlier to put up the stall. Lily decided to stick with Rachel as much as possible seeing as she was the only person who acknowledged her.

"I really do think Finlay's got the hots for you," Rachel whispered as they walked closely together on the narrow pavement.

"What on earth gives you that idea?"

"I've noticed the way he is around you. You know, breathing heavier, red sweaty face, and talking to you quietly in the ear."

"My, you are observant."

"Well, do you fancy him?"

"He's not my type really."

"I think he's cool."

"He's much too old for you. I think he may prefer an older woman somehow."

Rachel looked crestfallen, and a tinge of pity for the girl coloured Lily's heart briefly. It was a short-lived moment as they had arrived in the town square.

Lily furtively looked around to see whether she knew anybody in the milling crowd. She noticed a crowd of gangly youths gathered outside the baker's. They kept looking her way, making her feel uncomfortable.

As time marched on, she watched the decline of humanity around her as people seemed to agree with most of Walker's policies. She had to keep deceiving the group by handing out leaflets with a smile, and giving balloons to children, which made her feel dirty and damned.

Walker paraded around and showed no fear when some people yelled abuse in his direction; the antagonistic behaviour only buoyed him further and his swagger became more exaggerated.

Lily had lost sight of the group of youths when suddenly she felt something hit her on the shoulder. She looked at her arm to see a smashed egg oozing down her jacket sleeve. She had no time to say anything before the whole of the TEP group were pelted with eggs and over-ripe tomatoes.

Groceries rained down on them and verbal abuse serrated their ears. Some of the women clambered behind the stall as the well-aimed eggs stung their scalps and faces.

Some of Walker's mob men scuffled with the youths and a fight ensued. Teeth clattered and blood spurted. Cries of defiance and abuse swung from one group to the other. Walker's men rammed some of the youths into the surrounding walls, flattening their noses and splintering their heads. Another youth was sent crashing through a shop window, sending shards of glass onto the cobbled stones. Onlookers shrieked, and mothers gathered their children, herding them to safety.

The shrill sound of sirens rang in the air and Lily and Rachel crouched behind the stall whilst missiles continued to fly over them. Lily peered over the table top and witnessed the police separating the brawling crowd. She noticed that Walker had moved to the edge of the action, grinning at the unfolding events. His coat was surprisingly clean.

She watched as a policeman walked up to Walker and entered into a discussion, whilst the fighting men and youths were kept apart and arrested. The guilty parties were taken away in police vans.

"That was exciting," gasped Rachel. "Do you think we'll have to leave now?"

"I do hope so," replied Lily.

Rachel raised her eyebrows and cocked her head.

"You don't mean that."

"I'm not a fan of violence, that's all."

Rachel shrugged her shoulders and handed Lily another apple. As they stood there crunching on the fruit, Walker strode over to them.

"You both look a mess," he said as he eyed them up and down.

"Are we staying?" asked Rachel with her doe-eyes gazing up at him. "Only Lily is scared by the fighting," she continued as she pointed a finger at her.

"I wouldn't have thought you'd be intimidated by a few fists and missiles."

"Looks can deceive," said Lily.

"Indeed," he replied before he moved on to talk to the few men that were left.

"Oh, he so fancies you; you're so lucky."

Lily wanted to tell her how lucky she herself was not to be involved with him, as he would damage such a tender young thing. *He used to like them young*, she thought to herself. She hoped his tastes had changed, for Rachel's sake.

She was so lost in her own thoughts that she didn't hear Rachel say that they were to pack up and return to the headquarters.

They packed up rapidly with the shoppers eyeing them suspiciously, whilst the remaining men stood around smoking and kicking their heels on the cobbles. By the time they got back to headquarters, both women were red in the face and gasping for breath. Lily quickly stashed the paraphernalia away, wished Rachel a good weekend, then moved quickly to leave.

She met Walker half way down the stairs and as she squeezed passed him, he grabbed her wrist, gripping it too tightly for comfort.

"I'm watching you," he whispered in her ear. "I'll know if you're lying about tonight. I'll be at your place tomorrow at seven instead."

As he gave her wrist another squeeze and twist, he whispered. "Don't toy with me, bitch." He released her and marched up the stairs, two by two.

Lily's heart pounded in her ears as she continued down the stairs and pushed her way out of the door. The cooler air buffeted her in the face, making her gasp for breath. She could feel the memory of tears in her eyes but her resolve ordered her to keep going and take one step at a time. She had to deal with the evening ahead first. Tomorrow was another day for another plan.

Chapter Seventeen

Faith flitted around putting the finishing touches to the ostentatious table setting. She always demanded perfection and her home was a reflection of her inner machinations to control her environment.

Hugh had run a few errands for last minute necessities, such as bouquets of pure white lilies and collecting Faith's silk dress from the dry-cleaners. He was glad to be out from under her feet.

Faith had every confidence in her menu for the evening. She'd prepared a smoked trout mousse to go with asparagus tips for the starter, followed by beef wellington and seasonal vegetables. For dessert she'd made profiteroles and a chocolate sauce. They were to commence with champagne and canapés to celebrate the success of the clinic.

"It's all looking so wonderful," said Hugh as he eyed the immaculately dressed table. He moved towards Faith to hug her, but she backed away protesting that he'd mess up her expertly tied up chignon with corkscrew tendrils framing her face and the nape of her neck.

Hugh's shoulders drooped as he stuffed his hands in his trouser pockets. There was so much he wanted to say to his wife but he knew it was futile whilst she was on an entertaining mission. He had no choice but to laze around in his study and fling himself into his brown leather chair. He drummed his fingers on the desk whilst he thought about the evening ahead. He hoped that Nathan would be on his best behaviour, especially as Faith had gone to so much trouble.

He moved on to thinking about Lily. He wondered how she would be in the social setting rather than the comfort zone of the clinic. He wondered whether she'd be the same efficient, quiet woman, or did she hide an outgoing and vivacious personality that only came out after dark.

Faith popped her head around the study door. "It's time you had a shower and got ready; they'll be here in an hour."

He obeyed without question or bad grace. Faith was always right, in his mind.

Lily was the first guest to arrive. She stood outside the house twirling her hair around her fingers as she waited for the door to be answered.

"Hello, Lily, do come in," said Hugh as he leant in and kissed her on the cheek, as he blushed.

"Faith, this is Lily, the clinic wonder woman."

"I'm not really," said Lily timidly.

"I know Hugh greatly appreciates your work. It can't be easy working for two men."

It was Lily's turn to blush ferociously as she clasped her hands tightly together in a prayer-like position.

Hugh was handing out long-stemmed, crystal champagne flutes when Nathan's taxi pulled up on the gravel driveway. Lily was glad of the distraction. She loathed being the centre of attention.

Nathan breezed in and greeted everyone with his boyish charm and his glinting hazel eyes that resurfaced periodically. Faith smiled cordially, but kept her distance. Hugh suggested they move to the conservatory where a table of canapés awaited them.

"You look vaguely familiar, Lily. I can't think where I've seen you before."

"I think I just have a familiar-looking face without actually being so." Lily hoped that Faith hadn't spotted her on the TEP stall.

Surrounded by the splendour of Hugh and Faith's home, Lily felt uncomfortable and out of place. She clung onto the crystal flute for fear of spilling or dropping it. Her cheeks were pink and she could feel the pin-like prickles on her skin.

She felt like a fraud amongst the group whom all appeared to have balance in their lives. But she remembered that the façade could hide a host of problems. After all, she was one such successful actor in the play of riddles.

"You look pleased about something, Lily," said Hugh. "Care to share?"

"Oh, it's nothing. I was just thinking about my garden. You have such a beautiful one."

"It's all down to Faith, really." Hugh smiled at his wife but she seemed miles away in thought.

Faith stood up to retreat to the kitchen and asked Lily to go with her.

"You know, I'm sure we've met before," Faith started. "I'm not normally wrong about that kind of thing."

"I'm sorry to disappoint, but I have no recollection of you. And I mean that in the nicest possible sense."

They both laughed nervously and Faith's shoulders relaxed. Although knowing that Nathan was in the next room she could never totally relax.

"How are you finding working for the two men?"

Lily found the term "men" jarred in her mind as she always thought of them as doctors.

"I'm enjoying it immensely, they're both very kind."

"What, even Nathan?"

"Well yes, I mean, don't you find him kind?"

"Perhaps I just know him too well to see him in that manner."

Lily shrugged at that remark and then followed Faith into the dining room where the starters were already laid out.

"You must sit down now, I won't allow you to help; you're not at work now."

Lily smiled and appreciated Faith's sentiment, even though she sounded a touch condescending. Faith placed Lily next to Hugh and opposite Nathan, whilst she herself sat next to Nathan.

The meal exceeded expectation in taste and presentation. Lily tried to eat as much as she could, whilst trying to hide as much as she could in little piles. All she could think about was the extra jogging she'd have to do.

Lily felt excluded from a lot of the conversation as the others got lost in their pasts when they all met and experienced a hedonistic lifestyle. Lily learnt that the men went to Ridgemore Hospital in London and that Faith met them towards the end of their studies. Faith used to work as an advocate for a mental health charity, where she supported people who'd been sectioned. Through her work, she'd been invited to a soiree where she met Hugh and Nathan.

"You've been measured with your alcohol intake Nathan, are you unwell?" Faith asked.

"No, I'm just behaving as requested," he replied, casting a swift glance in Hugh's direction. "Besides, I'm not an alcoholic; I'm just a periodic heavy drinker."

"Is that what you call it?" sniped Faith.

The negativity in the room was palpable, so Hugh made a diversion.

"Shall we move back to the conservatory for coffee?"

He made a cafeteria of fresh coffee whilst the other three sat quietly looking at their own reflections in the conservatory windows.

"So, Lily, tell me about yourself," said Faith.

Nathan diverted his gaze from the reflection of himself in the window, and turned towards Lily expectantly.

"I've had quite a dull life really. I've lived all around the country to follow work. That's about it, really."

"No children, no husband, no ex, and no boyfriend?"

"No to all four. I'm happy as I am."

"Fair enough," said Nathan. "I feel the same way."

"Yes, but the difference is that you've had a wife." Faith tilted her head as she looked at him.

Hugh walked in just in time to hear the last comment.

"I think Faith misses Carol's company," he offered.

"That's not true. You really don't know me at all, do you?" Faith hid her face behind her coffee cup.

Nathan was perturbed by the outburst and Lily cringed in her seat. Faith's face was puce and showed signs of strain around her red-rimmed eyes. Resisting the urge to leave the group and retire to bed, Faith opened the box of chocolates Lily had kindly brought and passed them around. After a few chocolates and a refill of coffee, Nathan decided it was time he headed home.

"Shall we share a taxi?" he asked Lily who was sitting bolt upright in the armchair.

Lily thought she saw relief flicker in Hugh's eyes, and she felt sorry for him but she wasn't sure why. Hugh got up and phoned a taxi for the pair whilst he paced up and down the hallway.

"I've had a lovely evening," said Lily as she put an arm through her coat sleeve.

"It's been a pleasure meeting you. Don't take any funny business from Nathan when you're in the taxi."

Lily had no idea how to respond to that and hoped that a smile would suffice.

The sound of the taxi horn was a merciful noise, and the goodbyes were brief.

Nathan and Lily sat together in the back of the taxi as a quiet unease permeated the atmosphere. Lily felt the paradoxical sentiments of feeling safe in the company of Nathan as well as hating the very sound of his breathing so close to her. She wanted to scratch his face and rip out his heart to see whether it was the wizened morsel he purported to have. *You've forgotten all about me*, she thought to herself.

The taxi arrived at Lily's house first and she offered to pay her share, but Nathan was adamant he would pay. The generous offer bestowed upon him one of Lily's enigmatic smiles that occasionally graced her face. A smile that was long forgotten.

For a brief second, Nathan thought she might invite him in for a coffee. But the offer never came. Lily darted inside her house, fearful of being watched

The house felt cold and empty compared to where she'd just been, but she had no time to feel sorry for herself.

She resisted going to the knife drawer in the kitchen, choosing instead to go to the bathroom to splash cold water over her face.

As she looked in the mirror, the haunted look in her eyes reflected her empty soul. She missed the girl she used to be, but maybe tomorrow she would be a step closer.

Chapter Eighteen

Nathan was unusually hangover free, considering he'd been socialising the night before. He had promised Hugh he'd behave and he believed he'd been the personification of perfection. He had found the evening rather dull, with the most successful part being the food.

However, his normally relaxing Sunday morning was spoilt by his concern about Walker getting onto the council and exerting his new found power. He massaged his temples and closed his eyes in an attempt to soothe away the searing, swelling tension that was rotting his mind.

Perhaps he should discuss his options with Hugh, although Hugh seemed preoccupied with his own life. "Or should I say wife," he uttered to himself.

He made himself some coffee and collected the Sunday paper from his doormat.

As he picked up the paper he saw an envelope lying on the doormat. Trepidation filled him as he picked it up, and although the envelope bore no name, he knew it was for him.

The envelope felt lumpy and he guessed it was another piece of fabric. He tore it open and was repulsed to find a lock of matted strawberry-blonde hair. Nausea swept over his stomach and throat. So much so that he could taste vomit in his mouth.

As quick as his fingers had grasped the hair did he throw it on the floor and stare at it in horror. He took slow, steady breaths to regulate his heartbeat and emotions. He cautiously picked it up again and studied it. He knew then that the sender must be the woman herself. *If only I could remember her name.*

Nathan moved to the lounge and flopped into the chair, casting his mind back to his days on Poplar. He couldn't recall any names, and the faces were blurred. He certainly had no recollection of hair colour. His main memory was of the young woman with the pale grey eyes. He remembered her eyes as they were an unusual colour and spoke volumes. But to his chagrin he ignored every word.

The hair looked naturally blonde, and so he racked his brain to remember any recent encounter with such a woman. He knew he was a bit of a sex junkie and most of the women he bedded were blonde, but bleached that way. Perhaps she bleached hers now? He shuddered to think that he may have inadvertently slept with her.

He placed the hair back in the envelope and put it with the piece of nightie fabric. He wondered whether Walker had been blessed with the same personal delivery.

The solitude of the day made him aware of a mounting resentment and crushing inadequacies. He recognised that he was still afraid of Walker after all those years. Recognition that both angered and shamed him.

Lily had done an extra-long jog to compensate for the previous calorific evening. As she stood in her kitchen with sweat running down her neck and scrawny chest, she placed her hands over her ribs to feel the bony protrusions lift up and down as she panted.

The urge to cut her flesh was building up and pulsating to every nerve ending, but she knew that Walker must not see her with fresh wounds. So to satisfy her craving she placed rubber bands around her wrists and pulled on them hard until she allowed the band to snap back onto her wrist. The action sent messages of painful comfort to her brain.

She sipped the hot lemon water whilst she contemplated the evening ahead. She wondered whether Walker was falling for her and that made her feel sick. She needed to draw him in to move things along.

She took out a bottle of sleeping tablets left over from her past and began to ground six tablets with a mortar and pestle. She then scooped the powder into a small paper cone ready to use later.

She then decided to distract herself by preparing the meal. She set out two casserole pots to cook the stew in. The first one would contain a small amount of beef, and the second would contain cat meat.

It was a chance find that led Lily to that recipe. During her morning jog she came across a cat in the road with its head caved in after being hit by a car. She scooped it up and wrapped it in her sweatshirt. Although it would most likely do Walker little or no harm, it would give her pleasure to watch him devour the meat.

With the stews simmering away gently, she then painted her finger and toe nails a fiery red colour. Her bony hands and feet looked strangely comical, yet satisfyingly menacing, with the red painted claws.

At six thirty, Lily poured herself a large glass of red wine and put some classical music on in the background. She spritzed more perfume on her neck and décolleté and then added a slick of gloss on her lips.

Standing by the fireplace, she took a few large sips of wine and then stared at her eyes in the mirror. She wondered how it would feel to leave her eyes naked to the world. However, she wasn't ready to give too much away too soon. The emerald green contact lenses had to remain in place for now.

Like clockwork, Walker arrived at her house exactly at seven. Lily's cheeks flushed as she walked towards the front door. She could see the frame of his giant outline through the stained-glass panel.

She opened the door to admit the once again empty-handed Walker.

"Good evening, Finlay, do come in."

He strode in and walked straight into the lounge. She followed him calmly but remained standing whilst he made himself comfortable on the sofa.

"Would you like a beer?"

"Glad to see you are catering to my needs."

She went to the kitchen and poured him a beer to which she then added the white powder from the paper cone. She poured herself a wine and then she placed everything on a tray, including a bowl of extra-salted peanuts.

Walker quaffed his beer and threw handfuls of peanuts into his mouth. Lily sat serenely watching him.

"I don't know much about you. Have you ever been married?" she asked quietly.

"Women are for spending time with but not marrying."

"Why's that?"

"Because as they age they become ugly, moaning, bossy bores."

"Is that how you see me?"

"Not yet, but give it time."

"Let me get you another beer whilst I put the greens on."

Lily returned with his glass and handed it to him. She sat back in her chair and watched him with her enquiring eyes.

"How will you feel if you don't get elected?"

"Haven't given it a thought, 'coz I know I'll win."

Lily could hear the water boiling in the pan so she excused herself and went through to serve up. She lit the candle in the centre of the table then called him through. She observed him tuck into his meal when he asked, "What meat is this?"

"Beef."

Walker loaded his fork with meat and dumplings and washed it down with yet another beer. She watched as he rubbed his forehead and stifled a yawn. She continued providing him with tainted beer and offered him more food, which he gradually refused with a wave of a quivering hand.

Lily gazed straight into his eyes whilst stroking her hair. His eyelids looked heavy as though they were thunder clouds bearing in over the shoreline. The sound of the doorbell pierced the soporific atmosphere. She chose to ignore the intrusion and hoped that whoever it was would go away.

She buried her face in her wine glass to mask her discomfort when the bell rang again, only for a bit longer.

"Aren't you going to answer that?"

Reluctantly, she left the table and went to the door.

"Doctor Rine," she said quietly. "What are you doing here?"

"I don't really know, I think it might be the scotch." His voice faltered slightly and his arm pushed against the door frame to steady himself.

"Well, it's not terribly convenient; I've got a friend round for a meal."

"Sorry, I'll go. I just wondered . . . it felt like things were left unsaid last night in the taxi. Do you know what I mean?"

"No, not really."

Her spine tingled as she sensed Walker's presence behind her.

"I really must go. I'll see you in the morning." She felt rude closing the door in his face but she didn't want Walker's presence to be detected. She smoothed down her dress and her hair before returning to the kitchen. She saw that he'd helped himself to another beer which he was drinking steadily.

"Sorry about that, it was just my neighbour."

"At this hour?"

"His mother's dying and he needs someone to talk to at times. I'll see him tomorrow."

"Proper little angel, aren't you."

She didn't like his tone of voice so she just smiled and cleared away the plates. She served up her homemade sherry trifle and placed the bowls on the table.

"How about an Irish coffee? We can drink it in the lounge," she ventured.

"You like your alcohol, don't you."

"Only when socialising."

"Talking of which, how was last night?"

"It was interesting," she blushed.

"Did Doctor Rine behave himself?"

"That's a bizarre question, but yes, everyone was pleasant."

Lily made the Irish coffees and suggested they move to the lounge. She made a point of sitting on the opposite end of the sofa whilst they drank their coffee. She sat stiffly, her neck straining to hold her head up high. In her peripheral vision she saw Walker yawn but he'd only drunk part of his coffee.

"Not to your taste?" queried Lily.

"The cream makes it a bit poncey for me."

"It's just . . ." She stopped short as she saw an unexpected fire behind his eyes.

"It's just what? Just more alcohol for me to consume to make me sleepy?" He turned towards her and leaned over her diminutive figure with his grotesque frame, breathing alcoholic breath in her face.

"I . . . I don't know what you mean."

"Really," he replied as he grasped her wrists and twisted them outwards. Lily's face contorted with pain, and as she tried to pull away from him, his grasp tightened.

"I don't know what your game plan is, but you don't know what a force I am. And for the record, a man my size needs a lot more to knock him out."

Lily felt herself go limp like a rag doll, which only seemed to anger him further.

"Fight, woman," he yelled as the back of his hand caught the side of her face.

"Why are you doing this?" she stammered, as she felt her split lip with the tip of her finger.

"Because I can. Now tell me why you're plying me with drink." His menacing eyes tore into hers and compelled her to answer.

"I thought you might like me and I haven't been with a man for years. I was nervous and thought I could put you off wanting to go to bed with me until I was ready. It was silly really."

He moved back into the sofa but continued holding her wrists.

"You're a stupid woman; I will have sex with you when I want to. It's not up to you."

Lily's throat closed up and she felt sick. Her hands began to feel numb as the firmness of his grip had impeded the circulation.

Just at that moment, his cell phone rang. He let go of her wrists and reached for his phone. "What? I said I wasn't to be disturbed."

Lily tried to hear the inaudible voice on the other end of the phone whilst she rubbed her wrists and thought about her next move.

"You're in luck, woman, I'm needed at HQ."

She didn't want to delay him by asking why, so she stood up shakily to see him out. Walker caught the coffee table with his leg, knocking over a glass, spilling Irish coffee and double cream all over the floor.

He followed her into the hallway and pushed past her before throwing the weight of his body against hers and pinning her to the wall. She gasped for breath as his hairy forearm pressed against her throat.

"Now listen, you little bitch. I say what happens and when. As long as I am interested in you, you have to do as I say, otherwise the journey gets heavy going. Understand?"

Lily nodded as much as she could and blinked her eyes slowly to confirm she understood his demands. As he moved away from her, she exhaled loudly and slumped down the wall.

Walker left the house and closed the door firmly behind him. As she heard his footsteps recede she allowed the hot tears to tumble down her cheeks and the gut wrenching sobs to burst forth from her mouth.

It had all gone so wrong. He wasn't knocked out by the drugs so she could finish what she'd started. She was Walker's victim once more.

She picked herself up and proceeded to the kitchen to take a sharp knife from a drawer. Slowly, she ascended the stairs and locked herself in the bathroom.

Chapter Nineteen

It was a warm day, but due to her self-inflicted wounds, Lily was wearing a long-sleeved blouse to work. The slices in her arms were quite severe and she required several layers of bandages to soak up the seeping blood.

She'd wanted to stay off work but as Nathan had called on her the previous day, she felt it would look like she was trying to avoid him if she didn't go in.

She arrived at the clinic and concealed herself at her desk, hoping to avoid the doctors. When Nathan entered, she greeted him without raising her head. He hesitated near her desk, thinking they may have a brief chat, but she looked engrossed in her paperwork.

Nathan entered his room and slumped in his chair. He was feeling anti-social and not relishing interacting with patients. However, he was concerned about Lily. She was distant and vague, and she wasn't wearing appropriate clothes for the current climate. He was wondering whether she was showing signs of being depressed.

He'd observed Lily's ever decreasing appetite, and his unease for her was growing. He hung around the kitchen at lunchtime, hoping to see her for the talk he never managed to finish the previous evening. A hint of embarrassment about that visit clung to his mind.

At last, Lily entered the kitchen and flicked the switch on the kettle. It was only when she turned towards the window, and the sunlight caught the side of her face, did Nathan notice the shadow of what looked like a bruise on her cheek bone. She'd obviously expertly covered it with make-up, but it was still subtly visible all the same. He also noticed that her bottom lip looked swollen and bore the mark of a newly formed scab.

"Are you okay, Lily? You look like you have a bruised cheek and cut lip, would you like me to take a look?"

She instinctively raised her hand to her cheek, feeling embarrassed that he'd seen it.

"No thanks, Doctor Rine. I'm ashamed to say a had more to drink than I should last night and I walked into a door." She turned to make her hot lemon water and to hide her flushed cheeks.

Nathan didn't believe a word, but sensed she'd closed down. "I'm sorry I interrupted your evening last night," he said in the hope of gleaning more information.

"Think nothing of it, Doctor Rine, you didn't interrupt anything special."

"I thought we'd agreed at Hugh's that you'd call us by our first names."

"Sorry, it just doesn't come naturally." She cast her eyes to the floor before picking up her mug and disappearing.

Nathan opened the kitchen window to allow a refreshing breeze to waft in. His daydreaming was interrupted by Lily calling out that he had a visitor in reception. Disgruntled by demands on his lunch break, he slowly ambled out and came face to face with Walker.

"And what can I do for you?" asked Nathan, clenching his fists behind his back.

"A word in private," replied Walker as he moved closer to Nathan, but not before darting his menacing eyes towards Lily.

They moved to Nathan's room and closed the door.

"I've spoken to some of the women you've slept with recently, and they all appear to have the same story about how you raped them. Now wouldn't it be harmful if that came out?"

Walker was leaning against the door as he spoke in his low gravely tone. Nathan knew what Walker was capable of, going on past experience. It all seemed so futile.

"I see you still play dirty."

"You exude fear just like you did back then. You are no opponent for me."

"No one would believe me capable of such atrocious actions."

"I've had you watched to know that you get drunk then hook up with drunk blondes. I know more of your behaviour than you do." He paused to emit a low laugh. "I am a stain on your blemish-free career. I will never be totally out of your life. I'm in the black and grey shadows that exist in your life." Walker rocked on the balls of his feet, extending his height even further.

"And one last thing. If I catch you hanging around Lily out of work hours, she'll suffer at my hands. You don't want that on your conscience, do you?"

"What's she got to do with any of this?"

"Nothing, but she's great leverage for my demands." And with that, Walker left the room and walked out of the clinic whistling inanely.

Nathan stood behind his desk shaking and sweating. He remained standing and rubbing his neck, with Walker's words of warning running around his head.

Lily had locked herself in the staff toilet with her ear pressed to the door to make sure she could hear Walker leave. With her breathing shallow her head began to spin. Her cheekbone throbbed as a reminder of his visit, leaving her feeling an emotional mess.

Nathan was sitting in his chair with his head in his hands. He had begun to wish that he had never been to Poplar and that he was in a less high-profile career. He wished he could think of a way out of Walker's web.

He cautiously opened the door and went to the kitchen. Lily jumped as he entered the room.

"I didn't mean to startle you," he said as he reached out to touch her arm. She flinched and backed into the wall. Feeling cornered, her eyes became wide and her mouth opened to release a silent scream.

Her reaction puzzled Nathan. He didn't wish to harm or frighten her, but it looked like he was doing both.

"Lily, what's wrong, please . . ."

She raised her hand and shook her head. "It's not you. I'm just feeling under the weather." She paused to swallow hard. "I was wondering whether I could go home?"

"Shall I get Hugh to drive you home?"

"No need. The fresh air will do me good."

Hugh entered the kitchen as Lily was leaving. Her head was bent down, so all she saw were his shoes.

"What's wrong with Lily? Have you upset her?"

"No," said Nathan indignantly. "I'm not the misogynist pig you make me out to be."

"Sorry. I'm just a little fractious at the moment."

Nathan raised his eyebrows and turned to look at their tiny garden. He noticed that Lily had been feeding the birds by hanging fat balls on the tree branches. The sight made him smile.

"Will Faith be able to cover reception this afternoon?"

"I should imagine so. Has Lily gone home then?"

"She's not feeling well."

"Nothing serious, I hope."

"You know how reticent she is about disclosing how she feels."

Hugh nodded and switched the kettle on. "Fancy a pint in The Crown after work?"

"Sure, but what about Faith?"

"She won't want to come."

Faith obligingly covered the afternoon surgery, but emitted cold vibes towards both of the men. Nathan could see that Hugh was finding the strain of the discord unbearable and it was a relief for everyone when the clinic closed.

As Faith whisked outside to return home, the frosty atmosphere disappeared with her. The doctors were only minutes behind her as they headed to The Crown.

Hugh brought a couple of pints to the table where Nathan sat observing people milling around the bar. Some looked lonely and lost whilst others thrived in being the loudest and the centre of attention. The people were unfamiliar to him, not like the patrons of The Spread Eagle. There he had an abundance of women to sleep with, only now he wondered how many of them he could trust.

The anonymity of casual sex allowed him to enter into that intimate sphere without the commitment. However, at nearly fifty he suspected more was expected from him. Sleeping with the twenty- or thirty-something women was an extravagant waste of time and moral fibre, let alone dangerous in light of Walker's involvement.

Unlike his friend, Nathan had squandered his marriage to a totally respectful and reasonable woman who demanded nothing more than attention and love. He gave her neither, and it didn't make him proud.

"I don't want to stay too long. I can't bear the thought of Faith having more free time to spend with another man," said Hugh.

"I really can't imagine Faith having an affair; there must be something else. Is it the baby issue?"

"She came to terms long ago about her infertility, and so did I, eventually. She's just not connecting with me."

"She did look preoccupied today."

"God, even you've noticed."

"Look, why don't you buy her some flowers and take her out for a meal. Be romantic and spontaneous."

"Hark at you. Nathan the bloody agony aunt!"

Nathan laughed at the comment, but deep down he wished he'd listened to his inner voice years ago. Hugh downed his drink and said that he needed to return home.

They left The Crown together and Hugh headed home whilst Nathan headed for The Spread Eagle.

Lily felt uneasy at home. She sensed Walker's eyes following her every move. She had spent the afternoon sitting curled up on the sofa with her knees under her chin, rocking back and forth. Her lip looked more swollen and her pallor had increased, highlighting the bluish tinge around her cheek bone.

As the afternoon turned into early evening, she felt a heightened sense of vulnerability. She cautiously moved from room to room checking that all the windows were shut and locked. The front door was secured with a bolt and chain.

She decided to try and eat a couple of lightly buttered crackers with a glass of water. The crackers only added a tasteless dryness to her already parched mouth.

The phone sent out its shrill tone. She picked up the receiver, feeling her calves tense as she did so.

"Hello," she uttered.

"You left work early so I missed you. I might come round later so don't go out," said Walker before he hung up.

Lily stood for a few minutes listening to the disconnected line before passing out.

A few minutes later, she woke up on the floor with the telephone receiver dangling over the table. She put her hand to her forehead and felt a warm streak of fluid on her fingertips. When she looked at them, she saw blood. Her head was throbbing and her elbow hurt from colliding with the floor.

She knew what would happen if Walker came round later and she was not prepared for that. She would have no time to drug him, not that that had worked before. She also had little time to get him drunk, although she suspected she'd need a brewery to do that.

As she tenderly bathed the cut on her forehead she noticed how she'd become a shadow of her former self. Her cheeks were sunken and hollow, and her bruised cheekbone protruded under her skin like the front of a battleship.

She had always contemplated killing herself, but she never found the strength to cut herself enough to bleed to death and she never had enough anti-depressants for an overdose. As she contemplated it once more, she knew her thoughts were pointless. She needed to do this one thing before she could say a peaceful goodbye to the world.

Her whole body shook with shredded nerves, and her vision blurred as she tried to focus on the clock. Time was against her.

She just knew that she couldn't face Walker that evening, let alone face the hours ahead wondering if and when he'd show up. The cut on her forehead had stopped bleeding and was forming a crust. She smoothed down her hair, grabbed her jacket and her handbag and then moved to the front door. She peered through the glass to check that no one was there and then she cautiously stepped out and locked the door behind her.

Her steps were rapid and determined whilst she continually checked for unwanted attention all around her. She remembered the pubs the doctors frequented and she was desperate to find them. She hadn't thought about what she'd say, but that didn't matter.

She arrived at The Crown first. A crowd of smokers dressed in suits stood outside talking loudly and blowing noxious fumes into the evening air. She walked through the group with her head bowed down and gripping onto her handbag.

Inside was quieter and dimly lit. As her eyes adjusted she scanned the room for the men. She prowled around checking out all the alcoves and bar stools. They were nowhere to be found.

She negotiated her way back through the smokers union and made her way down to The Shambles towards The Spread Eagle. The cobbled streets were littered with couples and groups searching for entertainment. She felt lonely and invisible, much as she had felt throughout her life.

As she passed the Minster, light refracted through the leaded window panes and Lily wondered whether her god would save her. *He hadn't bothered before, so why would he now?* she thought bitterly.

Another group of smokers stood outside The Spread Eagle, only Lily felt less comfortable around them in their leather biker jackets and chest length beards. With a deep breath of courage, she walked through the throng that parted for her. She was sure one of the men with a beer-barrel gut winked at her.

Inside was noisier than the previous pub. People were almost shouting to be heard over the jukebox playing Green Day.

People were standing in every available space making it hard for Lily to see the people who were seated. And then she saw him.

Clasping her hands together and taking a deep breath, she approached

Attic of the Mind **117**

Nathan who hadn't yet seen her. She followed his gaze and ascertained that a blonde at the bar had caught his eye, which didn't surprise her.

"Hello, Doctor . . . Nathan," she said so quietly that he didn't hear her. She moved into his view and then he saw her. His eyes widened as the recognition hit his brain.

"Lily, I didn't take you for a pub goer."

"I'm not. I was looking for you."

"Really?" His eyes darted around the pub to see who was watching them.

"You never told me what it was you wanted to say in the taxi."

Nathan pulled out a stool for her to sit on and then he offered to get her a drink, which she accepted. They sat there in a contemplative quietness which was in juxtaposition with the rabble around them. Nathan felt paralysed by the fear of saying the wrong thing to her, which confused him as he didn't usually care what people thought of him in his private life. He knew he needed to be more accommodating of other people's emotions, and perhaps he should start with the strangely enigmatic Lily.

"I feel perhaps we got off on the wrong foot and I've given you a bad impression of myself."

"More than you realise," she muttered.

Nathan found her response quietly incoherent and decided to embrace her indifference.

"I'm not a curmudgeonly guy really."

Lily smiled shyly and sipped her red wine. Her minute face disappeared into the bulbous wine glass so Nathan was unable to read her facial expression.

"Perhaps I wasn't putting my point across succinctly. I believe you dislike me, and I'm not sure why."

"I don't like people, generally. They tend to be two-dimensional, flimsy beings with little regard for their fellow men." She took another sip of wine. "I'm a bit of a recluse really. If I didn't need the income I wouldn't work."

Her bluntness and clarity of thought astonished him; he hadn't seen her like that before. Perhaps she was more like him than he realised, as he, too, liked to be on the fringe of society observing the diverse behaviours of mankind.

They were both so busy checking out who else might be in the vicinity that they didn't notice the other doing the same. They were both suspicious of any man who was overly muscular with a shaven head.

"Was there something else you wanted?" he asked.

"Well, I just wondered whether you'd like to come back for coffee and cake," she blushed ferociously.

He was taken by surprised. "Er . . . okay, why not?"

Both parties finished their drinks, awkwardly gulping down the liquid before putting their coats on.

Unbeknownst to one another, they were both trying to be nonchalant about whether they were being followed. Both had some relief at not being alone, but Lily knew Nathan wouldn't be able to shield her forever.

There were less people milling around the streets, and the Gothic architecture of the Minster looked more austere in the fading light. Nathan felt ill at ease, and arriving at Lily's reminded him that he could be putting her in grave danger.

"I'm sorry, but I can't come in. I've remembered some paperwork I must get done for tomorrow."

She didn't believe a word. He was never that diligent about paperwork when in the clinic. She wondered whether he'd recognised her and was scared away.

Her hand shook as she tried to put the key in the front door, eager to get inside. She was annoyed with herself for not leaving the hall light on.

Once inside, she fumbled around for the awkwardly positioned light switch and then locked the door carefully behind her. The house felt cold and was not the haven a home should be. She knew it wasn't too late for Walker to come round, so she decided to go to bed and leave the house shrouded in darkness.

She crept upstairs, listening for every alien noise the house could throw at her. Relief washed over her as she switched on the bathroom light and found the room to be just as she left it.

After brushing her teeth she spat out the toothpaste and rinsed out her mouth. As she raised her head she saw in the mirror the shadowy figure of Walker standing behind her.

Chapter Twenty

Lily spun around to find Walker towering above her. She caught her breath as the adrenalin surged around her body.

"I said I may come round later, but you went out all the same. That was very naughty of you."

"How did you get in? What do you want from me?"

"I'd have thought that was pretty obvious. Don't play the coy bitch with me."

Walker's imposing size appeared to increase as he blocked her exit. Everything sounded muffled as her hearing was impaired by the rushing of blood streaming through her ears. *Fight or flight*, she thought to herself, *fight or flight?* Her diminutive figure would be no match to his colossal mass so she decided to make a dash for freedom.

She pushed herself off from the washbasin and tried to dart past him. As she levelled with him he shot out his arm and grabbed her around the shoulders. His arm cut across her throat causing her to choke and gasp for breath.

"Don't be a stupid cow," he rasped as he swung her round to face him.

He clasped one hand across her mouth to stifle her screams. In the process of the struggle, the sleeve of her nightdress was torn so it hung off her shoulder.

With all the strength she could muster, she raised her knee and gave him a sharp blow in the groin. For a brief instant he was overcome by the intense pain radiating across his lower body.

He released her long enough for her to stumble out of the bathroom and head for the stairs. She tripped down a few steps and caught herself on the banister to regain her balance. She could feel Walker's presence close behind her and his grasping hands brushing across the back of her neck, only just missing the opportunity to grab her hair.

The loudest sound in the world at that moment to Lily was the beating of her own heart. As she hurtled towards the kitchen she could see salvation was within her grasp.

She just managed to get her fingertips to the knife drawer handle when Walker grabbed her by the upper arm and catapulted her against the kitchen wall. As she hit it, her teeth smashed together, just catching her bottom lip. Blood gushed out as if in surrender to the violence, and her life proverbially flashed before her eyes.

Walker raised his fist and swung it towards her face. She ducked towards her right so that his fist connected with the wall. He grunted on impact, but undeterred he pushed his palm under her chin and rammed her head upwards so that the top of her scalp grated against the wall. His other hand began to wrestle with her nightdress until he finally managed to rip it from her shuddering body.

The wall felt icy cold against her back, and any resolve she had to fight him had dissipated into a puddle on the floor.

The flash of exhilaration and malevolence in his eyes sent waves of tension rippling through her body. He then pulled away slightly and grabbed a handful of her hair directing her in a downward motion. She screwed her eyes up and held her breath, wishing that he would just kill her.

She could hear Walker's deep breathing and gnarling when suddenly the doorbell rang. Walker yanked her up and pinned her against the wall with his spade-like hand pressed firmly across her mouth.

The doorbell rang again so Lily, out of sheer desperation, bit into his fleshy palm and then screamed with all the decibels she could dredge up.

Nathan heard her scream from inside, so he banged his fists against the door, calling out as he did so. The door was locked so he wrapped his scarf around his fist and smashed it through the stained-glass panel. Shards of glass sprayed everywhere and splinters stuck in his scarf.

"Lily, Lily," he shouted as he unlocked, unbolted, and unchained the door.

Walker could hear Nathan getting closer, so he whispered in Lily's ear, "I'll be back you fucking bitch." And with that he bolted out of the kitchen door and disappeared into her garden.

She slid down the wall and held herself in a ball shape. No sound came from her mouth and no tears wet her face.

Nathan rushed in, crunching on the fragments of glass as he did so, and found Lily crouched on the kitchen floor.

"Good God, Lily, what's happened here?"

He removed his jacket and draped it around her shuddering naked body. He felt awkward and shocked.

"I'll call the police and then get you checked over at the hospital."

Lily managed to shake her head whilst keeping her eyes fixed upon the floor. "No police, I couldn't cope, please no."

"Let me get you at least more comfortable," he said as he attempted to take hold of her elbow to lift her up.

She flinched at his touch and recoiled away from him.

"I must help you in some way, this needs to be reported," he said as he crouched down to her level. He saw the congealed blood in the crook of her mouth and as he raised his hand to wipe it away, he saw the terror in her eyes. He took out his mobile and called the police.

Lily began to shuffle around. Pushing herself against the wall for support, she levered herself up and held Nathan's jacket tightly around her. With a painfully slow manner, she moved one foot in front of the other until she made it to the lounge.

Nathan dashed upstairs and found a dressing gown in her bedroom which he brought down and handed to her. As she stretched out her arm to take it, he noticed the slash marks around her wrist and up her forearm. Some looked recently inflicted whilst others were mere memories of past episodes.

He began to see her fragility that she had so carefully preserved from prying eyes. He wondered what else he did not know about her.

They sat in aftershock silence, awaiting the next wave of fear and apprehension to wash over them.

"I don't think you should be alone tonight," he said as he looked for a reaction from her. "I'll sleep down here." He kept looking at Lily but she seemed locked in a dark world where she had no control.

"Did you see what he looked like?"

Lily shook her head solemnly. She couldn't divulge anything to him as she had no reason to know a man such as Walker, it would open too many thorny questions which would require complex answers.

"Are you hurt anywhere? I hope to God the police find the bastard."

Tears began to well in her eyes as he spoke the emotive words. They bubbled up to the surface then rained down her cheeks, with each teardrop screaming the words she couldn't speak.

The police arrived and interviewed her in the presence of Nathan. Lily gave them scant clues and refused to go to hospital or be seen by the police doctor. They were stumped by her unwillingness to cooperate, but they knew that sexual assault cases were notoriously difficult, so they didn't push her. They left her contact details should she remember anything else.

Once the front door was temporarily repaired, Nathan managed to persuade Lily to go to bed with his assistance and then he grabbed some blankets and returned to the lounge.

He noted how sterile her home was and how it didn't offer up any clues to her background or lifestyle. She was an enigma.

The sofa wasn't quite long enough for him, so he curled up into the foetal position and tried to blot out the images of a broken Lily on the kitchen floor from his mind. Darkness brought temporary reprieve for him, but for Lily, who was sitting bolt upright on her bed, it was the beginning of another nightmare.

After an uncomfortable few hours, Nathan awoke with various parts of his body aching. He cursed his aging body. He strained to hear any movement upstairs, but the house had a deathly hush about it.

He called up to her but there was no reply. Warily, he mounted the stairs, calling her name gently several times. Her bedroom door was ajar, so he tapped on it and called to her. When no reply came, he pushed it open further so he could peer around.

Lily looked in a catatonic state, unable to connect with reality, as she sat up in bed.

"I'm going to make some coffee and I'll bring it up to you."

She remained mute and statue-like. He waited a few more seconds before descending to the kitchen.

Whilst navigating himself around a kitchen he didn't know, he called Hugh and told him they'd need Faith to cover for Lily for a while. He said he'd explain later.

As he searched through the cupboards for what he needed, he noted that there was very little in the way of sustenance. Cereal, bread, soup, crackers, and salad appeared to be the only sources of food available.

He returned upstairs to find a more engaged and coherent woman.

"Thank you for your help, I'll be okay now," she said.

She cupped her hands around the mug of coffee which she normally did not drink first thing. However, she inhaled the strangely familiar and comforting aroma, which reminded her of being a child sitting with her parents as they drank the black nectar.

"I can stay if you want. Hugh and Faith will cope."

"Really no, I'm fine. I've taken up enough of your time."

He wondered whether she was stronger than she looked, but then he reminded himself of the self-inflicted scars he'd seen and decided that she wasn't.

"Lily, you must know that I blame myself. If I'd come back for coffee you'd have been safe." He waited for some sign of redemption but it never came. He couldn't blame her.

"I'll pop back at lunchtime; perhaps I could bring you something to eat."

She smiled meekly and shook her head. Somehow, Nathan wasn't surprised. It felt wrong to leave her, but he didn't feel he could impose himself on her; she was not a child after all.

He returned home for a quick change and then he headed half-heartedly to the clinic.

Chapter Twenty-One

Nathan arrived slightly later than intended at the clinic to find a stony-faced Faith and some disgruntled patients waiting for him.

"Yes I know, sorry, Faith," he said as he dashed through the reception towards his room.

Hugh was receptive at lunchtime, mainly because he wanted to find out what had happened to Lily. Nathan recounted how she was attacked last night and that he needed to call in and check on her.

"Bloody hell. Are you sure she's okay being alone?"

"I offered to stay. But I want to check on her now," he called back as he headed out of the main door.

"What's going on?" asked Faith as she entered the kitchen.

"Lily was attacked in her home. It was lucky he was calling to see her, she could have been killed," replied Hugh as he retrieved his sandwiches from the fridge.

"Is there anything we should be doing for the poor woman?"

"Nathan seems to have it under control," he replied quietly.

As he pounded the pavement, Nathan began to worry that Walker had seen him with Lily. Was the attack a warning? He marched as fast as he could to get to Lily's house. He arrived to see that the front door was boarded up. A scar of evidence showing that last night wasn't a dreadful dream. He checked around to see if he'd been followed.

He rang the bell and waited. He wondered whether her reticence to open up was because she was still ridged with fear. He bent down and called through the letterbox to identify himself. Finally, he could hear the door being unlocked.

He saw how her translucent face did nothing to hide the battle scars of the previous night. Each wound silently shrieked out her pain.

"As promised, here I am."

Lily motioned for him to enter and then she returned to the kitchen. On the table, he saw a mug of water with a slice of lemon floating in it.

"You really should try and eat something," he said gently as he placed an egg and mayonnaise sandwich in front of her. He looked into her eyes and saw how the green looked even more vibrant against the harshness of her pale skin.

"Have the police been in contact?"

"No. Anyway, it won't come to much as I couldn't identify him."

Nathan looked around the room and saw evidence of a struggle embedded in the wall. He didn't think the police would be able to identify a punch mark but he was anxious that the perpetrator was caught.

Nathan made a coffee.

"I know what you're thinking, but I'd rather just move on from this episode. He won't come back since you scared him off, I'm sure," she said with a weak smile of false reassurance.

He wasn't so sure. "Would you like me to call in after work?"

"No, thanks. I'll be back at work tomorrow." She saw Nathan looked aghast. "I'll cover the damage to my face with make-up so don't worry."

"It's not that, I just don't think you'll be fit enough."

"I'd rather be at the clinic where I'm not alone and my mind will be occupied. I'll go crazy here on my own."

Nathan rubbed his chin and watched her carefully. She seemed sure of herself despite her ordeal. What she said made sense.

Once Nathan had left, Lily was overpowered by the sense of violation that engulfed the house. Every window and door seemed vulnerable to admitting hostility into her home. She beat her fists against her stomach as she thought how she'd let this monster back into her life. As she contemplated drowning herself in the local river, the telephone rang. She walked slowly towards it and picked up the receiver.

"Hello," she said quietly.

She sensed someone was there, but they weren't talking to her, they were just listening. She put the receiver down and backed away from the phone. She stared at the phone with her back against the wall, as though Walker was going to crawl out of the receiver.

She kept the house silent so she was able to hear anything untoward happening. She could hear dogs barking in the street and in the back gardens, taunting her with their incessant yapping. Wind blew the trees and shrubs in her garden, and clouds brushed across the sky. An eerie scene was set in her mind.

The phone rang again. Her hands trembled as she picked up the receiver and whispered into it.

"Lily, its Faith. Just phoning to see how you were and if I could do anything for you?"

Lily so wanted to say how crushed and defeated she was, but without the back story, it meant nothing.

"I'm fine, really."

"But what happened exactly? Nathan was very vague."

"I disturbed a burglar; I shouldn't have tried to intervene."

"Goodness that must have been frightening. I can call round if you'd like?"

"I'm going to rest now as I want to be back at work tomorrow. So if you don't mind, no, I'm okay thanks."

She sensed Faith's concern but self-preservation was Lily's utmost concern at that moment in time. She didn't want to risk opening up to Faith as she thought she could do.

She moved to the kitchen to make herself some toast, and whilst there, she removed the tatty box from the bottom cupboard. She picked her way through the remaining pieces of fabric, medical notes, remnants of hair, and leaflets about the hospital. Her internal destructive anger urged her to send Walker another souvenir of his sordid past. His power loomed over her too much. She needed to distract him away from her, at least for a while.

The toast was unwelcome in her dry mouth, so she just nibbled on it in mouse-like fashion. She recalled a session she had had with her psychiatrist when she talked about wanting to take her own life.

"Suicide is not the solution everyone thinks it is. You can still have a life, if you're willing to open yourself up to opportunities," he used to say as he gazed at her from across his large mahogany desk. Those words had stayed with her for all those years, and reminded her that suicide would only hurt herself as no one else would care or miss her. She didn't want the people from her past to get away from being punished that easily.

She sat at the table turning the pieces of fabric in between her fingers. She closed her eyes and smelt the cloth and she was instantly transported back to the ward in the hospital.

She remembered how brutal and sadistic Walker was with her. He threatened her so that she was too fearful of disclosing what was going on. He told her that no one would think anything of it if she threw herself off the fire escape or hung herself in the bathroom, because her notes recorded her suicidal ideation and intent. She remembered how his eyes glinted in the semi-dark, and she knew that he was capable of carrying out his threats. For all she knew, previous so-called suicides could have been his work. He could write anything in her notes to demonstrate she was psychotic or severely clinically depressed.

She thought about the young junior doctor, and how he could barely look her in the eye when on rounds with the Consultant. She knew that he'd seen something that night, but he'd never made the effort to find out what or report his concern.

Walker was over-bearing and powerful to the patients and staff alike. She'd witnessed nurses in tears after one of his rants, and junior doctors tiptoeing cautiously around him so they could get through their rotation successfully.

With her eyes still firmly shut, she could still smell the sterile environment mixed with the aroma of urine and fear. She knew that Walker was also abusive and aggressive with the male patients as she'd often heard their muffled cries and seen their haunted stares.

And now she was his victim once more, only this time she wasn't trapped in his world. She had to find a way to weaken him. She decided to send some more nightdress fabric along with a leaflet about the hospital to the TEP HQ. She hoped that when someone opened the envelope it would raise awkward questions for Walker.

However, this time, she decided to add a typed note which read, "Remember me? I remember you. How long will it take for your sordid past to come out?"

She carefully enclosed the note, leaflet, and fabric into a typed envelope so it wasn't distinguishable from other letters. She needed someone other than Walker to be the recipient of her daring post.

The telephone rang again, but Lily's mood had become more defiant so the intrusion didn't frighten her this time around. She found Rachel on the other end, finding out where Lily had got to recently.

"It's voting this coming Thursday, so we could do with your help for the final push."

Lily felt bad about lying to her about not feeling well. She saw Rachel as a surrogate daughter, one that she could have had in a different dimension. She didn't care for her dire political viewpoint and the major fact that she found Walker an attractive proposition. As a mother she would have guided her daughter towards more enlightened ideologies. Lily sighed as she put the envelope in her handbag.

As the day drew to an end, her thoughts turned macabre as she wondered whether she'd have another unwanted visit from Walker. Nathan didn't call around or phone, which didn't entirely surprise her seeing as she had declined his offer earlier.

Before climbing the stairs to bed, she grabbed a kitchen knife to keep by her bedside; not for self-harming but for self-defence. She lay in bed with the side light on and her eyes wide open, she knew she was in for a long night.

The telephone next to her bed rang.

"Hello?" She listened to nothing but silence, but as she listened carefully she was sure she could hear someone breathing. She listened for a few seconds and then she replaced the receiver.

She picked up the knife and clutched it to her chest and waited for the darkness to dissolve into daylight.

Chapter Twenty-Two

Lily had just finishing applying several layers of make-up to camouflage her wounds when the telephone rang. She picked up the receiver and just listened.

"Lily, are you there? It's Nathan."

"Hello, I'm just getting ready for work."

"I was phoning to say don't rush back, only come back when you're ready."

"I'm ready now." She spent a few more moments insisting that it was the right thing for her to do and then she hung up.

As she passed the post box on the way to work she dropped the envelope in and smiled to herself. *Maybe this time I'll get you.*

She hadn't realised how slowly she'd walked as she found herself arriving at the clinic at the same time as the normally tardy Nathan.

"You've done a remarkably good job of your face," he commented as he retrieved his keys from his pocket.

Hugh hadn't yet arrived, so Lily put the kettle on and opened the waiting room windows. She turned around to find Nathan standing there looking ashen-faced.

"Have we got anything to clean graffiti off a wall?"

She gave him a puzzled look and then went to his room to see what he was talking about. There she found the word "coward" painted in dark blue capital letters on the cream coloured wall behind the desk.

Lily's face blanched as she wondered who could have written it, and how had they managed to enter the surgery. She was now beginning to feel unsafe at her work place too.

The paint had dried and they were unable to make the word disappear. Nathan began to sweat profusely as he realised that he could not see patients in his room with that on the wall as it would fuel gossip and curiosity in the community.

"We could move the pictures and posters from the waiting room to cover it up," she said. She didn't wait for his answer but just got on with the task in hand.

Hugh arrived just in time to see the pair removing the posters.

"I've got new ones to put up," she told him without being asked.

"Are you sure you're well enough to be here? Faith would happily cover for you again," Hugh enquired.

"I'm absolutely fine thanks," she replied, trying not to sound too sharp.

"How far have the police got?"

"No news as yet," she replied as she gave Nathan a quick glance.

He followed her look and asked, "Nathan, could we have a quick chat please?"

"Yep, let's go to your room," Nathan said as he steered Hugh in that direction.

Hugh began to pace around the room with his hands in his trouser pockets. "I couldn't help wondering why you were at Lily's the other evening?"

"I didn't know I had to ask your permission, what's your problem?"

"Look, Lily's a decent woman and a bloody good employee. I don't want you ruining it all."

"And how would I do that exactly?"

"Oh, come on, you know what you're like with women."

Nathan guffawed. "She doesn't like me much, so you have nothing to worry about."

"Pleased to hear it."

"Really? And why's that, fancy her yourself, do you?"

Hugh's red face came within inches of Nathan's face until he thought better of it and pulled back. "Time to get on with the clinic," he said as he turned away from Nathan.

Nathan left the room with a smirk on his face and returned to his room. He found Lily putting up the last poster on heart disease on the wall.

"It's the best I can do," she said, seeing his face.

"You've done more than enough, thanks." He saw that the large letters had been mostly concealed, but parts of them still protruded. At least the word couldn't be made out.

Several of Nathan's patients had commented on the dark markings, whilst others were less than complimentary about the jumbled arrangement of pictures and posters.

In between patients, Nathan seethed with anger towards Walker. "How dare he taunt me so," he muttered. He also wondered how Walker had got in when there was no sign of a break in. *How did he know the security code?*

When lunchtime arrived he breathed a deep sigh of relief.

Lily was just about to lock the front door when a foot jammed the gap. She looked up to see Walker standing there. Her weakened hands released their grip on the door, allowing it to swing back open again.

"Pleased to see me?" he said as he reached in and grabbed her tiny wrist. "We have unfinished business so I'll see you tonight." He gave her wrist a quick twist before releasing it, asking if the doctor was free.

Lily nodded whilst she held her wrist; she was too traumatised to think about alerting Nathan. Walker knocked at Nathan's door, but without waiting for an answer, he breezed straight in. Nathan looked up from his paperwork to see Walker standing over his desk.

"What the hell do you want?"

"Nice to see you, too," replied Walker as he plonked himself in the chair and swung his feet up onto the desk.

"I trust I'll be getting your vote on Thursday." Walker let a wide grin expand across his face and then he put his hands behind his head as he lolled back in the chair, balancing on the back two legs.

"As if you need to ask. The sooner you lose and leave this town the better. You're like a bad smell lurking around every corner."

"Do I sense bitterness, Doctor?"

"Your antagonising actions leave me feeling little else." Nathan was standing and rising up and down on the balls of his feet.

"What's that bloody mess on your wall?"

Nathan couldn't take anymore. "I'm not in the mood for your jokes. Now get out of here, you festering pool of shit."

"Charming," said Walker as he rose to his feet and lunged forward, grabbing Nathan around the throat.

"I want to make sure you keep a low profile, if not, you'll wish you'd got away whilst you could still walk." His eyes went the deepest shade of black and Nathan could see the image of his fearful face reflected back at him.

"And by the way," he continued, "there's more to come, so brace yourself." He then pushed Nathan back into his chair, almost tipping the chair and Nathan backwards.

Nathan watched as Walker left the room. For a man in his late fifties he still had an impressively broad back and shoulders. Nathan rubbed his throat as he considered his options.

Lily was startled to find Walker waiting for her in reception as she made her way back from the kitchen. She stopped in her tracks and let him invade her personal space. He stretched out and touched her cheek and then he ran his hand down the side of her face and under her chin.

"It would be a pity to damage such an angelic face," he said, and with a mocking slap, he strode out of the clinic.

Nathan appeared in reception just as Walker left. There was a distinct smell of fear in the room that neither person alluded to.

"Shall we go out and grab a bagel? I could do with getting out of here and you look like you could do with it, too," he suggested.

Although the thought of eating made her want to heave, she didn't want to remain in the clinic. Nathan left a note for Hugh and then they left together.

"What did that man want? He was a bit intimidating," asked Lily.

"He was just vote-hunting."

"You're not voting for him are you?" Her remark made her blush.

"No, but I believe there's lots of local support for him."

"More's the pity," she uttered under her breath.

Nathan bought a couple of salt beef and mustard bagels and handed one to Lily. He bit into his so that the mustard oozed out and clung to the sides of his mouth like a clown's smile.

Lily ran her finger around the edge of the bagel and licked the butter from the tip of her finger. She picked at the salt beef but barely touched the bagel. Nathan noticed every movement she made. He wished he'd offered more compassion to patients of the past who suffered with similar conditions. *Maybe it's time I started?*

"Why was that word scrawled on your wall?" she asked as she checked his reaction in her peripheral vision.

"Probably just some silly kids. Don't worry yourself about it." He finished the last morsel of bagel and threw the wrapper in a bin.

They sat in the dappled sunlight in the public garden and watched the blackbirds as they picked and probed the lawn hoping to find their own lunch.

"What's your passion in life?" he asked.

"Excuse me?"

"Well, the closest thing I have to a passion is medicine, that and watching war movies. So, what about you?"

"Apart from world peace, you mean?"

He gave her a wry smile. "You're not being serious."

"That's because my passion is unknown to me. I strive to get through each day unscathed and to be stronger than the day before."

Nathan frowned and rubbed the back of his neck. He couldn't grasp the underlying meaning to her cryptic nuances and his concern for her being depressed grew deeper.

"No hopes or aspirations for the future?" he continued.

"No."

"Tell me, Lily, are you sleeping well, I mean since the attack."

"Are you asking me as a work colleague or as a doctor?"

"Touché. You're my employee so it's my job to ensure you are okay."

"I'm fine, really I am. We should be getting back," she said as she looked at her watch.

They began to stroll back, and Nathan looked around to see if they were being watched.

"I don't hear you talk about many friends," said Nathan.

"I don't do friends," she replied before stepping through the door.

He stood still for a moment and then he shook his head before following her inside.

At the end of the day, Hugh was surprised to see Nathan still hanging around.

"No pub to crawl to then?"

"I've a few phone calls to make and then I'm going home," replied Nathan who had actually paid a decorator extra money to work after hours, and so he needed to stay behind to let him in.

With both Hugh and Lily gone, Nathan found he didn't like being at the clinic alone since the break-ins, and he was relieved when the decorator finally arrived.

Lily dawdled home as she felt safer in the street than in her own home. Her neck and jaw stiffened with tension the closer she got to her street.

As she walked up to the front door she could hear her phone ringing. *And so it begins.*

Chapter Twenty-Three

Just as she reached the phone it stopped ringing. The intensity of her heartbeat and rapid breathing almost transgressed into a panic attack.

She wandered around the house to check that everything was still in its place and the fortress was secure. She hadn't forgotten Walker's promise to return.

Hunger gripped her so she took a few handfuls of succulent green grapes to nibble on.

Tomorrow, Walker or someone would receive the letter at HQ and she hoped that it would distract him for a while at least. She wondered how many other women he'd harassed and whether he'd already set his sights on the unsuspecting Rachel. She thought about confiding in Rachel, even to warn her, but it was far too risky, especially as Rachel thought Walker was eminently appealing. She couldn't trust anyone with her secret.

The police would probably not believe her if she admitted it was him who attacked her. Walker would talk coherently to the police and she would be blamed due to having a psychiatric history. He'd probably say she was a stalker with an unhealthy fixation on him.

As she sat at the kitchen table staring at the craters of war on the wall, the doorbell rang. She sat bolt upright and held her breath. The doorbell rang again, and then after a few minutes she heard the letterbox flap move. She remained seated and gnawed on the skin around her left thumb.

After a few minutes of silence she crept along the wall of the kitchen and then the hallway. The front door was still boarded up so she couldn't see if someone was still standing there. On the doormat lay a leaflet for the Green Party and with a deep sigh she realised it was the last political push before the election on Thursday.

Her shoulders relaxed and she returned to the kitchen and made a salad. The radio played classical music softly in the background and the air felt unseasonably humid as though a storm was approaching.

Lily felt too anxious to soak in the bath so she had a quick shower so that she could once again be vigilant. She put on a cool, floor length white cotton nightdress and wrapped her hair in a towel.

She sat in the lounge and began flicking through the TV channels, when the doorbell rang once, then twice, and then someone just leant on it so the shrill sound tore through the air.

She felt powerless to resist the noise and the pull of her own morbid curiosity. She walked to the door and stood behind it so she could ask who was there. She waited for an answer but none came.

Her fingers hovered over the lock which she turned slowly. She then reached for the bolt but left the chain on. As she slowly opened the door, she peered around. Through the gap she saw a shadowy figure standing there. As she looked up, she saw it was Walker.

She quickly tried to slam the door shut but he jammed his foot between the door and the frame. He placed one of his huge hands around the door and then rammed his broad shoulder against it which snapped the chain like a cobweb.

The only sound she could hear was his heavy breathing and her own heartbeat throbbing in her head. She tried to scream for help but her mouth wasn't responding to the command. Fear crushed her where she stood, and she reverted to being the helpless patient once more.

Walker closed the front door behind him and locked it before turning to face her. She'd moved a few paces back but then found herself rooted to the spot and staring wide-eyed back at him. He continued to stare at her with an unsettling grin on his face whilst he flexed his biceps.

"No saviour around tonight, then?" he said.

She could feel beads of sweat congregate on her top lip as she summoned up the courage to speak.

"Why are you doing this to me? What have I ever done to you?" she spoke quietly, and her eyes were drained of all emotion.

"Dear Lily, you are but a pawn in the madness of life. I can do what I want with you."

Her toes curled at his words and she had to put her hand on the wall to steady herself.

"Where do you find the blackness in your heart to do such things, Finlay Walker? What has happened to you in your past to make you treat people this way?"

He stepped closer to her so that she could see up his flaring nostrils. "Power is everything, and you, my poor insignificant Lily, have none."

"I could go to the police and have you arrested."

"You've seen the police already but they didn't come looking for me. I'm a pillar of the community with my charity work. I'd kill you before you could harm me."

He stepped forward until she could feel his breath on her forehead. She resolutely remained in her position as she knew that any effort to escape would be thwarted by him in seconds. He reached out and traced the outline of her face with his fat finger. He then leant forward until his mouth hovered over her delicate ear.

"Here stands before me a woman who's in complete denial about her situation, but I imagine that's the safest place to be, eh Lily?"

His hot, rank breath warmed her ear and made her wretch. Her whole body quaked at his close proximity. She then felt his teeth on her lobe and closed her eyes in anticipation of the pain.

"Now where were we?" he rasped.

Twenty minutes later, Walker was drinking a coffee in Lily's lounge, watching the late evening, local news. Suddenly something on the screen caught his eye.

He pulled his mobile from his pocket. "What the fuck's going on down there?"

Lily stood in the doorway with her arms folded across her stomach, listening to Walker and watching the images of a building on fire on the TV.

"See you again," he said before raising his hand and slapping her hard across the face. She watched him walk out, aware that one side of her face was stinging.

She slid down the wall and slumped into a mound on the floor, as fat, salty tears flooded her eyes. The writhing of the tormented elements could be heard coming from above, and lightening flashed out its warning before the rumble shuddered through the house

Suddenly she knew what she had to do. He was never going to harm her ever again.

Nathan managed to get home in time before the deluge fell from the sky. The light from the storm cast eerie shadows around his home. In an effort to balance his mind he put the Indian takeaway on a tray and plonked himself in front of the TV to watch something trivial.

As he channel flicked, he fell upon the local news programme. He sat there happily putting loaded forkfuls of aubergine curry in his mouth and washing it down with Tiger beer.

He only had half an eye on the TV when an item attracted his attention. He watched the events unfold as a forkful of food hovered before his gapping mouth. A local camera crew were at the TEP HQ where flames were licking at the sky through the windows. Firemen were dousing the fire, whilst in the foreground was Finlay Walker being interviewed by an over-enthusiastic reporter in a poorly-fitted jacket.

Walker was looking directly into the camera saying that he feared nothing from the fire or from anyone trying to harm him or his campaign.

Nathan felt like he was being talked to directly, and although he knew he'd nothing to do with the fire, Walker may not be so charitable. He put his tray on the floor and then finished the bottle of beer in two large swigs.

The news programme was live so Nathan knew where Walker was at that precise moment, but that surety wouldn't last for long.

As the reporter took over and spoke into the camera, Nathan watched Walker in the background talking to two bulldog-like men who appeared to be taking commands from their leader before leaving the scene.

Nathan switched off the TV and then moved around the house to switch off all of the lights, leaving himself in the semi-gloom of the street light. Paranoid and irrational behaviour overtook him. He and Walker were locked enemies, so anything could happen.

He rummaged through his thoughts to see if he had something suitable to defend himself, but of course he didn't. *I live in Hallbury, not New York*, he thought to himself.

He'd never been in a fight. He recalled his halcyon days as a medical student where the closest he had got to combat was the annual tug-of-war between the two universities. He felt ill-equipped and his nerves were ripped up by the unknown.

He heard sirens in the distance and a car drove past with the bass beat too loud. The next noise he heard was the doorbell ringing. His outdoor sensor porch light allowed him to see the outline of two tall shadows through the diamond-shaped pane of glass in the front door.

With the house in darkness he was able to creep into the deep cupboard under stairs, shut the door and hide under the huge amount of coats and jackets he had acquired over the years.

He started to sweat under the intensity of the pressure and when he heard a pane of glass shatter at the back of the house, he clamped his hand over his mouth to muffle his breathing.

He could hear two men whispering and tramping about the house. He heard them move from room to room and then go upstairs, heavy-footed with malicious intent.

Once they thought he wasn't at home they began trashing his house. He could hear furniture being upended, pictures being ripped from walls and ornaments smashing onto the floor.

The sound of running water came from upstairs, but he had to remain still as he heard them thunder back down the stairs. Their footsteps echoed around the rooms, punctuated by sounds of smashing glass.

The neighbour's dog began barking and jumping up at the fence. Nathan heard the men laugh as they unlocked the back door and left.

He waited until the dog was silent and the only noise left to hear was the running water. Sweat trickled down his back soaking the waistband of his boxer shorts. His muscles were stiff and his back felt rigid as he slowly emerged from the cupboard.

The silence was deafening except for the sound of gushing water. Nathan dashed upstairs and sloshed about in the water that was pooling on the bathroom floor. He turned off the bath and sink taps, and then pulled out the plugs, cursing the mindless damage they'd caused. He threw towels on the floor to soak up the excess water, but just ended up with a sodden mess.

He could still hear water, so he raced downstairs where he found a similar picture of destruction in the kitchen. The lounge had the added complication of broken glass, mirrors, and crockery which had become embedded in the sofa and rugs.

Although he was feeling distraught and irate, he knew it could have been much worse had they found him; his face could have been smashed to pieces like the fragments of the mirror that lay in the Victorian fireplace.

Nathan wondered whether Walker would be satisfied with only environmental damage. Perhaps they would return for him later?

He ran back upstairs, two steps at a time and grabbed an overnight bag from the top of the wardrobe into which he stuffed clothes and toiletries. He picked up his mobile and quietly left by the front door, locking it carefully behind him. He looked up and down the street and then pulled the hood over his head before marching off as fast as he could.

He had made a hasty decision to get to Lily's house, so as he arrived there he realised he hadn't let her know beforehand, nor weighed up the consequences of his actions.

The house was in darkness but it didn't deter him from ringing the doorbell. It occurred to him that she could be nervous after the attack, so he bent down and called to her through the letterbox.

Lily came to the door in her dressing gown, her pallid face a backdrop for her saucer eyes.

"Sorry to bother you, but I've had a flood in my house, rendering it uninhabitable. I wondered if I could use your couch for tonight whilst my place dries out."

She hesitated before ushering him in. She was curious about the flood and wanted to hear more.

"That's what you get with old water pipes."

"I see. Don't take this the wrong way but why here? Why not stay with Hugh and Faith?"

"Between you and me, I think they're having marital issues; I'd only be in the way."

"Are you sure it's not because Faith doesn't like you that much?" She blushed and twirled a strand of hair between her finger and thumb.

He smiled at her brutal honesty. "You've noticed then."

"It was blatantly obvious. What did you do to warrant that?"

"I don't rightly know but I think she feels I'm a bad influence on Hugh."

"Naughty boy syndrome," she said with a half-smile. She moved to the kitchen to make some drinks.

"I don't suppose you have any beer?"

"Matter of fact, I do." She pointed to the fridge and motioned for him to help himself. She poured herself a red wine and then went upstairs to dry her hair.

Nathan moved to the lounge and settled on the sofa with his beer, when the doorbell rang. He could hear the hairdryer upstairs so he went to the bay window to see who it was. The bell rang again but Nathan couldn't see who was standing there so he tapped on the window. His heart almost missed a beat as Walker stepped into view.

The men stood there looking at each other through the glass, perplexed and irritated at the surprise encounter.

"What are you doing in there?" mouthed Walker.

"None of your business."

Walker glared at him as the muscles in his jaw flexed. "You do remember what I said, I wager?"

"What do you want?"

Attic of the Mind **145**

Walker held up a TEP leaflet and mouthed "canvassing." He then walked away without looking back.

Nathan's imagination went into overload. Was Walker stalking him? He then realised that he had inadvertently put Lily in danger. Perhaps this was what Walker wanted all along?

Chapter Twenty-Four

Lily had a better night sleep with Nathan sleeping downstairs. He, on the other hand, awoke with a stiff neck and cramps in his calves. His night had been filled with traumatic thoughts about Walker's visit and the possible harm that could come to Lily. He didn't know if she was safer with or without him.

He wandered into the kitchen, rubbing his neck, in search of black coffee, only to find Lily sipping hot lemon water and nibbling some toast. They eyed each other awkwardly and then she nodded towards the counter where a pot of freshly brewed coffee was waiting for him. After pouring a large mug of the black liquid, he turned to her.

"Thanks for letting me stay the night."

"No problem, hope the sofa wasn't too uncomfortable." He smiled and shrugged his stiff shoulder before returning to the lounge.

The pair walked to work but hardly uttered a word to one another in the stilted atmosphere. As they arrived, Hugh's car was already there.

"There's a distinct smell of fresh paint coming from your room, it didn't need painting already, surely?" said Hugh as they stepped through the door. He stood with his hands on his hips looking like a father figure chastising his child.

Nathan brushed off the comment and headed for his room, whilst Lily stood blushing until Hugh disappeared too.

Nathan was relieved to see that the inflammatory word had vanished from the wall.

Election night had arrived and the town was buzzing. Polling station signs hung on the gates of primary schools and community centres. Nathan and Lily arrived to find just four people in the queue in front of them so it wasn't long before they were in a cubicle. They both felt a nauseous sensation as they read the name Finlay Walker on the ballot paper. With their votes cast, they walked away, hoping for the best but fearing the worst.

"Did you manage to sort out the repairs for your house?" Lily asked.

"Yes, it's going to take a few days of work, they start tomorrow."

"Do you need to stay another night?" she asked quietly.

"I don't want to put you out."

"It's fine, I don't have any plans."

And so it was agreed that Nathan would stay over again. Lily's internal conflict pulled her in two directions as she felt protected by his presence, but as he was the same man who abandoned and ignored her all those year ago, could he be trusted? She couldn't decide.

Nathan decided to be more altruistic and bought a Chinese takeaway for their evening meal. She was touched, but not softened by his gesture. She appreciated the crab and noodle soup whilst Nathan polished off sweet and sour chicken with a side order of dumplings.

He'd also bought a bottle of Jack Daniels as he felt badly in need of an alcoholic crutch. He felt an immense sense of relief as he sat back in the chair and sipped the smooth liquor.

He swirled the drink around the glass and breathed in the oaky smell. He thought about how he needed to be more accommodating of other people's emotions. Those were the exact words and sentiments of his ex-wife many moons ago.

"Would it be okay if I took a bath now?" he asked as he rose wearily from the chair.

"Sure, take your time."

Lily pottered about in the kitchen, relaxed in the knowledge that she wasn't alone for yet another night. Her mood was also lifted by the knowledge that as it was election night, and that Walker would be occupied waiting for the results. She poured herself another glass of red wine and headed for the garden. The air had an oppressive humidity to it.

The light from the bathroom cast a soft glow onto the patio area and she let her eyes close for a minute so she could appreciate the stillness of the evening.

"I bet you didn't expect to see me," said a voice behind her, as a large hand rested on her shoulder.

Lily recognised the voice and his touch straight away. She turned her head slowly and looked up towards Walker's face.

"Shouldn't you be at the HQ?" she asked slowly.

"Yes, and so should you. You were so keen to help the cause, you should be there for the results."

His hand moved from her shoulder and curved under her arm. He lifted her from her chair, knocking over the wine glass in the process.

"Get ready," he hissed in her ear.

"I can't, I'm not alone."

"I'm sure the good doctor can manage without you. He won't be around you forever, you know. He won't be able to help you. You're nobody to him."

He forcefully guided her into the kitchen with one hand over her mouth, and prompted her to get her bag. He then dragged her back out through the garden and down the rear alley. He walked closely by her side with a firm grip on her arm so she felt unable to get away or scream, so strong was his power.

Lily was experiencing what was happening to her as though she was watching a movie. She watched herself become totally overcome by the monster of her past.

As they arrived at what was left of the HQ, Walker shoved her up the stairs with a brusque hostility.

"Don't think about leaving. You're being watched," he said as he pinched her arm before releasing it.

She felt as though she was in the midst of a hellish nightmare that smelt of charred wood. Rachel's face offered some gentle relief.

"Great to see you," said Rachel, her voice bubbling with enthusiasm. "This is so exciting, don't you think?"

"Yes, quite."

Lily's eyes darted around the sooty room and she noticed several of the burly men dotted around the room were watching her. Their discretion was infinitesimal. She monitored her breathing to halt the light-headed feeling from swamping her mind.

"We've got to go to the community centre in an hour. Won't it be wonderful to see Finlay make his acceptance speech?"

Lily nodded and then looked intently into Rachel's eyes. "I need to pop to the toilet; I'll be back in a minute."

"I'll come too, girls together and all that."

That scuppered Lily's plans but then she wondered whether it was time to trust Rachel. They moved through the throng of men with their thick-set faces and sweaty armpits. As they reached the toilet door, Lily turned to Rachel.

"I'm sorry but I've got to go now, my friend will wonder where I am." She started for the stairs when Rachel moved swiftly and stood in front of her, blocking the way. They stared at one another, and then Lily saw the transformation in Rachel's demeanour and eyes.

"I think you'll find that Finlay wants you to stay."

Lily's eyes widened. "But you don't understand, I've got someone at home, I must go back."

"I don't think you quite understand, Lily, you're staying here. Now let's go back." Rachel stood tall with her arms pressed against each wall.

"You just wouldn't listen. Finlay wants to own you, and he knows what's best for everyone."

"You don't understand. I have to leave. He's already hurt me and he'll continue until he's made to stop. Please, Rachael."

"I don't believe you. How dare you talk about him that way."

"You idolised him. He's not what you think he is . . ."

"Stop it. Now, go back in the room."

Lily was startled by Rachel's outburst, but she still needed to get out. She was about to push her down the stairs when one of Walker's cronies stepped out from the room and grabbed Lily by the arm. He swung her back to where Walker was waiting for her.

Nathan felt refreshed both mentally and physically after the long soak in the bath.

He descended the stairs and wasn't surprised that Lily had taken herself up to her room. She was as anti-social as he was. Content with his own company, he grabbed the bottle of whiskey and returned to the lounge.

He looked around the room and saw she had an eclectic library in the alcoves either side of the fireplace. He chose a book by P.D. James and settled on the sofa with his feet dangling over the armrest. He stayed like that for a couple of hours until he'd finished the novel. Already feeling stiff and sensing that it was too early to sleep, he decided to see if Lily was up for some company.

The stairs creaked gently as he tiptoed up them. His familiarity didn't extend to knowing which ones creaked and which ones did not. He could see that her bedroom door was ajar but that no light was on. With his new altruistic persona, he left her in peace and returned to the lounge to read another book.

Lily was escorted to the community centre where she found herself surrounded by TEP members whilst Walker stood upon the podium awaiting the declaration.

She felt numb to the occasion. She was never left alone and she couldn't even go to the toilet without Rachel standing guard outside the cubicle.

"Why are you doing this to me?" she whispered into Rachel's ear.

"You should feel honoured that he's chosen you. I wish he'd notice me more."

Lily's shoulders drooped and she looked at the floor, letting her eyes trace lines around her feet.

A hush descended on the room as the speaker stood up to make the announcement. Lily looked up and saw that Walker had a subtle smile on his face and a glint in his eye. *Good God*, she thought to herself, *he's won.*

As the announcement stated that Finlay Walker of The English Party was elected, the group surrounding Lily erupted with cheers, whistles, and shouts of triumph. They raised their arms in an attempt to salute his success and then Rachel turned to Lily and said, "You're so lucky, I'm so envious."

"You can have him, he's not my type."

Lily looked pleadingly at Rachel who was too busy waving to Walker. She was immune to her silent cries for help.

The room began to spin, and the last thing Lily remembered was the roar of the supporters and wondering whether Nathan had noticed she was missing.

Nathan fumbled around for the alarm clock as the shrill noise interrupted a dreamful sleep. He knew his body couldn't cope with another night on the sofa, age was against him. He listened for sounds of movement above him, but all was still quiet.

He eased himself up from the sofa, rubbing his lower back with both hands. His mouth felt repugnant and sleep crusts clogged his eyes. He wanted to use the bathroom before Lily awoke, so he wandered upstairs quietly. He noticed that her bedroom door was now shut.

Lily was stirred from her sleep by the sound of the shower running. Suddenly, she sat bolt upright as she remembered the events that took place during the night. Walker's fervent mouth after his acceptance speech.

Like lava from an erupting volcano, memories began flooding back to her at an alarming pace. She remembered Walker and Rachel, the election results, and then being transported back home by some TEP men and Rachel. It was Rachel who helped undressed her and put her to bed. She remembered losing the power of speech and being overwhelmed by a sensation of powerlessness. She still felt sluggish and deduced that she had been drugged over the course of the evening. Quite why, she couldn't work out.

She swung her legs over the side of the bed and waited for her head to readjust to the seemingly strenuous movements. When she stood up she had to hold onto the bedside cabinet to assist her frail legs. As she got to the door Nathan appeared from the bathroom.

"Morning, Lilith. Shall I make a pot of coffee?"

She nodded, still unable to annunciate any words.

"You look rather pale, are you feeling all right?"

His kindly words sunk into her disjointed brain and she could feel tears in her eyes waiting to roll down her hollow cheeks. She wanted to beg him for help but she couldn't find the words. She wanted him to read her mind and her eyes, but that was asking too much from a man who couldn't do that years before.

She struggled to get ready as she found her mind and body were working in slow motion. By the time she got to the kitchen, she found Nathan sitting at the table with his coffee and some toast. She faltered on her feet but managed to control herself by holding onto the table. Nathan wasn't blind to her predicament so he got up and poured her a coffee whilst she sat down.

"You're very quiet. Look, I know you don't like me that much, but if there is something wrong, you can talk to me."

"I'm fine, just feeling a bit fragile, that's all."

"Don't come in today. It's the weekend tomorrow, so three days convalescing should go some way to getting you better."

"No, I'd rather be at work."

Nathan rose to his feet. "Nonsense, you look dreadful. I'll take my stuff with me and I'll see you Monday."

She watched helplessly as he gathered his belongings and left the house, talking to Hugh on his mobile. The suffocating silence bombarded her numb brain and the tears she had wanted to shed had now evaporated.

Nowhere felt safe anymore; her home and workplace had been violated by Walker and the TEP. She checked that the tatty box had not been disturbed, and she was comforted to find that it was still in the bottom cupboard and everything inside was intact. She toyed with the contents and gained the strength and resilience to carry on.

She wasn't the innocent, deeply depressed nineteen-year-old anymore; she was a stronger forty-four-year-old who had the capacity to overcome Walker this time.

Chapter Twenty-Five

"Is there something wrong with Lily? I'm working here more frequently than I'd anticipated," said Faith as she switched the computer on.

"I think it's all to do with the attack. Nathan is probably better placed to tell you than I am."

"To tell you what?" said Nathan as he entered the surgery.

"What's wrong with Lily? I'm missing too many lunch parties."

Hugh looked across at his wife with disappointment in his eyes.

"The attack shook her up, but she looked extremely pale this morning."

"This morning? Again?" said Hugh as he moved closer to where Nathan was standing.

"Er, yes, I stayed another night as the repairs aren't finished."

"Weren't we good enough?" Hugh asked.

"I didn't want to trouble you both, besides, I live closer to Lily."

Hugh retreated, red faced into his room and Faith busied herself, avoiding any eye contact with Nathan.

The phone rang in Nathan's room, it was Walker.

"I thought you'd want to congratulate me on my political prowess."

"Not really."

"That's a pity. Where are you sleeping tonight, not with the pretty Lily again, eh?"

Nathan gritted his teeth; Walker was invading his personal life too much for his liking. "I don't want her to come to any harm. It's not her fault I'm staying there."

"Who's fault is it then?"

"If your men hadn't damaged my property I wouldn't need to sleep elsewhere."

"That's a slanderous comment, Doctor."

"You surely can't deny the action of your thugs. I saw them. I was there."

Walker laughed a throaty laugh down the phone. "You were there but you didn't stop them. Still a coward, I see."

Nathan wanted to throw the phone across the room. "What's your point with all this anyway?"

"The point, good Doctor, is that I am enjoying playing games with you. I'm having fun." He laughed again and then hung up.

Nathan was aware of his sweaty palm as he rubbed the back of his neck. *Whoever set fire to the TEP office should have waited until Walker was in there.*

At lunchtime, Nathan thought he would go home to see how the workers were getting on. As he passed the reception he noticed a rank smell in the air which Faith was hurrying to conceal with air freshener.

"Good God, it smells ripe in here," said Hugh, who appeared from his office.

"Not everyone has the same philosophy about personal hygiene," she replied as she waved her arm around, spraying liberally as she did so.

As Nathan left the clinic and walked along the narrow pavement, Walker's words spun around his head. He could see how Walker was enjoying taunting him and he wondered what would happen if he stood up to him.

He arrived home to find the men still working on the kitchen ceiling with the light fitting discarded on the kitchen table.

"Some blokes were looking for you earlier," said the man who was perched on the ladder.

"Did they say who they were or what they wanted?"

"No, they just said they'd call back later."

Nathan's heart sank. A sensation he knew he'd have for the rest of the afternoon.

He contemplated calling in on Lily on his way back to the clinic, but his lunch hour was running out.

Hugh and Faith were eating their sandwiches in the tiny courtyard behind the kitchen, as Faith disliked communal gardens.

"You looked rather put out when Nathan said he stayed the night at Lily's," she said as she glanced sideways at her husband.

"Did I?"

"You know you did. Have you got a soft spot for her?"

"Don't be ridiculous. Anyway, it's you that's been distant from me of late, not the other way round."

"That's typical of you to reflect the blame back at me for the decline of our relationship."

"Oh, so you admit there's a problem?"

"The problem is you, it's always been you."

"What do you mean by that? God Faith, we've stopped communicating and replaced it with bickering. What are we going to do about this?"

"I'm not sure there is anything we can do. You will always be you . . ."

"What the hell have I done?" he interjected.

"Nothing, really. You're right, perhaps it is I who has changed. And perhaps there is nothing we can do."

"You're not very clear. Talk to me, damn it."

Faith stood up and walked back inside with her half-eaten sandwich. Hugh remained, stony faced, and fed his to the birds before returning inside.

Nathan walked in and caught sight of Hugh's clenched jaw and red face.

"Problem?"

"Working with Faith isn't going so well," he replied, shoving his hands in his pockets.

"It's not going to be a permanent situation."

"Ah, but how do you know that, or are you and Lily keeping secrets from me?"

"Don't be so bloody paranoid."

Faith's return halted the conversation and each person fragmented towards their own work area, leaving a frosty residue in the air.

Nathan approached his desk and saw a leaflet sitting on the computer keyboard. He picked it up and saw that it was an information leaflet on Poplar Ward. He could feel the pulsating of his heart in his temples as he stormed into the reception area.

"Was the front door left undone at lunchtime?"

"No, why?" replied Faith.

"What about the alarm?"

"There was no need, we were in the courtyard."

"Damn this," he said as he marched back into his room. He decided to call Walker later.

Nathan found that he envied some of the patients who were the same age as him or older, because their lives seemed simple and trauma free. He knew that if he went to the police, he either risked imminent death in a painful manner, or Walker would counterclaim that he was part of the abusive ring and that he stole drugs for his own use. He couldn't walk away as Walker would always be on his trail. He had to find a way of rectifying his past mistakes to afford himself the quieter life he sought.

When the opportunity arose, Nathan called the town hall, where he finally got put through to Walker's new office.

"I'm asking you to stop harassing me at home and work, otherwise I'll have to go to the police and suffer the consequences. You're leaving me no choice, Walker."

"Feeling a little stressed, dear Doctor?"

"Stop with your cynical platitudes, you bloody arsehole. I'm not playing your games anymore."

"Brave words, Doctor, but empty all the same. You'd risk your career, pension, and status on trying to prove the improvable? Plus your partner in the practice would also suffer, not to mention your employee."

"Nothing matters, apart from those close to me. They could get police protection."

Walker guffawed. "You watch too many police dramas. Do you really think the police have the resources to do that?"

"Once the word is out," continued Nathan, "a cloud of doubt will shroud us both, we'll both lose out. And you know how the papers like to go digging once they smell a sensational story."

"I have many people protecting me. Who protects you, good doctor? I guess not even the beautiful Lily could protect you. And besides, I could easily have Lily murdered and frame you for it. How do you fancy a life-sentence?"

Nathan rested his head in his hand as he reflected on Walker's words. He could risk the lives of Hugh and Lily. He'd seen what Walker's men could do to property. He heard Walker laugh before he hung up.

Walker was still sitting at his desk when his secretary brought the post in, already opened.

"Not sure what this is, Mr Walker, it looks like some sort of prank," she said as she handed him a piece of fabric and an anonymous note.

"I suppose I'm to expect these kinds of things more and more now that I'm completely in the public domain," he replied as he screwed up the note and threw it in the bin along with the fabric.

He then picked up the phone.

"It's me. I've got a job for you."

Chapter Twenty-Six

Nathan returned home thankful that the week was over. He opened the front door to the smell of fresh plaster and the heavenly peace of no workmen. He slung his bag and jacket on the floor. Suddenly a canvas hood was rammed over his head and all he could hear was his own muffled rapid breathing, which failed to mask the sound of the front door being closed and locked.

He tried to speak but someone's muscular arm was wound around his neck and pressing on his throat. Gasping for air, he valiantly tried to speak, and claw at the arm around his throat. He kicked out blindly, thrashing around in the hope of catching someone. Out of the darkness, someone else threw a hefty punch at his stomach, winding him violently. He doubled over and dropped to the floor where he received several heavy-booted kicks to the kidneys and head.

Pain racked his flinching body and he became disorientated by the blows meted to his head and torso. He could hear the men grunting as they swung their legs and clenched fists. He could feel blood trickling from his throbbing nose, and as his teeth clattered together, there was an ominous grating sensation followed by a mouthful of blood which he hastily spat out onto the inside of the bag.

He tried to protect his head and face with his arms, but they'd become so numb that he wasn't sure where they were in relation to the rest of his body.

The next minute he was lifted up and carried upstairs. He sensed they'd reached the top of the stairs before he was forced to his knees. Without warning, his head was shoved down the toilet by one man, whilst the other man flushed the chain. Water engulfed his head and soaked the canvas hood so that it clung to his mouth and nostrils. He felt like he was drowning.

He struggled for air, whilst spluttering blood and bleach-tainted water out of his disfigured mouth. The hand on the back of his neck continued to push him down firmly, so much so, he felt his head would be severed from his neck at any moment.

The toilet was flushed again, and that time he thought he might actually die. His chest hurt and his head spun from the lack of oxygen. Suddenly, his head was yanked upwards whilst he remained kneeling. He became aware of someone's head close to his.

"If you think this was bad, imagine how slow and painful we could make your death in a place where no one would hear your screams."

He then felt another presence at the other side of his head.

"So now you have a choice; either shut up or risk this for yourself and that Lily woman."

Nathan was then shoved to the floor with a foot on his shoulder blade and kicked another couple of times in the ribs and lower back. The hood was then pulled from his head and the men thundered downstairs and slammed the front door behind them.

Nathan remained on the mercilessly cold, hard floor whilst he coughed and choked on the fluid in his lungs. Very slowly, he tried unsuccessfully to sit up by using his swollen hands on the toilet rim. He tried to open his eyes, but one was so swollen that it remained closed. Although the vision was blurred out of his other eye, he could just make out the visible bruise marks and boot-sole marks appearing on his arms.

His breathing was shallow due to the pain in his ribs, and he suspected at least one or two of them were fractured. With great care, he managed to crawl to the bath, where he used the side to heave himself up enough to see the car-crash vision staring back at him in the mirror. He knew that it would take more than a weekend for his injuries to diminish and for his head and face to regain their natural size and shape. There was going to be no way of hiding the attack from Hugh, who'd find the whole event abhorrent, and would probably get the police to be involved.

But Walker had been clever. Nathan couldn't identify the men and they never implicated Walker. No link and no proof. Walker had won another round in his particularly nasty game.

Nathan managed to stem the flow of blood from his nose by inserting clumps of cotton wool in each nostril. His teeth, however, where another matter.

His two front ones were loose and were the source of a steady stream of blood that pooled in his mouth. He hoped that by only eating liquids for a couple of days they would reset themselves in the gum without the intervention of a dentist.

He hobbled downstairs and shakily poured himself a large scotch which he knew he shouldn't do as he was in shock. He knocked it back, and found the taste of the blood to be potent and bitter. He peered around the room through his half decent eye to see whether they'd also damaged his home. It looked like all the pleasure had been reserved for his body. He took a deep breath and refilled his glass. He winced as he raised the glass to his split lips.

He eased himself into the battered leather chair and picked up his mobile to call Hugh. Faith answered the phone, and as she called Hugh, he attempted a few more deep breaths to facilitate his speech.

"What can I do for you?"

"I'm in a bit of a bad way, can you come over?"

"What, now? Can't it wait until tomorrow?"

"Not really, I'm badly hurt. Could you bring your first aid kit too? I'll explain when you get here."

Hugh went quiet, but then agreed to go with reluctance resonating in his voice.

Twenty minutes later, the doorbell rang. Even though Nathan suspected it was only Hugh, he peered through the bay window first. With pitifully slow footsteps, he made his way to the front door.

"Good God man, what the hell's happened to you?" said Hugh as he looked aghast at his friend's swollen and almost unrecognizable face.

"Had an unpleasant encounter with two blokes; I think they were sent by Walker."

Hugh guided Nathan to the kitchen and sat him at the table where he began to assess and treat the injuries.

"This is completely out of hand, Nathan. You've got to go to the police now."

"And say what? I've got no bloody proof, have I?"

"You've got these horrific injuries for starters. You'll be taken seriously now."

Nathan remained silent whilst Hugh soaked some gauze in saline solution to wipe away the incrusted and congealed blood from his face. Hugh only broke the silence to say he thought some ribs and his nose may be fractured, maybe even his cheekbone.

"A trip to the hospital would probably be the best course of action."

"I can't go there as they'd only ask how I got the injuries. I can't really say I walked into a door, can I? Besides, Walker has threatened to hurt you and Lily if I go to the police. I can't risk it."

Hugh's furrowed brow said it all, "Shit, he means business." He checked Nathan's bruised body. "You can just say you were beaten up in the street and you didn't see your assailants. It's not that hard."

Reluctantly, Nathan agreed and gingerly walked to the car with Hugh's help.

The injuries were as they expected and the police were called. Nathan gave them the story Hugh had suggested, so there was very little for them to go on. Hugh didn't like Nathan's ease at lying so well; it made him wonder how much he could trust his friend, and whether he'd already trusted him too much?

"Come back with me, you'll feel safer and Faith's cooking is more nutritious than takeaways."

"Does Faith know about the history between me and Walker yet?"

"Good God no, we'll say you got mugged near The Spread Eagle like you told the police; that's clearly quite believable."

Nathan wanted to raise his eyebrows but found that he couldn't. He knew he had no other choice. They returned to his house and packed a weekend bag before making a hasty retreat.

He didn't relish a weekend in Faith's company, but it was preferable to another beating. He believed he wouldn't live through the next one.

Hugh drummed his fingers on the steering wheel as he, too, wondered about Faith's reaction to the concept of their last-minute surprise guest.

Chapter Twenty-Seven

"My word, what has happened to you?" exclaimed Faith as she met the pair in the hall.

"I was mugged near The Spread Eagle," replied Nathan who found the deceit easy to recount, much to his chagrin.

"I said he should stay with us for a couple of nights, darling."

Faith looked at Hugh and shrugged her shoulders before she disappeared into the kitchen to make them tea.

"The proverbial hot, sweet kind, I suppose," whispered Nathan.

"Don't be mean; she's being nice so be nice back."

They sat in the lounge waiting for Faith to return. The air was filled with the smell of herbs and garlic, which reminded Nathan that he hadn't eaten. Sadly, his two precariously fixed front teeth would ban him from eating anything thicker than tomato soup.

"Did they take anything?" asked Faith as she entered the room with a tray of drinks.

"Who?" replied Nathan.

"The muggers, of course."

"Oh no, I fought them off, hence the injuries."

Hugh didn't enjoy being the audience to the dishonesty directed at his wife, especially when he was part of it.

"Let's not dwell on that incident. Anything worthy of viewing tonight on TV?"

"I don't know, darling. I've got choir practise."

"Tonight?"

"We've got that concert coming up, remember? Anyway, you've got each other for company."

The men sat and watched Faith leave the room. It was then that Nathan witnessed emotional pain etching itself on his friend's face. "Why the worried look?" he asked in a hushed tone.

"There's something going on with her, she's not been her usual self. I can only think she's having an affair." Hugh slumped back in the armchair and looked deep in thought.

"You could always check-up on her."

"That way leads to the slippery road of destruction. I have to be able to trust her, otherwise the marriage is worthless."

Faith popped her head around the doorway to announce her departure. Hugh held his hand out to her, but she just blew him a kiss before leaving. He looked down at his brogues whilst he sifted through the range of emotions scattered around his mind.

"So what are you going to do about Walker?" he finally managed to ask.

"I'm not sure, but I know I can't let him see that I'm intimidated."

"And are you?"

"Of course I bloody am!" he exclaimed, incredulity rising in his voice. "He's got enough men to beat me, you, and Lily up simultaneously. This is a no-win situation. I feel like I hold your lives in my hands."

As the evening progressed, Nathan found that his body and face hurt even more. The bruises had swollen to such an extent that his skin felt it could stretch no further. His head began to swim and Hugh noticed how pale his friend was looking underneath the black and purple mounds.

"You look like you could do with going to bed. The pain relief they gave you should kick in soon." His neck reddened at his choice of words.

"If you don't mind, I'd like that. Sorry I'm not much company for you."

Hugh carried the overnight bag to the spare room, whilst Nathan hobbled slowly behind him, finding each stair considerably difficult to mount.

Hugh left him alone and then returned to the lounge to rummage through some maudlin thoughts about his marriage. With his hand slapped across his forehead, he tried not to think about Faith with another man as it made him feel physically sick.

Lily had eaten a small egg salad with a fresh tomato and basil sauce. She remained seated in the kitchen listening to the classical music playing softly in the background.

The stained-glass panel in the front door had been replaced, so there wasn't the constant visual reminder of the fear she lived in.

She hoped that Walker had still received the fabric and note at the town hall, but she knew she would need to step up her campaign if she was to feel less controlled by him and was to achieve her desired outcome.

She took the tatty box and picked up another photocopy of the Poplar Ward leaflet. She then typed a note on her laptop asking the recipient to look into Walker's background as a charge nurse there. She then typed one word—Abuse—and then addressed the envelope to Rachel at the party HQ.

Pleased with her work, she decided to go for a jog. Dressed in black sportswear, she picked up the envelope and left the house.

Her route took her past the post box and then onward towards Nathan's house, which she noticed was in complete darkness. In some streets, people were arriving at houses with balloons on the gates, undoubtedly for a party. In other streets, she saw couples arriving home, laden down with supermarket shopping bags.

She kept jogging at a steady pace as she enjoyed watching snippets of life carry on around her. As she arrived in her own street, she could see in the distance a lone figure standing outside her house. Under the street light, the figure looked tall and broad, and with a sick feeling in her stomach, she concluded that it was Walker waiting for her. She stood still for a moment. The hair on her arms stood on end whilst she realised that she couldn't let him frighten her in her own home.

So, with gentle, rhythmic steps, she jogged toward her home and towards Walker who'd turned to face her.

"Finlay, what a pleasant surprise."

"I thought you'd think so."

"Do you want something?"

"At this time of day, of course I do. I want to come in."

Lily put the key in the door, focusing on not letting her internal tremors become visible. Walker followed her in and closed the door behind him.

"How's Rachel?" she asked.

"That's a strange question, why do you ask?"

"Oh, you must have noticed that she has a crush on you."

"I hadn't noticed."

"Come now, surely you're flattered by the attention of a young woman."

Walker stepped closer to Lily who then found herself backed into a corner in the hallway. She averted her eyes from his.

"I have my own interests; one of them being you," he replied in a low gravelly voice that sent shivers up her spine.

"Anyway, would you like a beer?" she tried to sound nonchalant as she sidled past him.

"Of course."

Walker wandered into the lounge, looked around and then sank into the sofa. Lily brought him a beer, and an orange juice for herself.

"Sit here," he said as he slapped the seat next to him. She automatically obeyed him like a marionette. He placed his hand on her thigh, which looked tiny in comparison. He moved his hand up and down her thigh, and all she could do was bite on her bottom lip and fix her stare on the vase of flowers in the bay window.

She could smell his beery breath as he nuzzled into her neck and licked the rim of her ear with his fat tongue. She was disgusted by his actions, but she was unprepared to battle with him.

As she felt his hands wrap around her neck, she felt her strength and resolve evaporate. She tried to raise her arms into a defensive position but she was thwarted by her own fear.

"You have no will to resist me," he rasped in her ear as he applied more pressure with his hands.

She could feel her head swim with a million stars and as she closed her eyes, the same stars floated around the inside of her eyelids. Then his mobile rang. His hands remained firmly in position, as though he was oblivious to the sound and buzzing. It persisted in ringing, so he pushed her into the back of the sofa and retrieved his mobile from his pocket. He scowled until he saw who it was and then the scowl melted away.

"Yes?" he appeared to listen intently. "What, right now? Okay, okay I'm coming."

He shoved the mobile back into his pocket and stood up, then without even glancing at Lily, he walked away and out through the front door. She heard the door close, and then she vomited onto the wooden floorboards.

Walker's footsteps pounded the pavement as he headed home. It was a twenty-five minute walk, but if he moved fast enough he could cut down the time.

He was panting for breath by the time he reached the end of terrace property. He pushed open the gate, making sure that he closed it behind him and then he went inside.

"You know I don't like to be kept waiting, Finlay," said his sister Muriel who was three years his senior.

"Sorry, Muriel," he replied with his head hung low.

"Louder," she hissed as she struck him across his back with a short leather riding crop.

Muriel was almost equal to Walker in stature, and thanks to her hobby of lifting weights, her arms were more like fence posts than angel wings.

Walker fell to his knees and began to kiss Muriel's large booted feet as he begged her forgiveness. She lifted one foot and sent him reeling backwards with one swift movement.

"I don't want to hear your snivelling, Finlay. I want you to make me happy. You know what that means, don't you?"

"Yes, Muriel, yes," he replied as he lay curled up on the floor like a chastised puppy.

She bent down and pulled him up by the lobe of his ear. He daren't make a sound as she hated that. As he stood to his feet, whilst remaining in a hunched over position, he began to shuffle behind Muriel who was still pinching his ear.

They travelled upstairs and into her bedroom where she finally released him from her grip. As a parting gesture, she slapped him across the back of his head, and again, he made no murmur or moan.

"Now strip," she commanded as she stood over him with her hands on her rotund hips.

Walker obeyed as he knew he had no choice. He stopped having a choice when their mother left them when he was ten and Muriel was thirteen. Muriel had found her authority, and Walker had found a love that he would do just about anything to keep.

As Walker stood naked before her, she eyed him up and down and then she ordered him to remove her clothes. After years of such treatment, he'd managed to control his shaking hands as he took off her clothes before finally removing her underwear.

Muriel picked up a wide leather belt with a large brass buckle and proceeded to lash Walker's torso. She stood back to admire her work that had left satisfactory red road-like marks all over his back and chest. She then ordered him onto the bed. He shut his eyes and thought of Lily and then he thought of Muriel.

Chapter Twenty-Eight

The following morning, as Nathan lay in bed in the overly floral spare bedroom, he was distracted from his throbbing head by the sound of Hugh and Faith arguing downstairs. He couldn't make out what they were saying but he imagined it was in the realm of possibilities that he was the main feature in the *contra tent*.

He propped himself up on his elbow and winced before he managed to turn himself onto his side to sit up in bed. The physical pain was getting unbearable and his breathing still shallow. All the same, he levered himself out of the bed and shuffled his way to the bathroom. He splashed his still swollen face with cold water in an attempt to revive himself, only to find that patting it dry was excruciating.

As he was coming out of the bathroom, he heard the front door slam shut followed by the house falling silent. He hoped he wasn't alone with Faith. Fortunately Hugh appeared on the landing.

"You're up then, how are you feeling?"

"Rough and sore like a piece of meat that's been tenderised."

Hugh walked up to Nathan and peered at his facial injuries.

"It's going to take a while for you to recover; I'll get a locum in to cover you at work for the next week or so."

Nathan tried to shake his head but his neck muscles were so tight that he found he couldn't move.

"I'd rather go to work but I know you're right, thanks."

Nathan gingerly got dressed whilst Hugh made some coffee. Once dressed, Nathan dragged his aching body to the kitchen where he sat at the table with Hugh.

"Faith not around?"

"No, she had to go out."

Nathan sipped the lukewarm coffee through a straw which gave him much needed relief for his parched throat.

"I heard you both arguing, was it about me?"

"Why does everything have to be about you?"

"It doesn't, I just wondered, that's all."

"In case you hadn't noticed, there's an atmosphere between Faith and I. I haven't figured out exactly what's wrong."

Nathan sucked on the straw and watched his friend walk about the kitchen aimlessly. "Have you bought her flowers and taken her out for a meal?"

Hugh pointed to the vase on the windowsill and then said that Faith always complained she was too busy or too tired to go out in the evening with him.

"Well, what about a Sunday lunch in a gastro pub?"

"For someone who's already had a failed marriage and a string of short-term flings, you really relish advising me on my love life, don't you?"

"I don't want you making the same mistakes I did. I won't raise the issue again." He made slurping noises at the bottom of the mug with the straw as he finished his drink. Hugh offered him a refill but Nathan waved his hand over the mug.

"I'd like to go home now, if you don't mind."

Hugh wanted to discourage him from returning, but he could see that Nathan looked worn and weak and probably wanted the peace of his own home and his own bed.

"At least Faith will be happy when she gets home," Nathan said.

"Somehow I doubt that."

Nathan eased himself into the car and found that the seatbelt still put agonising pressure on his ribcage.

"Keep your mobile with you at all times and call me if you're in trouble."

"I'm not sure what you'd be able to do."

"I'd call the police, I'm no fighter." He shut the door and started the engine. "You do know if this starts to involve the clinic, I'll have to involve the police further in the matter," he continued.

An uneasy silence hung between them, so for the last five minutes of the journey Hugh put the radio on. As he pulled up outside Nathan's house, the tension in Nathan's neck muscles increased.

"Would you like me to come in with you?"

"No, I'll be fine." Nathan sighed and got out of the car, dragging the overnight bag behind him. Hugh waited to see him go inside before he drove off.

Once inside, Nathan peered around the house to check that everything was in its place and that all was quiet; once assured, he began to relax as much as his body would allow him to.

Sitting in the battered leather chair, he wondered whether Lily was okay. He hoped that he'd not put her in any danger by leading Walker to her house. He remembered Walker's threats, but Lily was nobody to him, was she?

The day was pleasantly warm and a clear blue mantle hung overhead. Lily wandered slowly around her garden surveying the plants and weeds that required her attention. She'd had a poor night's sleep awaiting Walker's return that never came. The garden held a therapeutic quality that helped maintain her mental equilibrium in times of trouble.

The telephone rang and stopped her in her tracks. She was unsure about answering it but the persistent noise urged her to pick up the receiver.

"Lily. It's Nathan."

She remained mute.

"Are you all right? I mean, I was just checking to see how you are feeling."

"I'm fine thanks, and you?"

"Not bad, but I wanted to let you know that I won't be in next week."

"Taking a holiday?"

"Something like that. Anyway, Hugh's getting a locum in." He paused to gather breath. "Well, if you're okay, I'll see you in a week's time."

"Okay, bye." She put the receiver down and felt puzzled about his call. As she began to walk away, the phone rang again. Thinking it was

Nathan again, she picked up quickly. "Yes, Nathan."

"Sorry to disappoint you, it's me."

She knew he'd call sooner or later. "Finlay. I was expecting somebody else."

"Yes, the good doctor, I see."

Lily blushed but said nothing.

"I shall be around later, so don't bother going out. If you're not in, I will find you."

Thinking that finally the time had come, she asked him what time he'd be arriving.

"When I choose to arrive."

The phone went dead. She dislodged the clouds forming in her so that she could start planning. She wasn't going to be submissive this time.

She dashed upstairs and retrieved the camcorder she'd bought recently, which was small enough to secret somewhere in a room. She couldn't decide which room to put it in, the bedroom or lounge. She thought the latter would be easier and more appropriate as they'd not ventured upstairs yet. The bookshelves in the lounge also lent themselves to be an ideal hiding place.

Once she positioned it amongst the books, she pressed record and wandered around, sat on the sofa, and lay on the floor before crawling all around. She checked what had been filmed and she saw that it caught most of her movements except for the floor.

She put some bottles of beer in the fridge and then made herself some hot lemon water. She sat cogitating over her plans for the evening and thought that finally she'd have some concrete, irrefutable evidence to demonstrate what a sadistic abuser Walker was. The police would have no choice but to arrest him.

She wandered back into the garden and for the first time in a long time, the sun shone in her heart as well as on her idyllic, yet wild garden.

The evening wasn't without its dangers, and she knew she'd have to provoke him without being antagonistic. A bottle of red wine was available for later to provide the bolster she'd need to put her plan into action.

She spent the rest of the day tidying the house and preening herself. It was almost seven thirty and she knew he could turn up at any time.

By ten o'clock, she had begun to wilt. Tiredness invaded her mind and body. She felt if he didn't come soon, she'd have to go to bed as her nerves were shredding more by minute.

She was on her third glass of wine when the doorbell rang. It was twenty past ten and she could only imagine that it was Walker. As she made her way to the front door, she could see the outline of a sizeable figure standing there.

She took a deep breath and opened the door. "Finlay, I've been expecting you."

He stepped inside without waiting to be invited, pushing her to one side as he did so. She closed the door and turned to face him but he was already in the kitchen helping himself to a beer.

"You only have rabbit food in your fridge; no good for a man like me."

"I'm sorry; I didn't know you needed feeding. I have some egg and salad."

"Beer will do me for now."

"Shall we move to the lounge?"

"What's your hurry? Got the good doctor waiting in there?"

"I thought we'd be more comfortable there, that's all." Lily could sense her cheeks tingling and warming, so she tried to hide her face behind her wine glass. "Are you concerned that he could be here?"

"He doesn't concern me in the slightest. I control you, not him."

"Control me?" she repeated as she shifted around in her chair.

"Yes, don't play coy with me, it doesn't suit you. I can tell you're afraid of me and you'd do anything to keep me happy."

Lily didn't like the way the conversation was going and she needed to get him to the lounge. As she attempted to get up, he grabbed her wrist from across the table. His speed startled her and she winced as he twisted her wrist.

"Have I done something wrong, Finlay?"

"You do nothing right, as far as I'm concerned."

He stood up whilst maintaining a hold on her wrist, and then he walked around to her side of the table. With his other hand he grabbed her hair at the back of her head and pulled it back so her throat was exposed and uncomfortable. She found it hard to swallow.

"You've always been a little tease."

He bent forward and began nipping at her neck with his teeth. His gesture was gentle to start with but he gradually bit her harder and harder.

"You're hurting me," she strained.

"You're not allowed to complain, I'm in charge."

He then dragged her upstairs whilst she struggled to get free, but that only made him grip her harder. She was cursing herself for not buying two camcorders, but she knew it was too late.

Once in the bedroom, he demanded that she undress. At first she refused, but after a couple of blows about the head, she gave in. As she stood naked before him, she vowed that he'd never do that to her again. Ever.

He then demanded that she undress him, and it was as she unbuttoned his shirt she saw the welt marks on his chest and abdomen. When he noticed her looking at them, he pushed her away and buttoned up the shirt.

"Trousers," he commanded.

She was repulsed by his very presence in her room. She vowed that although he might take her body, he could never take her mind. Her sanity would remain hers to destroy, not his, and that was a promise she made to herself.

When he left the house, she ran herself a deep bath. She gently traced her face and neck which felt tender to the touch. She lay in the bath and submerged herself. As a trail of tiny bubbles trickled upwards from her nose, her mind felt comfortably quiet and still.

It won't happen again, she said to herself; *I'm the one with the power.*

Chapter Twenty-Nine

On a regular basis, Nathan would take himself to The Spread Eagle for one of their succulent Sunday roasts. Sadly, on that particular Sunday, he realised that he could not go as his face looked like it had been in a fight with a bag of spanners. And besides, his teeth were still a little loose, so he could still only manage soft, pureed food.

Although he hated to admit it, he was feeling sorry for himself and he wondered what the gods wanted him to do. Was he to be eternally punished for not confronting Walker's behaviour? He was now in a quandary in that it was no longer just his professional career and integrity that were in jeopardy, it was also his life and the lives of others.

As he perused the kitchen cupboards for a tin of soup or baked beans, the doorbell rang. Danger had never announced itself to him before, it just appeared. In light of that, he fearlessly approached the front door. He couldn't see a figure through the diamond-shaped glass so he just opened the door. No one was there. He stepped out to take a look up and down the street, when his foot slipped and there, oozing around the sole of his shoe, was a dog turd. He cursed the idiot who'd left it there, and then he hobbled to the tiny patch of grass at the front of the house to wipe the unctuous stench from his shoe.

Muttering to himself he returned inside and closed the door. The putrid stench had pervaded his house and his nostrils. Didn't people realise that he was already suffering enough?

In a bid to boost his flagging morale, he ordered a creamy curry from the Indian takeaway and decided that he'd watch some war movies back to back.

By the time four o'clock had arrived, he'd eaten a moist curry with no rice and was about to start watching his third movie when the phone rang. His back and knees had stiffened with the prolonged lounging on the sofa, so he heaved himself up and shuffled to the phone.

It was Hugh asking if he was okay.

"I feel like I'm seventy years old, but I'm coping. Thanks."

"How about I come round, take your mind off things."

Nathan reluctantly agreed as he found that he was taking pleasure from his hedonistic day. But true to his word, twenty minutes later, Hugh arrived at the door.

"Holy crap. Bizarre smell in your house," he said as he stepped inside. "It smells like curried animal, what the hell have you eaten?"

Nathan explained the doorstep gift, which Hugh only seemed to half listen to. "I'm having a scotch, medicinal purposes only, of course. What can I get you?"

"I'll have a strong coffee."

Hugh proceeded to follow Nathan around like a lost puppy. His walk was unusually slouched and his scuffed his shoes along the floorboards.

"I've had a monstrous row with Faith."

"Another one?"

Hugh frowned at him. "She found out that I'd been checking up on her at the book group. She was volcanic with rage."

"Well, it's as you said, it shows you have no trust. Anyway, what was her explanation?"

Hugh followed Nathan back to the lounge, his nose still twitching at the peculiar smell.

"When she found out from Agnes what I'd been doing, she confronted me about my motive. I ask you. All of a sudden I'm the bad guy?"

Nathan stuffed a cushion behind his back whilst his friend recounted the recriminations that flew between husband and wife. Nathan had half an eye on the TV screen which was still playing a war movie. Although on mute, he could still follow the plot.

"So finally, she said that if I don't trust her, I can leave. Bloody great."

Nathan was caught out and his face reddened. Their eyes met fleetingly and then drifted apart to a safe distance.

"You can stay here for a bit until things cool down, which they will. Give her time."

"Sanguine advice from you. Thanks for the offer."

They sat in uneasy silence, with Hugh periodically checking his mobile phone.

Nathan's head began to pound again, but he could see Hugh was in emotional turmoil and that his own pain had to be put to one side for a change. It was a new concept for him, and he glimpsed an enlightening moment through the dense clouds.

"Why don't you go home, pack an overnight bag with clothes and beer and stay here. Let the air cool between you both." He looked at Hugh with the wide eyes of an expectant child.

Hugh sat fiddling with his mobile, unable to speak momentarily.

"It saddens me that it's come to this," he said as he put down the empty mug. "But it might be a good idea."

He rose and indicated for Nathan not to bother getting up. "I'll see you in an hour."

And then he was gone.

Like clockwork, an hour later, Hugh returned with a larger than expected overnight bag and another bag with rattling bottles. He looked pale and drawn, and his eyes were red rimmed and glassy.

"Take your stuff up to the spare room, then come down and have a beer, you look like you could do with one."

Hugh wasn't that hungry so he was content with just a ham sandwich, whilst Nathan finished off the sloppy curry. They sat quietly with another war movie playing on the TV. Hugh's eyes looked straight through the screen.

Nathan was overcome with alcohol and pain and decided to leave his subdued friend sitting in the lounge, nursing the same beer he'd had for over an hour.

Nathan staggered up the stairs and into the bathroom where he was greeted by his stubbly, multi-coloured face in the shaving mirror. He wished he could fall asleep and not wake up again until his face had regained its normal appearance.

After completing his ablutions, he went to bed where he fell into a peaceful sleep, thanks to Hugh's presence.

Hugh wasn't tired. He was emotionally drained, but not tired. His heart and mind were racing. His silent mobile lay on the arm of the chair like a pet hamster that had lost the will to turn the wheel. He picked it up and dialled Faith's number.

"Yes, Hugh?"

"I know I said I wouldn't, but I miss hearing your voice. I miss you."

Faith's silence shouted rejection in his ear, but like a child pushing the boundary, he kept persisting with platitudes of praise and words of woe.

"You've not given us much of a cooling off period," she said quietly.

"I couldn't help it. I don't know you anymore. You keep going out, not answering your mobile, and you misled me as to your whereabouts." He punched his thigh to stop himself from digging a bigger hole, but by the tone of her voice, he was already too late.

"I have to go, my lover's getting impatient."

"Don't be sarcastic, Faith. God, I'm sorry, I didn't mean—"

"Perhaps you are, but you need to show it more. Goodnight, Hugh."

He hit himself on the forehead with a sharp tap from his mobile phone. He knew that Faith would never really have an affair; but since she'd stopped focusing on him so intently, he had found the evil sap of jealousy rise within him. The air surrounding him was poisoned by his iniquity.

He thought back to the time when he first met Faith at the doctors' ball. She looked the epitome of allure in her lilac, silk ball gown, with her waist-length hair in a thick plait that traced the gentle curvature of her spine.

If he remembered correctly, it was Faith who approached him when he was standing with Nathan. He was surprised that she was addressing him as it was usually Nathan who attracted the attention of women at such events.

She worked for a mental health charity as an advocate and he remembered her being very passionate about her work. He found her intently fascinating, and it wasn't long before Nathan had wandered off, leaving the pair to discuss the legal ramifications of the mental health system.

If he wasn't mistaken, it was Faith who flirted with him and it was she who made him feel special. In fact, that was the way she treated him up until the time of the partnership between him and Nathan. He'd had minimal contact with Nathan up until that point.

The day he brought Nathan into their home seemed to be a day like any other, but looking back, it summoned subtle changes in his wife that perhaps he didn't pick up on at the time.

She was her usual polite and engaging self, traits that made him feel proud to be with her. She wasn't put out when Nathan stayed with them for a few weeks whilst he looked for somewhere to live. But as time passed, she stopped staying up with them in the evening, preferring to take herself to bed with a book or a headache. Perhaps he was so wrapped up in catching up with Nathan and machinating over their student days, that he'd allowed a distance to forge itself between him and his wife.

Nathan was looking for work, and so in between interviews he spent much of his time in the house. At that time, Faith was only working part-time as a charity coordinator and so they spent many hours together.

Nathan became a locum doctor and on one of his travels he came across the rundown clinic with an elderly doctor about to retire. He was so fired-up that as soon as Hugh walked into his home that evening, Nathan was talking double-speed about the place and the opportunity afforded to them both.

Hugh thought Faith would be delighted about the development as she'd always wanted him to have a partnership in a medical practice. Although she was pleased for him, she was subdued, *or was it reticent*, he thought to himself. As he reflected, he realised that he should have discussed it with her, involved her in it, but he was swept away by Nathan's enthusiasm and fortitude.

He wondered whether it was actually he who had let Faith down emotionally by deserting her for another, the other being Nathan. He didn't want to be on his own with his torturous thoughts so he walked upstairs and knocked on Nathan's door.

"Am I disturbing you?" he said as he peered around the door. "I just needed a chat to clear my head."

Nathan mumbled something which didn't deter Hugh from entering the room and sitting on the edge of Nathan's bed. His action roused Nathan.

"What are you doing? I really need to get some sleep, Hugh."

Hugh stood up quickly and hovered over the bed, feeling awkward and yet reluctant to leave, whilst Nathan drifted back to sleep. Hugh was just about to leave, when the sound of splintering glass pierced the silence. He stood stock still and listened fearfully, then turned to Nathan. He bent over him and shook him on the shoulder. Nathan roused with difficulty and was very irritable. He was about to reach out and clout his friend when he too heard some disturbing noises coming from downstairs.

Nathan sat up, suddenly sober. The two men stared at one another, wide eyed and palpitating hearts. An uneasy quiet shrouded the house. Regardless of the anxiety gnawing them, they knew they should investigate.

"Call the police," whispered Hugh.

Nathan got up and slung his dressing gown on. He ignored Hugh's advice, even though he knew his omission and actions could have dire consequences for his already battered body.

"Oh that's right, why bother the police when we can deal with it ourselves?" Hugh hissed.

Nathan shot him a glance and then opened the door slowly; he knew he could only open it halfway before the hinges would squeak. Once they'd squeezed through, they came to a halt on the landing.

They could hear an unidentifiable noise—rather like a hissing snake—coming from downstairs. They shrugged their shoulders at one another then they edged their way to the top of the stairs. They took one step at a time, Nathan first so he could make sure they avoided the creaking steps.

In his heightened anxiety, Hugh forgot to mirror Nathan's movements and landed on a creaking step. Suddenly someone darted out of the lounge and out through the kitchen door.

Nathan tried to pursue him, but his ribs hurt with the exertion. He stopped at the lounge door and clung to the doorframe whilst he tried to breathe.

Hugh switched the hallway light on and then all became clear. They could see a trail of black spray paint running along the wall from within the kitchen. When Nathan switched the lounge lights on, they were confronted with scrawled words sprayed on all of the walls. Hugh gasped as he saw the word "coward" sprayed in huge black letters. Some of the paint was running down the walls.

The men stood dumbstruck until Hugh handed the phone to Nathan.

"Hello, police, I've had a break-in."

Hugh could hear someone speaking to Nathan at the end of the line.

"No, I don't think anything was taken. Okay, see you then."

"What's happening?"

"A patrol car will be around within the next half an hour," he said as he walked over to the bottle of scotch sitting on the sideboard.

"I think I'll join you," said Hugh, holding out a glass.

They sat in the lounge surrounded by the grotesque graffiti, warming the scotch by wrapping their hands around the glass. Forty minutes later, the police arrived.

Nathan showed them around and then they returned to the lounge.

"And you say you've no idea who did this, sir," asked the young police officer as he scrutinized the wall art, "only the words seem very personal, sir, if you don't mind my saying so."

"I told you, we couldn't see their face, they were wearing a hoody." Nathan took another swig of scotch to moisten his arid mouth. "I'm a local doctor and so I get to meet a lot of bizarre people. Someone might have a grudge against me, for example."

Attic of the Mind **185**

"Such as what, sir?"

"I said 'for example.' I don't actually know what it could be."

Nathan could have happily bitten off his own tongue as the police officer gave him a patronizing stare. Hugh felt the need to interject.

"Perhaps it's connected to the assault the other day."

"I was going to bring that up, sir. Our records show the other crime against you. Are you sure you aren't a target for someone?"

"All right, officer, look, although I didn't see who it was, a traveller woman did come in last week requesting a termination. I think it may have something to do with that, a pissed off prospective father perhaps with Catholic values."

The officer stared at Nathan from over the rim of his glasses and the other officer remained quiet. Both officers waited for Nathan to finish his explanation. Nathan's cheeks flushed and his throat constricted.

"I'll give you a crime number for your insurance report. If you remember any other details, such as a name, sir, please contact me on this number," he said as he handed Nathan a business card along with the report sheet.

After the police left, Nathan let out a deep sigh.

"Why didn't you bring up Walker, instead of that bloody cock-and-bull story? You had the perfect opportunity."

"Oh yes, I should have said that Walker, the respected pillar of The English Party—the not-quite-far-right-or-racist party—sent his heavies round to beat the crap out of me for no apparent reason. That would have gone down well."

"Don't be so melodramatic, I have problems too."

"Yes, but yours don't have the potential to extinguish your life."

Hugh just sat there pursing his lips so they looked like a duck's bottom, which made Nathan laugh. Hugh gave him a quizzical look and then a smile broke across his face. "I really should be getting to bed; I'm meeting the locum doctor before clinic begins tomorrow."

Nathan nodded and waved him off whilst he poured himself another shot of scotch to drink whilst he surveyed the intruder's handy work.

He raised his glass to the wall, downed the shot and then made his way to bed.

Hugh was lying in bed, wide awake with fearful thoughts churning through his head. The welfare of his friend troubled him, and he could only see a horrific outcome for Nathan, and not much elation for himself, either.

Chapter Thirty

Hugh muddled through the first couple of days at work alongside the locum doctor and a quieter-than-usual Lily, whom he'd noticed was also wearing more make-up than usual.

The locum was a fastidious man who was heading for retirement and wanted very little commitment in his final years. He kept himself shut in his room at lunchtime, which left Hugh and Lily alone.

Neither person was invigorated enough to talk, so they sat together in the public garden, people watching.

"That young man's had his eye on the brunette under the weeping willow for the past couple of days. It looks like he's plucked up the courage to make a move," said Hugh.

"I do hope they get together, I'd like to see love's young dream blossom here. It'd be appropriate, don't you think?"

"I suppose so, but I hope he knows he's leaving himself wide open to potential heartache."

Lily heard the wistful melancholy in his voice, but she didn't offer any empty clichés. She wanted to ask if he was okay, but she didn't think it was her place to ask.

They watched the young man with shoulder length hair approach the brunette with an elfin crop. He appeared shy with his faltering approach, and the woman smiled with an openness that swept away any nerves he may have been feeling. He sat next to her on the bench and held out his hand, which she shook with enthusiasm.

"Poor soul," said Hugh as he watched the mating game unfold.

"I didn't take you for a cynic," she said with rosy, glowing cheeks.

"Neither did I," he replied quietly.

Lunchtime was over, so they ambled back to the clinic. Hugh found himself wishing he could sit with her in the garden all afternoon. And as for Lily, she wished the afternoon would go on forever.

A few patients moaned to Lily about not being able to see Doctor Rine, and had to resign themselves to seeing the locum. Lily didn't realise that patients actually liked Nathan. It was a revelation to her.

Hugh had a gap between patients and so he took the opportunity to ring his wife. Her mobile rang for what seemed like a long time before she finally picked up.

"Yes?"

"Darling, could I come over after work and sort out this mess. I miss you madly."

"It's not convenient. I've got extra choir practice due to the concert at the Minster this Saturday. You've probably forgotten."

Hugh's face grew red and he punched his thigh. "I hadn't forgotten. I'd like to go, of course. So when can we meet up?"

"Why don't you come for Sunday lunch? I'll have the time then."

Hugh screwed up his face and then tempered his tone before he spoke. "Okay, I'll come over at twelve. I'll see you Saturday anyway."

"You'll see me singing but I won't have time to speak to you," she said before hanging up.

The conversation left him baffled and irate at her dismissal of his needs. A mist fell before his eyes and rationality melted away. He walked out of his room and into the reception where Lily was hunched over some invoices.

"Do you fancy coming to the chorale society concert at the Minster this Saturday? Faith's in the choir."

She kept her head slightly bowed and curled her toes in her shoes. "That would be lovely, thank you," she said as she continued to avoid eye contact before returning to the invoices.

Hugh bounced back into the waiting room to collect his next patient, with more vigour than he'd had in days.

By Friday, Nathan's face had reduced to its near normal size, but it still retained hues of yellow and green tinges around the nose, mouth, and eye sockets. He'd organised a decorator to erase the offending words from the walls thus restoring his home to its former tranquil status.

Nathan was enjoying having Hugh to stay, but he knew it would have to end sooner or later, and he felt that the coming weekend would be the last. Hugh had called him to tell him about the plans for Sunday, and he anticipated that the lunch would be followed by an intimate moment that would push the pair together once more. *As it should be*, he thought to himself.

What had been most remarkable about the week was that he'd felt his normal self, something he'd not felt for some time. Once the battle scars on his face and walls had theoretically healed, he'd resorted to scanning the memories etched on his mind that were pleasant and carefree. Walker's threats were evaporated from his life for a week, and as the weekend approached, the contrast in his emotional wellbeing was magnified.

He picked up the local paper and saw an article on Walker, who was hosting a garden party for local businesses and charities. The local primary schools were going to perform a few songs to entertain the crowd. The paper was going to do a feature on it the following week. Nathan threw the paper down in disgust.

On some level, he felt like he deserved all the punishment meted out to him, but that didn't stop him from hoping that it would stop soon so that he could be emotionally free at last.

Nathan heard a key in the front door which initially froze his heart with fear, until he heard Hugh's voice.

"Do you fancy going to the pub? Might be our last chance for a while. I've got to focus on Faith a lot more for the foreseeable future."

Nathan could see how buoyant Hugh looked and sounded, and he didn't want to burst his bubble.

"Why not, but as long as we don't stay in The Crown all evening."

Hugh nodded and then picked up the takeaway menu next to the phone. "My treat," he declared as he waved it at Nathan.

Nathan's teeth had gradually settled back into the gums, allowing him to be more adventurous with food again.

Thirty minutes later, they were sitting around the table eating chicken korma and naan bread. Nathan had a vision of it being their last supper together, in which Hugh played the saintly figure and he played the Judas figure who would later be found hanging from a tree.

"What will you do if Faith rejects you on Sunday?"

Hugh put down his fork and looked at Nathan with eyes as big as saucers. "I can't believe you'd even entertain such an idea, let alone suggest it to me."

He stared incredulously at Nathan as he awaited an explanation or at least an apology.

"You seem to forget how my marriage ended. No announcement, no fireworks or banners; it just quietly fizzled out without me even noticing, until she told me she was leaving," mused Nathan.

His eyes misted over as he reflected on how his life could have been had he paid more attention to his wife, instead of flirting with every nurse and medical professional that came his way. He was always so self-assured and personable with the women who surrounded him at work. He wondered if he had donned his white coat and stethoscope at home, and behaved in the same way with his wife, would she have remained with him?

"Anyway, are you coming to the chorale concert tomorrow?"

"Do I have to?"

"No, I won't be alone anyway. Lily's coming with me."

Nathan sat up in his chair. "Are you crazy? What will Faith think about you taking another woman?"

"It's Lily, a work colleague whom my wife has met. Besides, she is far too skinny for me. I like Faith's womanly curves."

"But does Faith know that?"

Hugh rose up to grab a beer before he turned around to face Nathan. "I'm not you. Faith knows that I love her and that says it all." And with that, he moved to the lounge leaving Nathan feeling like a four-year-old boy.

Nathan meandered to the lounge with a bottle of beer and plonked himself in the leather chair.

"I think I should come, it'll look less intimate. You know it makes sense not to upset Faith right now, don't you think?"

"If you say so."

"Right, let's go," said Nathan as he ushered Hugh out of the door, leaving their bottles of beer half full.

The sky was clear as they walked to The Crown, and the birdsong echoed around the trees that lined the road. They passed groups of young people larking around and generally enjoying the zest of life.

"We used to be like that," Nathan said as he nodded in the direction of the youths.

"You still are in many ways."

"Explain yourself."

"You've had a string of women with no eye on commitment. You're an ardent pub goer and you take very little in life, bar your job, seriously."

"That's a rather damning character reference."

"You know the old adage, 'truth hurts.'"

"Ouch," said Nathan as he play-punched Hugh on the arm.

They arrived at The Crown which, compared to The Spread Eagle, had fewer smokers standing outside the entrance. Inside, there was a more sedate crowd, interspersed with the odd student who was being keenly watched by the owner.

Unlike Nathan, Hugh didn't frequent the pub enough to have a usual or favourite table and neither was he eyed up by several women dotted around the bar. The chances of the latter happening to Hugh were remote. He sent out I'm-unavailable vibes, as Nathan called them, to all around him.

Hugh had always been a one-woman man, not an occasionally two-timing lover like his friend. But their traits complimented one another in a strange way, although Hugh always hoped that some of his fidelity would rub off onto Nathan one day.

Nathan looked around at the relatively tranquil scene rolled out before him, and to his surprise the evening was more sobering and tiring than he'd anticipated. Before he knew it, he was requesting that they return back home as his head was beginning to thud after two pints.

Hugh didn't appear to mind, as his head was full of the anticipation of the rendezvous tomorrow with both women, but for different reasons he had not as yet worked out.

Chapter Thirty-One

The following morning, Nathan noticed that Hugh was acting like a boy who had over indulged in the sweet shop. He was ricocheting from wall to wall on a sugar high. He assumed and hoped it was because he was seeing his wife in the concert that evening, and not because he was being accompanied by the ethereal Lily.

Nathan was unclear whether he was going to the concert to keep an eye on Hugh and Lily, or whether it was to protect his own skin from Walker and his men. Either way, he knew he was in for a boring evening.

"I'm cooking a meal tonight as a thank you for letting me stay," said Hugh as he pulled out a casserole dish from the cupboard. "Chicken in white wine, my speciality. Although rarely appreciated by Faith, who didn't like the sauce."

Nathan felt as though he needed to temper Hugh's bubbling enthusiasm. "I thought Faith said she wouldn't have time to talk to you tonight."

"And?"

"It's just that you seem rather upbeat for a man who's only going to have a glimpse of his wife from a distance. There'll be no smooching tonight, my friend."

"It's not all about the physicality. It's enough that Faith will see that I'm there for her . . ."

"With Lily."

"Oh, do shut-up," he replied as he hurled a tea towel at Nathan who was grinning childishly.

At that moment, Nathan felt a pang of poignancy as he realised how much he was going to miss the companionship of his friend. But he also realised how much he should want his friend's marriage to be saved and strengthened. It occurred to him that he was beginning to see how it wasn't all about him. *A light-bulb moment,* he thought to himself.

Lily returned home after her morning jog, drenched in sweat. The sensation of sweat seeping out of her pores was almost akin to blood oozing out of her veins. However, it didn't achieve the same emotional cleansing that self-harming did.

She stood in the shower and allowed the powerful blast of water to bombard her scalp, before rushing down her still trembling body. Her ears were filled by the pounding sound of the water and all her senses were overcome by the power of the water; so much so that she didn't hear the phone ring.

Stepping out of the shower, she wrapped her body and hair in towels, and then sauntered to her bedroom, when she finally heard the phone ring. She picked up the receiver idly.

"Hi Lily, it's Rachel. Please don't hang up on me. I'm sorry about the other night, Finlay has ways of making me do things I wouldn't normally do."

Lily nodded her head and listened intently to the tirade of excuses and apologies, wanting desperately to forgive and trust her, but Lily held grudges and rarely forgave anyone who overstepped the mark. She didn't like being that way, but Walker had instilled that trait in her.

"What do you want?"

"It's the English Party's garden party this afternoon, and Finlay asked me to invite you. Please say you'll come, please do."

"Why is it so imperative that I attend, and why should I trust you?"

"I think Finlay genuinely likes you, he's just a bit gauge in demonstrating his feelings. It'll be fun mixing with the crowd and eating fine foods."

Lily could think of a million reasons not to go, but if Rachel was correct in saying that Walker had feelings for her, then she had to go. She agreed to meet Rachel at two o'clock at the library garden gates and then hung up.

She thought that the garden party would be a safe venue for her and she couldn't imagine anything awry happening there, as it was too public. A little voice in her head whispered worried thoughts that she casually brushed to one side.

Confusion began to swamp her mind as she tried to analyse Walker's invite by proxy. She found herself thinking that if he really did like her, that perhaps he actually liked her when she was nineteen, that perhaps it wasn't abuse.

She shook her head to disperse her misplaced emotions. Of course it was abuse, she said to herself, and of course his intentions were ill thought through. *Walker only ever had feelings for himself,* she thought.

After eating some fruit, she got ready to go out. Dressed in a floral tea dress and ballet pumps, she felt appropriately dressed for the English Party event. She thought that Walker would be impressed and perhaps even pleased.

The weather was perfect that day for an outdoor event, and Lily found she had a spring in her step as she walked to the library. She passed excited children on scooters and bikes as they trundled along the pavement, doused in the warming sun. Couples strolled along, holding hands as though they were the only people in the world.

As she approached the library, she could see Rachel waiting anxiously hovering outside the garden gates.

"I was worried you might not come," she said as Lily reached her.

"Why ever not? I'd said I would come. Should I be worried about something?"

"Of course not."

As Rachel leaned in to kiss Lily on the cheek, Lily could smell her citrus perfume floating on her skin. On the balmy day, the scent was refreshingly clean, but Lily sensed that she'd need more than the scent of lemon to keep her feeling cool that day.

Caterers had been hired to provide a sumptuous buffet which left the English Party members to mingle and promote the party's manifesto. Lily could see the dominating figure of Walker standing by a wooden arch covered in climbing roses. He was talking to a small group of men and women who appeared transfixed by his words and by his commanding and dapper appearance. Lily smoothed down her hair before she was whisked away by Rachel to the buffet table.

"I just love smoked salmon sandwiches," she said as she put three on her paper plate and popped another straight into her mouth.

Lily didn't hear her as she was distracted by Walker. Although he was still talking to the small group, he was periodically looking in her direction. When his eyes met with hers she was compelled to continually keep watching him, until Rachel shook her from her reverie. Rachel was shaking her head as she looked at Lily's empty plate.

Lily obliged her by picking a small bunch of green grapes and putting them in the centre of the plate. As she stood beside Rachel watching the proceedings unfold, a hand pressed firmly on her shoulder. She knew who it was before she turned around.

"Glad to see you made it," he said as he looked down at her with a steely stare.

"I'm glad I've pleased you," she replied before she slowly put another grape into her mouth.

A photographer was cruising around the intensely floral garden, taking pictures and occasionally staging them with Walker as the main central subject.

"You can expect me later," he said in a low voice.

"I won't be in, I've been invited out."

Walker placed his hand around her elbow and gave it a squeeze with a pincer movement; but not so hard so as to make her face crease up.

"I don't expect you to be going out without my permission."

Lily fixed a false smile on her face. "I'm going with Hugh, the doctor, to watch his wife in a concert, that's all."

"Then I will come round after. I'll know when you're home." He released her elbow and walked over to the photographer who was hovering around the buffet area.

Lily put her empty glass down on a passing tray, carried by a white-suited waiter, and then picked up another glass of sparkling wine from the same tray. She was acutely inept at social functions. Her dislike of talking to strangers was debilitating.

Periodically, she'd be aware of being watched, and invariably she'd see Walker or one of the older brawny-looking men casting their eyes over her. Their stares came without a smile or softness to reassure her that they were just looking, not stalking. *At least Rachel isn't glued to my side.*

Lily finished her second glass of wine and decided to leave. As she walked towards the gate, Rachel appeared at her side.

"You're not going already, surely. Does Finlay know you're leaving?"

"I don't need his permission, Rachel. I've got somewhere else to go soon."

"I don't think you like Finlay that much and I don't understand why." She looked down at her dainty shoes. "I think you must be mad not to fancy him."

"And I think that perhaps you should see him more as a father figure rather than a potential partner; he's far too old for you."

Rachel's face turned a shade of scarlet and she looked directly into Lily's eyes. "I can think what I want. You, on the other hand, have to think more of Finlay. I won't let you hurt him."

Her pinched face looked severe and aged by ten years. It wasn't a face that suited her and Lily found the look menacing.

"Why is it so important to you that I should like Finlay?"

"Because he's made me the custodian of his emotional wellbeing, and to make sure he's happy. You make him happy, so you have to do what he wants."

"Happiness comes from within. No one else can make a person who is twisted or curmudgeonly feel that emotion."

"Finlay isn't either. He's a gentleman."

"Look, I really have to go. Finlay is coming to my home later, anyway. So you see, I'm not letting him down."

Rachel relaxed at those words and stepped back, leaving only the clean smell of her citrus perfume to remain in Lily's personal space.

As Lily reached the gates, she turned around to see Walker watching her from the lavender garden and Rachel still watching her from where they'd parted. She didn't raise a smile or acknowledgement to either. As she walked out through the gate she breathed in deeply and let out a long, shaky sigh.

Lily was surprised to see both Hugh and Nathan waiting for her outside the Minster. She could see that Hugh looked excited with his cheeks a gentle hue of red, and rubbing his hands together manically. Nathan, on the other hand, was looking bored with his arms folded across his chest.

"You never let me down, on time as always," said Hugh as he leaned in to kiss her on the cheek.

Lily and Nathan acknowledged each other with a nod and a brief smile. "How are you feeling," she asked him as she noted the fading green and yellow stains around his eyes.

"Much improved, thanks," he replied.

They joined the line of people waiting to go inside. They followed Hugh closely as he made his way to the front pew, so as to be as close to the choir as possible. Lily sat between the men with her hands clasped together in her lap, feeling like a weed in a bouquet of exotic flowers.

As the overhead lights dimmed, allowing the candle light to come into its own, a hush came over the audience as the choir glided out from the Vestry in their long billowing black skirts and white blouses.

"There she is," whispered Hugh excitedly as he touched Lily on the wrist. He didn't notice her flinch.

Hugh fixed his stare on Faith, hoping that any second they would lock eyes and forgiveness would flow between them. His eyes began to feel prickly and sore from minimal blinking.

Song after song, the swell of their voices reached the upper parapets of the Minster, and Hugh's intense emotions began to subside. Faith never seemed to search the audience looking for him, but he did notice that at one point during one rendition, that a semi-smile graced her lips towards someone other than himself.

Periodically, Nathan would let his head rock back and close his eyes, as though he was lost in the soulful music. Only he knew that he was bored rigid. To entertain himself he looked around to see if there was anyone he'd fancy taking home. The disappointment forced him to revert to closing his eyes and touching the parameter of sleep.

Lily noticed Nathan's closed eyes and wondered whether he was asking God for his forgiveness. The music caressed her withered soul but didn't abolish her persistent, searing pain. She had an uneasy feeling that several people were watching her. *Can they see what happened to me; do they know I'm damaged?*

She watched Faith submerge herself in singing, and realised that she was envious of her. Envious that her past was so pure, and envious that she had such a devoted man in her life. She wondered why some women had it all whilst others had nothing.

As the choir launched into the penultimate piece, Hugh strained to sit as tall as possible in the pew. He wanted to wave at Faith, but he knew she distained such behaviour. He began drumming his fingers on his knees and he wondered how she could ignore the heat of his stare.

As they embarked on the opening bars of the Hallelujah chorus, Hugh felt a rush of desperation flood his body. He wanted to climb over the people and the pews so he could rush up to his wife and hold her tightly in his arms; he missed her warmth so much. He didn't know how to contend with the wall she'd built between them both. He turned his head and whispered in Lily's ear.

"I can't attract Faith's attention. What can I do?"

Lily flinched at his proximity. But at that very moment, she saw Faith look straight at Hugh.

"She's looking at you now," she whispered back. But by the time Hugh turned his head, Faith had returned her attention to the conductor. *All is lost*, he thought to himself as he punched his thigh.

The conductor turned and took a bow and then he waved a gesturing arm at the choir behind him. The audience rose to their feet and applauded.

Hugh could still see Faith over the heads of the people in front, and he saw how she looked so serene. He missed her.

Fearing an overemotional and self-pitying evening with Hugh, Nathan turned to Lily. "Why don't you come back for a nightcap?"

Thinking of another hour of protection, she accepted the invitation. But unbeknown to her, Rachel was sitting a few seats behind her. She had a pinched expression on her face as she waited for the three of them to move down the aisle. As she followed behind, she retrieved her mobile phone from her pocket.

Hugh shuffled along behind Nathan and Lily, whilst periodically looking back to see if Faith was heading his way. He wanted to push against the crowd and go to the Vestry where he knew she'd be. He didn't want to cause a scene so he pressed forward with the others.

He resigned himself to spending one more night at Nathan's with a wretched heart, and he prayed to the unseen god that tomorrow would see him reunited with his wife.

Rachel watched the group from afar then punched the keys on her mobile phone to send a text message. A smile seeped across her face.

Chapter Thirty-Two

Lily felt uncomfortable in the doctors' company. She felt her past dragged her below the surface of humanity. She watched them both as though they were actors in a film and she was in the audience. She watched their movements and mannerisms and listened to their eloquent phrases. She felt that life had offered them more privileges than she had ever been offered. She recoiled into herself, finding it difficult to be in Nathan's home. But to leave would surely be more perilous.

The three of them sat in Nathan's rather neglected garden. Weeds thrived on the small square of lawn, and bedded themselves happily in the beds where purple campanula tumbled over the border edges.

"I was hoping to achieve more with Faith this evening," said Hugh.

"Don't be so dejected, I said it'd be difficult tonight. Focus on tomorrow," replied Nathan, stifling a yawn.

Lily hadn't been privy to Hugh and Faith's background story, so she didn't know what to say. She didn't think that she had the right to speak in the matter, so she turned her head slightly towards Hugh and gave him a subtle smile. He might have missed had he not been looking directly at her, and admiring her delicate aura.

"I ought to be going," announced Lily as she rose from the garden chair.

"So soon?" said Nathan.

"Yes, but I've had a lovely evening, thank you both."

Hugh waved a hand in a parting gesture as he remained entrenched in his chair, burden by his deflated mood. Nathan walked her to the door.

"Will you be okay getting home?"

"No worries. I'll see you Monday."

As she walked away and heard the front door close behind her, she suddenly felt very alone. A chill ran up her spine as she heard the echo of her solitary footsteps against the eerie silence of the late evening.

Her heart leapt every time she passed a tree that lined the street. Ominously dark shadows lurked behind every one. As someone approached her, she sensed the sweat seep out of the pores in her armpits and her mouth felt as dry as a desert. As soon as the person passed her by, her heartbeat returned to its regular rhythm.

As she neared her home, she scoured the street for anyone loitering in the vicinity, but all seemed clear. As she got closer to her house, her pace increased and so did her heart rate. She rummaged around for her keys and put them into the lock as swiftly as possible. As she entered the house, she closed the door and leant on it before letting out a deep sigh.

There was a cold silence in the house, and only the ticking of the clock in the hallway interjected the stillness.

She moved to the kitchen and switched on the light. As she did so, she saw a folded piece of paper propped up against the vase of flowers. The note bore her name.

With heightened trepidation, she reached out and picked up the note. It read, "You are back later than planned but I am waiting for you." It wasn't signed, but she knew who it was from.

She clutched one hand to her chest as she scoured the kitchen. Her ears strained to detect any sounds of movement. As she moved from room to room, her heart pounded in her throat and every dingy corner was filled with menace.

She knew she had to explore upstairs, but behind every door lay a threat that she wasn't willing to embrace. As she stood at the bottom of the stairs, she was filled with so much fear that her feet wouldn't respond to her mental commands. She backed away from the stairs and picked up the telephone.

"Hello, police," she whispered. "I have an intruder in my house."

She quietly and urgently gave her address, and then she removed herself to safety in the porch, where her screams for help could be heard by her neighbours. She crouched down and waited for the police to arrive.

Within a few minutes, a car pulled up outside her house and the two police officers got out and found a terrified looking Lily crouched in the porch. They advised her to remain just inside the hallway as they separated out to search the property. She kept her back to the wall and bit her bottom lip as she waited for some kind of skirmish to ensue. But when both officers rejoined her, she saw that they were both alone.

"Could you say again why you thought an intruder was here, Madam?"

She cleared her throat before she spoke. "As I said on the phone, I found a note on the kitchen table. I left it by the phone."

She moved to retrieve it and discovered that it had gone. "I left it here, I know I did." She looked on the floor and under the pile of post on the table.

The police officers looked at one another, and one of them rolled his eyes.

"We found no evidence of a break-in, including the back gate."

"You don't believe me do you?"

"It's not that, Madam, it's just that we can't find any evidence to support your claim."

One of the officers guided her to the lounge and suggested that she sit.

"Is there any reason for you to think that someone would be here? Is someone threatening you?"

Lily sat dumbfounded with her head in her hands. She remained mute as she knew that without evidence, she wouldn't be able to claim the mental torture that Walker was putting her through.

Her silence seemed to confirm the officer's negative suspicions, and so they both stood up and one put his notebook away before the other one spoke.

"We'll be off then, but don't hesitate to call if you're troubled again. We'll see ourselves out."

As they closed the front door behind them, Lily let out a strangled shriek and let the bitter tears flow down her sunken cheeks. He'd been there, she knew he had, and once again he'd slipped through the net without leaving any evidence.

Her whole body shook as the tears cascaded down her face and soaked her dress. The urge to cut her flesh was powerful and she saw no reason to resist. Perhaps, she thought to herself, she could cut herself deep enough to release her from her persecution.

She prised herself out of her chair and moved slowly to the kitchen where she let out a gasp as she found Walker standing there, looking directly at her with a smirk on his face.

"I knew you were here," she uttered as she blotted her cheeks with the back of her hand.

"So why did you call the police if you knew it was me?"

"Because you're frightening me with your games."

Walker paced around the table and stood right in front of her. He was so close that the tips of their feet touched.

"I know exactly what kind of person you are. You don't have the mental capacity to defend yourself against me. You're weak."

He threw his head back and laughed, and then he grabbed her by the shoulders and shook her frail body with convulsive movements.

"You never fooled me with your dyed hair and coloured contacts. I can see beneath your façade and see the pathetic person you really are. I see the clinically depressed, self-harming, and anorexic person you try to hide from the world."

He pushed her into the chair, and then ran his hand through her hair, gently tugging at it as he did so. He bent down and whispered in her ear. "I've never lost sight of you. Wherever you've moved to, I've been watching you closely."

"Whatever do you mean?"

"Stop the charade, Maria, it's getting boring. Think about it, you're not exactly scintillating company. You couldn't believe I was really interested in you, surely."

Desperation clouded Lilith's thoughts as she realised he knew her true identity. She eyed the knife drawer, but Walker was blocking her way. Beads of sweat formed on her brow and upper lip. Her breathing had become erratic.

"So what happens now?" she asked in a shaky voice.

"What happens is that your house gets burgled, you disturb the intruder and you get killed. A tragedy, really."

She wanted to scream to alert the neighbours, but her mouth was parched. After several forced swallows of saliva, she managed to speak.

"You wouldn't do that to me."

"I will have to because your games may get out of hand. Rachel is already curious about our association."

"Our association revolves around you abusing me."

"You need to reframe your beliefs. Your depression is twisting your judgement."

"There's no point in killing me, I've got no proof."

"Apart from the souvenirs you keep sending me." He sniggered as he watched her shoulders droop.

"There is someone more threatening than me."

"You are talking about the doctor, I suppose."

"Yes. People would listen to him more than me."

Her eyes looked doleful as she tried to look into his eyes without wanting to heave.

"Are you saying that I should kill the doctor instead of you?"

She paused for a few seconds, but then her mouth spoke without any reflection.

"I could help you," she whispered, closing her eyes tightly.

Walker bent down so that his head was level with hers.

"What did you say?"

"I could help you get rid of Nathan," she said softly, and a searing pain darted through her body as she said his name.

"Now there's a delicious thought," he said as he pulled up a chair. "But how do I know that isn't a ruse? How do I know you won't side with him when the time comes?"

"Because you'd be there and you'd kill me as well as him if I deceived you. The deal is that I keep my life and Nathan loses his. We then call a truce between ourselves."

"Get me a beer."

She stood up shakily and moved to the fridge. She again considered the knife in the drawer in front of her, but she knew she had little courage or strength to follow any action through against the giant of a man. She took him a beer, and sat down to make a deal with the devil.

"So, you're wanting rid of the doctor because he didn't protect you on the ward back then." He paused to take a swig of beer. "I know you've been sending him souvenirs too. He's no idea who you are, has he?"

Lily shook her head, staring constantly at the floor. "I never wanted either of you dead. I just wanted to mess with your minds." She blushed and bit her bottom lip to prevent herself from divulging any more deliberations.

Walker reached out and took her chin in his hand and lifted her face so his eyes could bore into hers. "You could never mess with my mind. But I think it's worked with the doctor."

He sat back in the chair and folded his arms across his vast expanse of chest. A smug look came over his face. "You're not as hard and tough as you'd like to make out, are you, Maria Langer."

"Maria is dead, she died with my past. Only Lilith Fields exists now."

"So your past is dead is it? The same past that screws with your mind on a daily basis. The same past that fills you with bitterness and eats away at your soul."

He grabbed hold of her wrist with one hand and shoved up her sleeve with the other. "Still self-harming, I see," he jeered as he released her arm with disdainful force.

She pushed her sleeve back down with an urgency that betrayed her discomfort at being found out.

She was instantly transported back to Poplar Ward, with the intense emotions crippling her ability to remain strong. She remembered how she felt when her self-harming was discovered by a nurse. She also remembered the great lengths she'd go to in order to find ways to cut herself. She would sneak into the men's bathroom to find a razor blade, or she would carefully remove a fragment of glass in a window she'd already cracked in the women's bathroom.

Her self-harming behaviour increased after Walker had worked a night shift, but no one had bothered to correlate the pattern with the events in her daily routine. But she knew the junior doctor had noticed something untoward about Walker's behaviour towards her and some of the other patients. But he failed in his duty of care and defiled his Hippocratic Oath.

During that time, the doctor's name and face had become emblazoned on her mind. She knew she'd never forget him, even though he'd forgotten her.

And now she was face to face with her abuser, planning to kill the junior doctor who ignored her pain all those years ago. She felt his punishment was perhaps too severe, but she wasn't in control of his destiny. She had to look after herself.

"I wonder if I can trust you," he said as his fat fingers lingered around her mouth and pawed at her fleshy lips.

She took his hand in hers and kissed her fingers, before she looked him directly in the eyes. "You should know me well enough to know that I honour my word. Let's make a plan to defeat him," she said before she kissed his fingers some more.

Chapter Thirty-Three

Hugh rammed his dirty and clean clothes into the holdall in preparation to leave. The day was reminiscent of Christmas Day when, as a child, he knew that untold treasures lay waiting for him under the tree. The obvious difference was that it was Faith waiting for him at their home, and his internal child was jumping up and down with anticipation.

"All set then?" enquired Nathan.

"Ready as I'll ever be. I don't really know how it got to this."

"All that matters now is that you fix it."

Hugh nodded as Nathan slapped him on the back. During Hugh's stay, Nathan's confidence had grown and he was experiencing the youthful invincibility that he had always known.

He had not received any troubling letters, no more undesirable packages on the doorstep, and no more intruders had invaded his personal space. He took all of that to be a sign that Walker had eased the pressure off him because his new position in life was eating up all of his time.

With his face looking as near to normal, Nathan decided to have Sunday lunch at The Spread Eagle, and perhaps even treat himself to a dessert of the female variety.

As Hugh drove off, Nathan bounced up the stairs to get ready to go out.

Hugh stood at his front door, unsure whether he should knock first, or just use his key. As he fumbled in his jacket for his keys, Faith came to the door.

"Hello, darling," he said as he stepped forward to kiss her. Faith turned her head slightly, so his kiss landed on her cheek. His shoulders drooped at the rebuttal but with his stoical manner, he followed her in. He presented her with a bouquet of white and red roses for peace and love. She accepted them with a graceful smile.

The house looked exactly the same as it did before he left a week ago. Hugh had expected to see any reference to him to have been erased, so she could live happily without any reminders of his existence.

Over the course of lunch, the stilted conversation circled their true feelings and the situation they found themselves in, until Hugh could stand it no longer.

"I'm sorry I didn't trust you, I was foolish. Please don't shut me out, please tell me what's wrong."

She purported that nothing was wrong with their marriage and that it was still to do with the fact that she didn't approve of his partnership with Nathan. In fact, she felt that everything that was wrong in their lives was down to the very existence of Nathan.

Hugh sat back in his chair, perplexed at her deep rooted contempt of his friend.

"I hear what you're saying," he began. "However, it doesn't explain why you despise him so much and where you were when you weren't at the book group."

"I just needed space to think."

"Well. Why the secrecy? I'm not unreasonable; you could have told me that."

"Not without having to justify myself which would have meant bringing Nathan into it, and I didn't want to do that. I know how important he is to you."

"Not as important as you are to me."

She smiled at his comment and reached over the table to take his hand, which she caressed with her thumb. "So, you're not in love with Lily then?"

Hugh looked vague and then Nathan's warning words echoed in his head. "Good God, no. She doesn't get out much so I thought she'd like to come with us. Besides, she likes you."

On the surface, Faith appeared appeased by his words, although her eyes lacked sparkle.

"If I take you back I want us to see less of Nathan. Do you think we can do that?"

"If that's what it takes," he replied, although he was still convinced that something wasn't being said. "But I still have to work with him, and you will also have to occasionally."

She returned her attention to the raspberries and clotted cream, seemingly ignoring his last comment. Hugh watched her surreptitiously. He wasn't sure what the problem was exactly, but he knew it had something to do with his wife and Nathan.

Nathan was relieved to be sitting at his usual table in the familiar down market pub. The eclectic mix of bikers, Goths, and tarts didn't disappoint him, and he'd already spied an interesting woman to take back to his place later. He tucked into his roast dinner washed down with a pint of beer.

He visually targeted the woman with honey-blond hair until she sauntered over to his table, pouting her rosebud mouth.

"Do I know you?" she said.

"No, I think you'll find that we are perfect strangers," he replied as he blotted the gravy from the corners of his mouth with the serviette.

On closer inspection he could see that she was much younger than he usually went for, but she appeared keen and he wasn't the type to disappoint. He deliberated whether he should ask her age, but he decided that if she was old enough to drink in the pub, then she was old enough to grace his bed.

He pulled out the stool next to him and indicated with his eyes that she should sit. They conversed about inane topics until Nathan decided that it was time he should mention the point of their casual union.

"Fancy coming back to mine?"

"Thought you'd never ask," she replied as she pushed back the stool and stood up; beaming at him as she did so.

They walked back to his house with urgency in their steps and their hands tantalisingly brushing against one another. No sooner had they entered the house, Nathan hurriedly pushed her up against the wall and began fumbling with her clothes. He found her slender body exquisite and it wasn't long before they were both naked in his bed.

Chapter Thirty-Four

Lily knew that she needed to get closer to Nathan for the plan to work. She wasn't the type of woman to push herself forward, and Nathan seemed like a lazy lover, so she'd have to make the play rather than wait for his advances.

Without her green contact lenses her eyes had more soul and expression, although much of the expression was that of pure agony. Her muted grey eyes reminded her so much of when she was called Maria that she had to wear the contacts to quash the bubbling torment.

Her recently re-dyed hair looked glossy but her physique lacked curves. She ran the palms of her hands down her torso and acknowledged the bony prominences as she brushed over them.

She wondered whether Nathan had ever thought of her as attractive. She smiled to herself at the absurd thought. However, she needed to catch his eye somehow before Walker lost his patience and decided to end her sorry life. She felt the task was awkward as they worked closely together but she had little choice in the matter. Walker had made that abundantly clear.

Her mind ached with pontificating. She knew she could only find relief by either self-harming or going for a jog. After an internal debate she chose the latter.

The Lycra trousers accentuated her emaciated shape which pleased her immensely. She liked the way her inner pain was reflected through her physical appearance.

Her route took her along tree-lined streets that echoed with clusters of families enjoying a Sunday afternoon together. The smell of roast dinner still clung to the air.

As she approached Nathan's street she considered a detour to avoid any chance of seeing him. Her feet, however, were undeterred and so onwards she jogged.

She kept to the opposite side of the street, when in the distance she saw a woman walking out of Nathan's house. Lily stopped behind a tree and peered around the gnarled trunk for a better view. To her dismay, the woman looked barely old enough, by the way she was dressed, to be out on her own, and her honey-blonde hair glinted in the dipping sun. The girl had a youthful bounce in her step and a beguiling aura that clearly entrapped any man she came into contact with.

She couldn't see Nathan, but she knew in her heart that the two of them had slept together. Perhaps he was lying in bed basking in the glory of his triumph. He was obviously feeling better, she thought to herself, as she continued on her route towards her house. Once she arrived home, she headed straight to the shower where she stood and reflected on the urgent matter of seducing Nathan.

Walker was making a pot of tea when his sister, Muriel, walked in.

"Pour me one," she said.

Her clipped manner sent a chilling frisson down Walker's spine. He steadied his nerves as he poured her a cup and passed it to her. His anticipation and fear was palpable in the room, but even so, he craved her attention. He needed her to demonstrate her love for him, a true and only love that compared to no other.

"Have you sorted out that bitch yet?"

"The plans have changed slightly, but in time she'll be gone."

"You'd better be right. I don't want anything spoiling what we've got."

He sat opposite her and studied her physique from behind his cup. She wasn't classically beautiful but she was striking in a powerful way. She had a strong jaw line which was emphasized by her short crop of dark brown hair that had a smattering of grey running through it. She wore little make-up, preferring to use only mascara and her signature deep red lipstick that made her wide mouth look like a grotesque slash across her face.

"If you fail me and I have to deal with her myself, you will find your punishment severe."

"It won't come to that, she's terrified of me and she'll do anything I say."

Muriel didn't like his cocky tone of voice and slammed her cup into the saucer. Her eyes glinted with an acrimonious stare that pierced his mind.

"Get upstairs and run me a bath."

Walker scraped his chair back and walked with bended back. He knew better than to tarry when she'd told him to do something.

Shortly after, Muriel appeared at the bathroom door, clad only in a flimsy dressing gown that clung to every curve and muscle. She slipped it off for Walker to hang up whilst she stepped into the warm bubble bath.

Walker knew what to do without being asked, so he rolled up his sleeves and proceeded to lather soap all over her body, ensuring that no part of her muscular frame was missed. He then moved on to washing her hair, making sure that he massaged her scalp in slow, circular movements. All the while, Muriel sat with her head tipped backwards, her eyes closed and occasionally murmuring with pleasure.

The pleasure was a mutual commodity, as Walker relished the time he was allowed to caress her. The love he felt for her swelled his heart and he wished it could remain so without her need to dominate and belittle him.

She climbed out of the bath and stood with her arms splayed out so that he could dry her. Once the water had disappeared down the plug, she ordered him to undress and take a shower. A cold shower.

"It's a cold one, as I'm displeased with your lack of action with that bitch. Think on, Finlay."

He stood beneath the torrent of cold water, resolutely resisting shuddering or whining. After a few minutes, his skin became numb and his mind sloshed around in his head. The rapid drops of icy water stung his tight scalp.

Seconds before he felt he may collapse, Muriel turned the shower off and stood back to gloat over his shivering flesh and diminished muscles.

"I hope that you have reflected on the issue, Finlay."

He bobbed his head and then gratefully wrapped himself up in the threadbare towel. He kept his eyes averted from hers, although he knew she was watching him.

"Now get yourself over to hers and make sure she's got no other trinkets from the past."

As she walked passed him, she reached out and slapped him across the face. Walker clenched his fists as the stinging sensation rippled across his semi-frozen face. His thoughts became dark and clouded; Muriel was displeased with him because of Lilith, so she would have to pay.

Lily sat at the kitchen table squashing the ham sandwich between her fingers. She broke off small pieces and slowly placed them in her mouth. She drank copious amounts of water to wash the morsels down. Food was her constant enemy.

When the doorbell rang, she thankfully put the sandwich to one side and walked to the door. She could see the vast shadow looming through the stained glass and she knew it was Walker.

The fight or flight reaction rushed around her quaking body. The mere sight of his outline was enough to catapult her back to Poplar Ward.

She took a deep breath and opened the door. Walker stepped inside, knocking her back against the open door. As she closed the door, he spun around and pinned her against the wall.

"I want you to give me any souvenirs you have left from Poplar," he growled.

"I've none left."

She had to squeeze the words out of her constricted throat and her eyes were seeing red pinpricks. He continued applying pressure to her fragile neck. "Why don't I believe you?"

"You have to. I've sent them all to you and Doctor Rine. Honestly, I swear."

He released her neck and then pressed his middle finger into her forehead. He pushed as hard as he could until his finger tip turned white.

Lily couldn't help reacting to the pain, which angered him, and so with a clenched fist he punched her in the stomach with force. Lily let out a breathy cry and bent over double, racked with pain. Her head was spinning with stars.

Walker pulled her up straight by her hair and pressed his face into hers.

"I'll ask you again, where are the other pieces?"

"I don't have anymore," she whispered, still struggling for breath. "I don't, I don't. I promise."

"Be warned, if I receive any more items or the good doctor complains about getting more, I will hurt you so badly that you'll wish you were dead."

Lily nodded her head as much as she could, all the while worrying what he may do next.

There was nothing gentle about Walker's treatment of her, and after he'd degraded her, he decided it was time to discuss their plan.

"Have you worked out how you'll get the good doctor here?"

"I was wondering why I can't go to him. It'll be hard to explain his dead body here."

"Because we won't get interrupted here. You never have any visitors, but that other doctor friend of his may call there."

It didn't feel right to her somehow, but she couldn't argue with him at that moment in time. Walker was looking at her expectantly, so she obliged by speaking.

"I'm going to be more sociable with him at work, and then invite him over for dinner."

"And if he refuses?"

"He won't, as he likes to be waited on by a woman. If I make him feel special and wanted he won't want to turn me down."

"So when is this taking place? It can't wait forever."

"This Friday, so not long to wait. What will you do?"

"I will come round and find him assaulting you. There will be a scuffle when I try to intervene, and in the process I pull him off you and throw him against the wall. He hits his head and breaks his neck."

Lily swallowed hard and smoothed down her hair. "But won't people think it's odd you are here?"

"We've become good friends because of the party; the members will vouch for that. You can give me your spare key in case you forget to leave the door unlocked."

"Then we call the police?"

"Obviously. It's a case of self-defence; they'll believe me."

Lily wrapped the cardigan tightly around her body, and gazed at the floor. Vile images of Nathan's corpse lying on her lounge floor flashed in front of her eyes. They made her feel sick.

As Walker left with her spare key, she ruminated over his visit and the days to come. She knew that tomorrow she'd have to begin using her proverbial feminine charm that she'd shut away since her late teens. She'd need Nathan to notice her quickly and effectively as her life was in jeopardy, more so now than ever as Walker had a key.

Chapter Thirty-Five

As Nathan entered the clinic he noticed something different about Lily. He couldn't say exactly what it was, but she appeared sweeter and more tempting in some way.

He brushed passed her as she dallied in the narrow passageway, and he smelt the delicate fragrance of vanilla and peach pervading the air around her. When she smiled at him he noticed her lips were pink and glossy, which accentuated the whiteness of her teeth.

She seemed expectant of some acknowledgement from him, so he smiled when she called out that it was nice to have him back. He entered the kitchen without a backward glance.

"Notice anything different about Lily?" he asked Hugh.

"No, not really. Why?"

"Not sure. It's just not like her to make such an effort with her appearance."

Hugh shuffled his feet before making a small coughing noise in his throat. "Could we meet at lunchtime?" he asked, avoiding eye contact.

"Sure, business meeting?"

"Kind of. Anyway, I've got calls to make," and with that, he disappeared to his room.

Every time Nathan came out of his room to call in his next patient, he'd catch Lily looking at him or notice her twirling a strand of hair around her finger as she spoke on the phone.

He found her mannerisms contrite and gauche, but he was intrigued all the same. He wondered whether she'd fallen in love and whether a dreamy-eyed man would be waiting outside for her that evening. He'd somehow never expected her to fall in love. She was almost asexual to him. Overtly sexy women were what he noticed, and Lily wasn't one of those.

The morning moved along swiftly and it wasn't long before Hugh was knocking on Nathan's door.

"I've asked Lily to bring us coffee and our sandwiches in here so we can have a working lunch," he said as he slowly paced around the room. "I'm in a bit of a quandary," he began as he gazed out of the window. "Faith has taken me back but with certain conditions attached."

"Sounds ominous."

"Well, the conditions are to do with you, so indeed, they are rather unpromising."

Before Nathan had time to mock Hugh for his pompous language, a knock came at the door and Lily sashayed in with a tray of lunch. She placed it on the desk and gave Nathan a sideways glance before she exited. She left a sugary sweet trail behind her that rippled Nathan's nostrils.

"Lily appears more coquettish today, don' you think?"

"I hadn't noticed. Unlike you, I don't view every woman I see as a potential bed partner. For now, we have more important issues to concern ourselves with."

Nathan picked up his shop-bought tuna and cucumber sandwich and bit into it. He stared at Hugh waiting for him to continue speaking.

"I've always been a bit naive when it came to women, not like you. I know something has happened between you and Faith, but I don't want to know what."

Nathan took a breath to interject, but Hugh raised his hand. "Don't deny or confirm anything, I can't bear to hear it."

Nathan swallowed his mouthful and looked at Hugh. The crow's feet around his eyes deepened as he smiled and shook his head. "You've got it wrong . . ."

"I said spare me the details, I know you too well, unfortunately. You are both important to me, but Faith has to come first."

Hugh drummed his fingers on the desk as he contemplated his limp sandwich.

"Anyway, Faith has asked that we spend less time together socially, and when Lily takes annual leave, we're to get in a temp as she'll only do the odd emergency day here."

"And how do you feel about all of that?"

"Numb, as I can't have my wife and my best friend together in my life."

"Well, tell her how you feel. And tell her what you want to happen."

"I want my wife to be in love with me again."

Hugh stood up and placed both hands flat on Nathan's desk. His face was red and shiny.

Just then, a knock came at the door and Lily popped her head around the door. "It's time for afternoon clinic, doctors."

Hugh spun around and marched towards the door. Lily stood to one side to let him pass. As he did, she glanced towards Nathan and cocked her head.

"Nothing to worry about," he told her.

She paused for a few seconds with her heart beating rapidly. She opened her mouth to ask him out for a drink, but her tongue stuck to the inside of her dry mouth. She walked away.

All through the afternoon patients arrived and departed, and Lily's ability to stay focused on her job had waned. As the last patient disappeared into the balmy evening, she shut down her computer and dawdled in the hope of catching Nathan on his way out.

After ten minutes she began to feel awkward so she called out that she was leaving. Only Hugh called out in return.

She left the clinic and hovered outside the door. She wondered how she was going to get Nathan to take notice of her as a woman, not just a work colleague. Then suddenly it dawned on her, she should go to his favourite pub and see whether he'd notice her more outside of the work environment. Her wardrobe would limit her ability to be overtly sexual, but she felt pressured to perform.

She dashed home with trepidation in her thumping heart, praying that Walker hadn't used his key to wait for her inside. As she put her key in the lock, she held her breath and listened intently for any sounds coming from within. She stepped inside and hesitantly called out his name. Silence was the only resonance to reach her ears.

She climbed the stairs two at a time and entered her bedroom. Her heart was racing and her hands were clammy.

Raking through her clothes she had to acknowledge that her wardrobe was, on the whole, staid and prissy. A pair of long forgotten skinny jeans lay on the top shelf of the wardrobe, so she slipped them on with a camisole that she normally wore under a blouse.

With a slick of lip gloss, smoky eyeliner, mascara, and blusher, her face was transformed from demure to captivating. She smoothed down her hair, spritzed some perfume along her collar bone, and headed for The Spread Eagle.

As she walked through the smokers hanging around outside the pub, she felt numerous pairs of eyes staring at her. They felt like criticizing eyes which made her want to run home and hide. But Walker had given her no choice.

Inside the pub felt a few degrees warmer than outside, and Lily felt sticky and uncomfortable as she prowled around the crowded room. She clasped her handbag close to her chest as she scanned the room frantically looking for Nathan. Stranger's eyes met her eyes, and the unwanted attention gripped her heart like a painful cramp.

Finally, she spied Nathan sitting at a table with a pint and a young blonde woman standing by his table, talking with him. Lily couldn't make out whether it was the same blonde she saw leaving his house the other day.

Lily froze as the noises in the pub became muffled and the people became blurred. It took her a few seconds to realise that someone was talking to her over her shoulder.

"You all right, love?" asked a beer-bellied man as he tapped her on the shoulder. She jumped and gasped out loud.

"I'm not that scary," he said as he grinned and displayed a set of crooked, nicotine-stained teeth.

"I'm looking for my friend, I can see him over there," she replied as she pointed in Nathan's direction.

"You're friends with the old playboy, are you? You ought to watch yourself with him. You'd have more fun with me." He invaded her personal space, making Lily's skin crawl, and she could smell his smoky breath, making her nose wrinkle up.

"I don't know what you mean, but I must go and speak to him," and with that she weaved her way through the crowd until she came face to face with Nathan.

He stopped talking to the blonde woman in mid-flow and stared wide-eyed at Lily. The blonde followed his eyes so that she, too, was gawking at her.

"Surprised to see you here," he said

"I can be full of surprises in private."

The blonde woman straightened her back and pouted in Lily's direction.

"Do you two know one another then?" she asked petulantly.

"We work together," replied Lily.

"That's all right then," said the blonde, relaxing her shoulders.

"Did you want something, Lily?"

She paused to consider her response, but only ended up saying that it could wait and then she bid him a good evening. As she retraced her steps back towards the door, the beer-bellied man winked at her and raised his pint glass. She returned a meek smile and then hurried out the door without a backward glance.

The task was much harder than she thought, and it was stilted by the fact that she didn't think she really wanted Nathan dead. She hadn't considered such a plan herself.

Toying with such sinister thoughts made her feel guilty, but at the same time she felt powerful in her mind.

The house looked mercifully quiet and empty when she arrived at the gate, and she wished her mind could be the same. Without a thought of Walker, she entered and raced upstairs to change into her jogging clothes.

Once out of the house again, she began to pound her feet along the pavement as though she was stomping on her sullied mind.

Unwanted notions of murder and death blinded her until she felt that nothing but her own death would be the solution at the end of the task ahead. The finality of ending her life seemed deliciously sweet but tainted, as she knew no one would miss her.

She thought how Hugh would probably miss her efficiency but not her as an individual. And Nathan would already be dead, not that he'd actually noticed her when he was alive.

Her father didn't even remember her now, not that he ever showed her much love and care when he did know who she was.

Her mother had also abandoned her through the shame of having a daughter who was mentally ill. She died without ever having rekindled the maternal love that was once there before the psychiatrists became involved.

Sweat was accumulating on the bridge of her nose, and dripping down from her forehead by the time she'd reached Nathan's street. Her mind had been so preoccupied that she hadn't noticed where she was, and she was taken aback when she came face to face with Nathan.

"We meet again," he said.

Lily looked around for the blonde, but she wasn't there.

"Surprised to see you alone," she replied, feeling braver.

"I am able to be alone, you know. Anyway, you never explained why you were in the pub. I know it wasn't for a drink."

Lily suddenly wished she looked better, acutely aware of her sweat-drenched body and glistening face. She tried to smooth down her frizzy hair which only compounded her feeling an undesirable mess.

"You look like you could do with a cool drink. Do you want to come in?"

Her initial thought was to decline the offer and to run back home at a fast pace. But then Walker's words infiltrated her head and she knew that she'd no choice but to accept.

It was the first time she'd entered his house, and it wasn't quite what she'd pictured. The air smelt neutral which matched the palette of various hues of white on the walls. The furniture was comfortable and lived in, and not showy or extravagant as she expected.

She followed him into a minimalist kitchen with red glossy cabinets. It didn't look like he did much cooking, and there was nothing in the house that pointed to the fact that he'd ever been previously married.

"Chilled white wine or fruit juice?" he offered.

She chose the former thinking that it would take the edge off her anxiety.

"We'd be more comfortable in the lounge," he suggested.

"The kitchen's fine," she replied before mentally kicking herself for being so clipped.

They sat opposite one another in quiet embarrassment as they sipped their alcoholic beverages. He noticed the dark shadows etched under her emerald eyes.

"You still haven't answered my question."

"You mean, why was I in the pub? I was looking for you." Her already red cheeks glowed more profusely, and she took another sip of wine.

"Whatever for?"

She took a deep breath. "I was wondering whether you'd like to come over for a meal on Friday." She pinched her bottom lip between her teeth until she felt the strangely pleasant taste of blood in her mouth.

"Well, this is a surprise; I didn't think you liked me.'"

"I know, I've been hard on you, which is perhaps unfair. The meal is a peace offering." She looked at him with her luminous green eyes and waited for him to respond.

"Okay," he pronounced slowly. "That would be very nice, I think." He stared at her for a few minutes, with his arms behind his head. "I still don't know much about you."

"Why don't we leave that until Friday, it'll give us something to talk about."

Nathan smiled and raised his glass to her, reminding her of the beer-bellied man earlier.

When he tried to top up her glass, she put her hand over it and professed that she needed to go home.

She marched home knowing that the final journey to the end of her sordid life had begun. *Peace will be mine at last,* she thought to herself.

After she'd gone, Nathan thought about her invitation and he looked forward to getting to know her more.

Chapter Thirty-Six

Hugh tiptoed around the bedroom, trying not to wake Faith, as she'd taken to lying in lately instead of rising with him to have breakfast together. He missed those early morning moments. They now seemed a thing of the past.

She looked angelic with her hair drifting over the crisp white pillow and the recently acquired furrows of worry erased from her face.

He moved downstairs quietly and ate some cereal before grabbing his packed lunch from the fridge. He noticed there were more bottles of white wine in there than usual.

He walked to the bottom of the stairs to listen out for sounds of her stirring, but all was quiet, so he blew her a kiss and quietly left for work.

Lily was already there when he arrived, and he could smell the comforting aroma of freshly brewed coffee. It didn't stop him wanting to walk straight back out of the clinic and return to his wife who seemed more in need than some of his patients. He was at work with loathing in his heart.

He sauntered into his room to check the post that Lily had piled on his desk. He perused them and then sorted them into piles for her to deal with later.

A gentle knock came at the door and Lily entered with a large mug of coffee. He smiled gratefully and then noticed how dejected she looked. A preoccupied notion had lodged in her eyes.

"Are you feeling okay?" he asked.

"I've a lot on my mind, but I'm coping."

"Anything I can do?"

She shook her head and disappeared from his room.

When Nathan arrived, she couldn't look him in the eyes for fear of letting him see the jumble of hatred and pity radiating from her own eyes. Her avoidance behaviour puzzled him as he thought the platonic date on Friday meant a new shift in the dynamics of their relationship.

"Morning, Lily."

"Morning, Doctor . . . Nathan," she corrected herself from below the reception desk where she was sorting out some files. As Nathan walked towards the kitchen, he glanced back to see if she was looking at him. He couldn't comprehend why it was so important that she liked him.

Each person spent the day working and avoiding one another as best they could. The atmosphere was jarred and prickly, but no one was willing to soften the mood with placating words or gestures.

Nathan was having his lunch in his room when a call came through. It was Walker.

"Long time no see, good Doctor."

"What do you want, Walker?"

"I just wondered how you cleansed your conscience enough to do your job, knowing that you have a tarnished past."

"I don't have to talk to you . . ."

"Well, before you go, have you ever wondered what happened to that female patient you ignored?"

"What if I have?"

"Do you ever wonder if she's watching you? Even now?"

A prickle of irritation skimmed across Nathan's skin and his clenched fist thumped the pile of papers on his desk.

"Are you trying to tell me something?"

"Just wondering, Doctor, just wondering," and with that he hung up, leaving Nathan listening to the flat tone.

Part of him wanted to believe that Walker was just trying to unnerve him, but another part of him was curiously disturbed. *What does Walker know*, he wondered.

In the reception, Lily had recognised Walker's voice on the line but neither acknowledged one another, as though when at work, they occupied a different reality where neither had met before. She hoped that once Friday was over that's exactly how things would be. The abuser sets the victim free. Free to be herself.

At lunchtime, she sat on the bench next to the bed of roses, tilting her head back and closing her eyes. She allowed her mind to be permeated by the serenity of nature.

A shadow drifted across her face and her peace was spoilt by someone making coughing sounds. Reluctantly, Lily opened her eyes to see a figure standing over her, with the sun forming an illuminated aura around them. She shaded her eyes to see Rachel standing there.

"Hello, Lily, just checking you're attending the English Party AGM tonight at eight."

"Not sure, I—"

"Finlay Walker expects you there, don't let him down."

Lily sat up more, only to see that Rachel had already left.

Late afternoon clinic was disjointed with non-attending patients and the two doctors mumbling to one another whenever their paths crossed in the waiting room. Lily sensed a veil of sweat coating her body as closing time arrived.

Therapy had taught her how to categorise and compartmentalise the troubling thoughts in her mind, leaving nothing to fester and demoralise her at a later date.

She couldn't be bothered to change for the AGM, so she made herself an egg salad and a mug of hot lemon water, and sat in the garden.

Thoughts about how Walker was going to kill Nathan entered her mind. Anxious sentiments surged through her heart. Suddenly, the salad felt like the enemy, and so she pushed the plate away and drank some water instead.

Moving around her house, she searched each room to anticipate where the evil act would take place. It both saddened and angered her that her house would be tarnished by Nathan's last breath.

With a jolt, she noticed it was quarter to eight so she grabbed her bag and rushed out of the door. Walker hated lateness. The streets and the people were a blur as she hastened to the HQ, her heart pumping oxygen and adrenalin around her body.

Her hand shook when she reached out to press the intercom. It was Rachel's light voice that answered and let her in. As she hurried up the stairs, she smoothed down her hair and skirt and took a few deep breaths to control her erratic heartbeat.

When she opened the door, she was surprised to see only Rachel standing before her. Before Lily could speak, someone kicked her in her lower back which sent her sprawling across the floor. Her handbag slid out of reach, and as she grappled to reach it, Rachel kicked it further away as Lily felt someone's foot between her shoulder blades, pressing her into the hard core matting on the floor.

"What's happening? Why are you doing this to me?" she said in between shallow breaths.

"Because we don't want you causing trouble for Finlay," said a deep woman's voice.

"How would I cause him trouble, I support the party," replied Lily as she tried to lift herself up on her forearms.

Rachel slid her foot under Lily's arms so she flopped down flat onto the floor again, banging her chin as she did so. She turned her head, scuffing her cheek on the rough carpet, as she desperately tried to see who the perpetrator was. The only thing she could make out was the outline of a broad, tall woman, but her facial features were blotted out in the gloomy light.

"Who are you?" she asked out of the corner of her mouth.

"I'm Muriel, Finlay's sister. And I want to make sure you've no more articles pertaining to the hospital."

Lily's head was spinning. She didn't even know Walker had a sister, let alone one who was just as aggressive and as frightening as him.

"You haven't answered my question," Muriel hissed as she applied more pressure to Lily's back, until it felt to Lily that her very soul was being expelled from her.

"I've already told him they're all gone." Her voice was beginning to falter and crack as she fought back the tears.

"I will have to check that out. I know where you live, you snivelling wretch."

Lily couldn't answer her as tears streamed down her face and pooled on the floor, wetting strands of her hair.

"Rachel, please help me," she begged as she felt two large hands grab onto her arms to lift her to a standing position with her arms pulled behind her back.

"Rachel," she called out again.

"I can't help you. I'll do what my mum asks of me, not you."

She's his niece, she thought to herself. But he was the abuser and she was the victim, didn't they get that?

She was about to tell them her history with Walker when she was hoisted up and frog-marched towards the wall. She then felt the weight of Muriel's body against hers.

"Any hint of trouble from you and you'll never see another day. Got it, bitch?"

"No more trouble," Lily replied through her flowing tears and runny nose that spewed into her mouth as she spoke.

"Dry your face, you look a mess."

She obliged and blotted her face with a tissue whilst she tried to cease her intermittent sobs.

"Don't go whining to Finlay about our encounter. If I hear you have, our next meeting won't be pleasant."

Lily agreed to do as she said, and wondered how much more unpleasant their next meeting could possibly be.

"Right, let's go," and with that, she pushed Lily towards the door and switched off the solitary light. They all exited together and parted directions when they reached the outside.

Lily stumbled and caught herself on the window ledge of a shop. She could feel carpet burns stinging her chin and cheek. She drifted home in a ghost-like state, oblivious to her surroundings.

Once inside, her body shook uncontrollably as she slumped onto the bottom of the stairs, unable to drag herself any further.

Her mind buzzed as she realised that Muriel and Rachel were related to Walker. She hadn't imagined him to be a family man. *What a misguided family they are*, she thought to herself.

After what seemed like an eternity, she managed to stagger to the kitchen to drink a glass of water in order to quench her nagging thirst. Her mind cleared enough for her to recognise that her personal battle had expanded beyond its normal range. Walker was well protected and she realised that she was fighting so much more than she'd originally thought. She was disturbed to think that his sister and niece perhaps knew about his past, and yet still protected him. "What kind of people do that?" she uttered to the dented kitchen wall.

Her life had become a bleak nightmare and she was keen for it to be terminated, but not before she'd finished what she started.

She scrabbled around in the cupboard and brought out the tatty box, which she placed on the kitchen table. She opened it and perused the contents which offered her the comfort and finality she ultimately sought.

Underneath the scraps of fabric and papers lay a revolver with four bullets in the chamber. She'd procured it when she met some deliciously deviant and resourceful patients in the psychiatric hospital. It seemed quite normal that suicide was the goal for most of them in there.

She caressed the cold, hard metal and twirled the chamber around to listen to the reassuring clicking. She smiled as she held it to her temple and pressed the barrel into her skin. "Not long now," she whispered to herself. "Not long now."

Chapter Thirty-Seven

"Fancy a drink after work? We can go to The Crown," asked Nathan as he and Hugh made their morning coffee.

"I don't think I should, really, it's still early days with Faith."

Nathan didn't really expect a different response from his friend. But he had to admit to himself that he missed Hugh's company more than he'd imagined.

The notion of not wanting to be alone in a pub was unsettling for Nathan, as never before had he been afraid to drink alone. He was used to finding female company for as long as he needed, but nothing quite matched up to the occasional beverage with another man. He let out a deep sigh for Hugh to hear.

He could hear Lily moving around in the reception and it occurred to him that perhaps she'd accept the invitation as she was trying to extend the hand of friendship. He picked up his mug and left Hugh standing alone in the kitchen.

"Would you like to go for a drink after work?" he asked her as she had her back to him. She jumped slightly at his presence and then slowly turned around. He noticed how milky her skin was, revealing tiny thread veins under the surface, and how her hollow eyes seemed to have a permanent frightened look behind her stare. He also noticed grazing on her cheek and chin. He wanted to enquire but somehow knew she'd have a plausible tale to tell which he wouldn't believe.

"That's kind of you," she started, before she realised that the plan would go better if they spent more time together.

"I'd like that." She feigned a smile then returned to her work.

He sensed some reluctance in her voice, but he shrugged it off as he wasn't used to women turning down his soulful hazel eyes.

Hugh overheard the conversation as he stood slightly back from the doorway, and his heart sank when Lilith accepted the offer. At that point, like many in the past, he wondered what attracted women to Nathan so much more than to him.

By the time the end of the day arrived, the sky was covered with a blanket of cloud, and Lily felt shrouded in a grey mist that was beginning to obscure her view of the world.

"Ready to go?" asked Nathan as he appeared in the reception.

"Yes. Is Hugh coming with us?"

"No, you've got me all to yourself," he said before flashing the smile he thought was so irresistible.

The pair headed out whilst Hugh hung back. He felt stupid thinking the way he did, especially as he had no right. Under the circumstances, to consider Lily in any other way other than a work colleague, was futile.

His shoulders drooped as he realised that he was dreading going home. He never knew what mood his wife was going to be in. She flitted between maudlin and anger. The latter frame of mind gave her an acid tongue with bitter comments that punctured his core.

He was experiencing the harshest loneliness of all, that of being lonely whilst in a relationship.

He did a final check around the clinic and then locked up. As he lumbered to his car and climbed in, he thumped the steering wheel with a balled up fist.

Although Lily did her best to hide her injuries, Nathan couldn't ignore them any longer.

"What happened to your face?"

"I fell down a few stairs yesterday, it's nothing."

"You shouldn't be falling down. Are you feeling dizzy or faint?"

"Really, I'm fine."

He expected little else from her and decided to move on to the topic of her past once they'd reached The Spread Eagle.

"What can I get you?"

"A glass of red wine, please."

He ushered her to his regular table and then he returned to the bar. He watched her sitting uncomfortably as she smoothed down her hair and fidgeted in her seat. It looked to him like she didn't want to be there, and he wondered why she had bothered.

"You promised to tell me more about yourself," he said as he placed the glass in front of her.

"There's not a lot to say. My mother's dead, my father has Alzheimer's and lives in a care home. I've never been married, I haven't any children and I've given up finding a relationship."

"Brief and concise," he replied. "But I'm sure there's more to you than that."

"I believe you'll find that your life has far more fascinating facets than mine, tell me about you."

"That could take some time, and I'm not sure that you'll like me anymore after hearing what I have to say."

"Why, what have you done that's so bad?"

"Well, I'm divorced, which should hint at my inability to maintain a meaningful relationship. Women hate that, don't they?"

"It depends on what the woman in question is looking for. Is that your worst crime?"

Nathan looked at her and saw an enquiring hopefulness in her eyes.

"I'm not sure what you're getting at. I've never been in trouble with the police, if that's what you mean."

Lily hunched over and her mouth was a thin line. She wanted him to disclose his guilt and his shame. Anger swelled in her.

"So life's hurt you, not the other way round."

"I'm not perfect and I know that, but I haven't deliberately hurt people. My wife left because I wasn't committed enough. I'm not the total bastard you think I am."

"That remains to be seen," she muttered under her breath.

Nathan shrugged his shoulders at her incoherent mumblings. "Anyway, this is a dreary topic, there must be other things we can discuss," he said as he ran his hand over his chin.

"Perhaps you can tell me what's going on with Hugh, he hasn't seemed himself of late," she said twirling a strand of hair around her finger.

"Well, that's awkward, as it puts me in the role of bastard once again." He grinned at her, but saw she looked ominously serious. He ran his fingers through his mousey brown hair and then spoke. "I'd be interested to know why you've taken such a dislike to me."

She shuffled in her seat and then took a gulp of wine. "I think it goes deeper than words can express."

"Very cryptic and conspiratorial, but clarity would be preferable. I'd like to think that we could be on different terms. Friends even." His last statement was over-emphasized.

"I feel as though we've met in a past life, and it wasn't a pleasant experience," she mused.

"I'm a man of science. Past lives don't fit into my scheme of things."

She smiled gently at him, and Nathan wondered whether he saw an air of pity in her gesture.

"I'd like to invite you to dinner this Friday."

Nathan's mouth gaped open briefly before accepting the offer. "What will you be cooking? Just so I bring the right wine."

"A surprise, the whole evening will be a surprise." A shadow crossed her face as she spoke and Nathan was sure he saw the light in her eyes dim.

"Do you believe in the concept of forgiveness if you are a mere man of science?" she asked.

"It depends on the depth of the misdemeanour. Conversely, bearing grudges can eat away at the emotional well-being of a person, until they're rotted to the core. I see enough of those cases in the clinic every day."

"What you say may be accurate to some degree, who am I to argue with a doctor? However, true forgiveness can be a great deal harder to execute, don't you think?"

"I've never had to forgive someone that much."

"Not even yourself?"

Nathan didn't answer straight away, and he didn't like the idea that his soul was being forcibly laid bare for her to scrutinise. He was seeing a profundity to her character that he didn't think she possessed. She was truly unlike any woman he'd known before, and he couldn't make up his mind whether he liked that or not.

Lily was feeling on edge because she was under the distinct impression that she was being watched. As much as she tried to brush it off as a paranoid element to her depression, she couldn't get the frissons that traversed her spine to dissipate.

As Nathan returned to the bar for some more drinks, her eyes followed him and then glanced around the other patrons out of curiosity. Bored of that activity, she moved to another pastime of picking the skin around her fingernails, when a disembodied hand rested firmly on her shoulder, and then the rest of the body drew level with hers.

"Not giving any secrets away are we?" whispered Muriel hoarsely in her ear.

Lily tried not to flinch or allow her face to redden, but she couldn't stop her throat from seizing up. "Just having a friendly drink, that's all."

"Remember what I told you and watch what you do. Remember, you wouldn't be missed if you were to disappear." And with a final squeeze of her hand, Muriel was gone.

"Who was that?" asked Nathan as he returned to the table.

"Just someone I met recently," she replied nonchalantly as she gazed passed him to scan the room.

"She looked kind of familiar. Do I know her from the clinic?"

"No, I shouldn't think so."

"Sometimes I think we keep bumping into doppelgangers to remind us of people we left behind on the way," he said rather wistfully.

"I think we should look to our history to see how past events shape our future, not retread our relationship issues with those we choose to forget."

She sounded a tad bitter to him, not like the women whom he was used to drinking with who were more concerned with having sex. He wasn't sure whether he was looking forward to wasting a Friday evening, but it was too late to back out, he thought to himself.

They both finished their drinks rapidly. And both were dreading Friday.

Nathan turned and observed Lily's stance. He could see she was alarmed by something by the swiftness of her footsteps, and the way she clutched her jacket around her body.

"Would you like me to walk you home?" he asked.

"No thanks. I'm fine."

He didn't quite believe her, but she had forcefully rejected his offer, so he trundled back home.

Lily entered her house and instantly smelt the fragrance of lemons. Her heart stood still and her lungs deflated. She hesitated by her front door, unsure whether she should progress further, all the while listening out for alien sounds.

After a few frozen minutes in the hallway, she crept towards the lounge with her hands rolled into fists. Her heart sank as she saw books scattered all over the floor and sofa cushions ejected from their positions.

Devoid of previous fear, she rushed to the kitchen to see a mess equivalent to a child's baking session. She frantically bent down to check for the tatty box in the lower cupboard and was almost euphoric to find the box and its contents untouched. She piled the pans up in front of it again and raced upstairs.

The contents of her wardrobe and drawers were strewn all over the floor and bed. In the bathroom, the cistern had clearly been searched in a desperate attempt to find the suspected hidden treasures.

Every room had been violated by, she suspected, Rachel and Muriel, making Lily seethe with rage. She hated them all, and wished she had more bullets.

Chapter Thirty-Eight

Fed up with creeping around his own home, Hugh clattered the crockery as he made himself breakfast. His theatrical adolescent anger worked well, as a few minutes later, Faith padded into the kitchen.

"My God, you're noisy this morning. What are you doing?"

"Making my own breakfast again, and trying to find the source of the rancid stench in here, I can't work out where it's coming from," he replied without looking at her.

"I can't smell anything."

"Well no, it's not really here now, but it was ripe when I came home last night. I thought it might be coming from the fridge, but how can it when eighty percent of the stuff in there is bottles of wine."

Hugh's voice skewered the air, and Faith held her hands over her ears.

"Faith, I'm talking to you."

"Stop shouting, I'm not a child. Leave me alone," and with that, she stormed off in her own adolescent strop.

Hugh threw his sandwiches onto the worktop and then slammed the fridge door. The bottles rattled in the door which then swung open again like the slowly opening lid of a coffin in a horror movie. There were more bottles in the fridge than they'd require for a dinner party, he thought to himself.

He closed the door slowly a second time, and leaned against it with his eyes screwed up tightly. No more could he be a coward, he thought to himself, he was going to have to broach the subject with her. He was losing everything in his life, whilst she was a bystander with her brain steeped in wine.

She'd hidden her alcohol dependency well, he'd give her that. But he could no longer stand by and let her behaviour ruin what they both had. Whether they had anything left together remained to be seen. He picked up the battered sandwich and headed for the door. He paused at the bottom of the stairs and blew her an unseen kiss before he left in his usual quiet fashion.

As he drove along the straight road that was lined by fields, he couldn't stop himself from wondering whether Nathan and Lily had spent the night together. He was aware that it was none of his business, but he also knew that he'd be vigilant for any clues of intimacy at the clinic, those little looks, those covert smiles, and the give-away glow. It would eat away at him all day.

As he pulled into his parking space, he could see Lily arriving alone. He knew it could be a ruse and that Nathan could be waiting around the corner so that they didn't look like they were obviously together. He sat in his car, drumming his fingers on the steering wheel to see whether Nathan would arrive within the next few minutes. After five minutes, he decided to go in, chastising himself for acting like a jealous idiot.

"Good morning, Lilith. How are you today?" he asked as he stepped through the door.

"Well, thank you. And you?"

"So-so," he replied. He hung around for a few seconds to see whether she'd take any further interest in him, but when she didn't, he moved to the kitchen to console himself with a fresh coffee.

Nathan blustered into the clinic ten minutes later, apologising profusely for his tardiness. The truth was that after leaving the pub with Lily, he doubled back on himself and returned to the pub to find some female company. Hence, he'd had a late night with a woman far too young for him. That morning he was feeling the stiffness and fatigue that can accompany someone whose years were amassing quicker than desired. He felt strangely sordid following the previous night's activities.

He grabbed a mug of coffee and disappeared into his room to check his post that Lily had reliably put there every morning since her arrival. Much of the post was mundane that required filing by Lily.

The last envelope he came across was marked "private and confidential." As he slit it open, a photograph slid out, upside down onto his desk. He turned it over to see a picture of the outside view of Poplar Ward with the tall, thin trees lined up along the austere red brick building. He poked his fingers into the envelope and fumbled around to see if he could find a note, but it was empty, and nothing was inscribed on the back of the photograph.

When there was a knock at the door, he shoved the photograph into the pile of post. Lily walked in requesting any filing. When he handed her the pile, the photo fell onto his desk picture side up.

They both froze with their eyes fixed upon the picture before Nathan whisked it up and shoved it in his top drawer.

"Just these, thanks Lily," he said, ruffling his hair with one hand whilst picking the phone up with the other. The final gesture signalled her time to leave the room.

Hesitantly, she walked out and closed the door behind her. She remained motionless outside the closed door, with waves of panic reverberating up and down her body. She prayed he wasn't calling Walker about the photograph as it had nothing to do with her. But who, she thought?

She listened at the door, but she couldn't hear him talking at all. Unaware of her surroundings, she hadn't heard Hugh come out of his room to catch her standing there. He made a small coughing sound to alert her to his presence. She just bowed her head and hurried away with her face a deep shade of crimson.

Hugh could only think the worse of Nathan, and he was angry that Lily may end up leaving them because of a foolish one night stand. There was no time to challenge Nathan right there and then as the first patients had begun to trickle into the clinic.

Lily quivered in the reception as she envisaged phoning Walker to tell him that she had nothing to do with the photograph. She picked up the receiver and her fingers lingered over the keys. She remained in that position for several seemingly long seconds, until she calmly replaced the receiver. What good would her action do, she pondered? If Walker was sending Nathan his own collection of items, then he would already know and just laugh at her pitiable naivety.

A patient entered the reception and distracted her briefly from the unease that was gnawing away at her nerves. The respite didn't last for long, as every time the phone rang, she'd break out in sweat until the voice at the other end of the line was as innocuous as she hoped for.

She decided that she'd stay in the clinic at lunchtime to protect herself from unwanted attention. Lunchtime was easy to deal with, but she knew that going home was going to prove difficult to manage. She envisaged lying awake all night, anxious about a potential visit from Muriel or Walker.

The culmination of years of planning was to arrive the following evening, and she hoped that in between time, the issue of the photograph would go unnoticed.

"How was your evening with Lily?" asked Hugh as he breezed into the kitchen to fetch his lunch from the fridge.

"Fine thanks, why?"

"It's just that she looked upset when she came out of your office this morning. You didn't do anything stupid did you?"

"Stupid? Like what?"

"What do you think I mean? Did you sleep with her?" Hugh's eyes were fiery and his eyebrows arched as he glared at Nathan.

"No, I bloody didn't. She's not my type, if it's, in fact, any of your business."

"Anything which affects this clinic is my goddamn business."

Both men stood to attention facing one another. Hugh clenched his fists, and instead of punching Nathan as he felt like doing, he jabbed his own thigh a few times before he left for the solitude of his own room.

Nathan remained alone in the kitchen, mulling over what Hugh had just said. *Why was Lily upset*, he wondered?

His cogitation was interrupted by noises coming from the reception area, which made the hairs on his neck stand on end. *First the photograph and now an intruder*, he thought to himself. "Hugh should be grateful not to be a part of all this," he muttered as he quietly went to check out the noises.

He moved quietly down the narrow passageway and cautiously peered around the door which was wide open.

"God, it's you," he gasped as he spied a startled Lily.

"And who did you think it would be?"

"No one in particular, I was just being vigilant. Anyway, it's lovely outside; I'm surprised to find you in here."

"I had some jobs to finish before the afternoon rush."

He looked across at her and thought how waiflike she looked in the midday sun. Her fragility was accentuated by the austere light and there was something haunting about her. She interrupted his trance-like state by addressing him with her gentle voice.

"You're still coming over tomorrow evening?"

He paused longer then he felt polite, but it was too late. She looked at him with her injured features as he grappled with the words in his head.

"Of course I am. You said eight didn't you?"

"Eight is fine," she said as she looked away, wishing she was in the garden, and wishing that tomorrow would never arrive. A small voice echoed in her head that she may not be alive tomorrow. Only Muriel knew the answer to that.

Nathan returned to his room and sat at his desk. He took the photograph out of the drawer and turned it over and over with his fingers.

His mind was drawn back to his time working in the hospital, and as he traced the outline of the building with his finger he was once again walking in the grounds and entering the ward. Before he knew it, a grotesque succession of images and smells drifted past his senses.

He could smell the cleaning fluid that was used to wipe every surface. The antiseptic aroma would almost burn his nostril hairs. The cries of patients as their twisted minds distorted their thoughts, and auditory hallucinations rang in his ears as though he'd heard them for the first time that morning. He closed his eyes and mentally reviewed all the pitiful images and re-examined that alarming night that sent him down the road of self-loathing and self-destructive behaviours.

His lack of compassion and empathy towards those less fortunate had led him to be the lonely man he had become, instead of the hedonistic, laid back but decent man he used to be before he worked in that hospital.

His foot tapped repeatedly on the floor as it all flooded back to him, and he realised that the only way to cleanse his soul was to go to the police and come clean about the past. He knew that time had no bearing on the severity of the crime and that he'd have to inform the General Medical Council of his conduct.

But perhaps the person he dreaded telling the most about his plan was Hugh. Although Hugh would praise his decency, it would have consequences on the clinic and hence, their friendship. He comprehended that in the end, he'd have to leave the partnership and the area. "All will be lost in the end," he uttered to himself.

He realised that it wasn't the right time to talk to Hugh as he seemed perturbed about something. He decided that he'd invite him over on Sunday so that he could begin his battle on Monday. Proof or no proof, he was going to deal with the matter like the man he used to be before Walker put the fear of God in him.

He turned his thoughts to Lily and he wondered what had upset her so much. Had she expected more from their platonic drink? Didn't he make her feel special like she had hoped or needed? "Bloody questions, and bloody women," he quipped.

His mind ached from the mental journey, and an overwhelming sensation of doom careered around his body. He took one last look at the photograph and then placed it back in the drawer.

All afternoon the photograph taunted him, almost more than the previous pieces. He found himself only half-listening to his patients, concentrating more on the significance of the photograph amongst the other gestures. On their way out of the clinic, patients commented to Lily that the doctor appeared distracted, and was he unwell? All Lily could do was smile and apologise.

On the drive home, Hugh reflected on the recent changes in his wife, and deduced that she was hiding matters that needed bringing out into the open. He hated the way he'd avoided conflict for fear of hearing something so damaging that he might not survive; but he knew he was unhappy with his life. He needed to address issues in order to move forward, with or without her.

The notion of being without her in the future scared him. He'd come to terms with not being a father, although he felt that she'd got over the fact much quicker. But he'd always seen himself becoming a husband.

He pulled up onto the gravel drive and drew up next to Faith's car. He was pleased to see that she was at home. He sat for a few minutes to compose his thoughts, knowing that if he approached her with accusatory remarks, he'd achieve very little, except perhaps an argument. He didn't want a fight and he hoped she didn't either.

As he got out of the car, he could hear Faith's raised voice, but he couldn't make out what she was saying, or who she was talking to. His heart pumped faster as he approached the front door. He opened it as quietly as possible, hoping not to alert her to his arrival. He was disappointed to find she was arguing with someone on the phone, which she promptly slammed down as soon as he stepped through the door.

Her face was flushed and her eyes had a wild and glossy stare. It was too late for her to hide her emotions, and she knew it.

"That sounded heated, who was that?" he asked in a quiet tone.

"No one really, just some set-to at the chorale society."

Hugh raised his eyebrows and then put his briefcase down.

"So what was to be left to you then?" he asked as he repeated the snippet he heard before she abruptly terminated the call.

"We have a troublemaker in the soprano section, so I said that I'd deal with her, try and smooth things over."

It hurt Hugh to see how easily she could lie to him so convincingly. Secrets and lies were things that he couldn't abide in a relationship, even though he, too, was keeping secrets from her.

He spied a glass of wine next to her on the console table, and he opened his mouth to pass a comment but then closed it again. "What's the point?" he muttered to himself.

Attic of the Mind **247**

Faith picked up her glass and moved in a subtle zigzag manner to the lounge, where she collapsed onto the sofa, sloshing some wine down her top as she did so. She stared vacantly out the window as though oblivious to his presence.

He shrugged his shoulders and then got himself a beer. He sauntered to the conservatory with a bottle and a novel, keen to get lost in both. The fantasy world had so much more to offer him than the drab reality that excluded him from every joy possible.

Lily had got over the first hurdle of anxiety, which was entering her house. She locked the door quickly and paused before entering the kitchen. There was a faint smell of lemon in the air.

Whilst she waited for the kettle to boil, she checked that the tatty box was still hidden behind the pans, which it was. The growing noise from the boiling kettle irritated her as it could have been masking any potential background noise she needed to be aware of. She switched it off before it reached its optimum temperature so she could listen to the house.

A petulant breeze had lifted, scurrying fat clouds across the dimming sky, and rattling the original sash windows in their frames. She wanted to venture into the garden, only the fading light cast shadows in the dark corners, and the strangely atmospheric light made the shrubberies look as though they were alive and ready to pounce.

Threatened by the garden, she decided to put on some classical music, very softly in the background. She then picked up a novel to absorb her mounting tension.

After reading the same line over and over again, she had to accept that she was too distracted to absorb the words and sentiments intended by the author.

When her main enemy was only Walker, Lily concluded that she could cope, although she was fearful at times, but she was able to shut him out of her mind after years of practice. It was a technique she'd acquired when she was nineteen.

But now that Muriel and Rachel had entered the game, she was unable to blot out the trepidation and menace which they exuded. Was it possible she was more afraid of Muriel than Walker because Muriel was a woman?

She'd never really taken to forging friendships with either gender, but she still saw women as being more readily available to being companions *du Coeur*. Muriel eroded her vision of women so that they were almost the same aggressive beasts as men.

Lily was saddened by her new found fear, and longed for her miserable passage of life to be expunged.

She decided that the cathartic and necessary next act would be to write a suicide note that would explain to those who found her, and the few that perhaps cared why she'd committed such a heinous act. It would also point out why Walker deserved to be punished for his deeds.

She thought that she should also explain Nathan's part in the misery scene, and although his part may appear miniscule to onlookers, an explanation was called for. The elucidation would also involve Walker's part and reasoning for Nathan's demise. She decided not to muddy the waters by mentioning Muriel and Rachel; they would be tarnished enough by Walker's story once it was in the public domain.

Her pontificating was interrupted by a rattling sound coming from upstairs, which she convinced herself was just her bedroom window complaining about the wind. She remained downstairs for several minutes until the rattling noise unnerved her so much that she had to go and investigate.

She opened the knife drawer and took out the meat carver with its long, wide blade. She moved silently down the hallway, hugging the wall with her back and then proceeded to tip-toe upstairs.

Her eyes moved rapidly from the stairs to the landing and then to the doors upstairs to check for signs of movement. Her heart thumped so loudly in the background silence that she thought it would be audible to anyone else present in the house.

As she slowly crept towards her bedroom, from where the noises were coming, her breaths became shallow and beads of sweat threaded across her skeletal face.

Her hand gripped the door knob, and as she turned it cautiously, she gripped the knife so tightly in her other hand that her knuckles turned white. She held her breath so she didn't mask someone else's rasping noises.

The grey atmosphere made it difficult to decipher unwanted shadows within, so she tentatively reached out and switched on the light, worrying that as she reached out, someone would grab her wrist. Scanning around, she saw that nothing had been touched or moved, and no one was standing behind the door, which her furtive imagination had played out in her head.

She repeated her stealthy movements in the spare bedroom until finally she reached the bathroom door, which would complete her tour. She pulled the light switch next to the door and found the bathroom empty. As an immense relief washed over her, she leant against the cool white wall tiles, and inhaled a cleansing breath deep into her lungs.

It was only as she stood there that she noticed the shower curtain wasn't tucked back neatly as normal. She suddenly felt flushed with a transparent layer of sweat that coated her body, so she re-positioned the knife in front of her once more and stepped closer towards the bath. With one arm outstretched, she whisked back the curtain and brandished the knife as aggressively as she could.

Her mouth fell open and she dropped the knife as she saw a crude drawing of a pair of eyes, drawn in what looked like red lipstick on the stark white tiles.

She spun around to check that no one had appeared behind her, and then she clasped her hand around her gapping mouth as she began to sob with uncontrollable, stuttering sounds.

The knife lay at her feet with the blade glinting in the remorseless electric light. Slowly, she bent down to retrieve it. She ran her finger along the edge of the blade, feeling the coldness of the steel against the tender flesh of her finger tip.

Her pent up emotions were bringing her body to bursting point. She desperately needed to relieve the pressure before she exploded.

Very slowly and deliberately, she stretched out her left arm with the palm facing up, and with the knife in her right hand she began to draw the blade over her alabaster skin in vertical lines.

She pressed down on the knife so the blade popped into her flesh and slit it open like the sail on a ship being ripped in two by stormy weather. As the blade progressed along her arm, syrupy cherry blood seeped out along the cuts and slowly oozed down her arm.

Splashes of red dripped onto the pale vinyl floor as though her body was crying tears of blood. After half a dozen slices, she began to feel numb, a numbness that felt calm and reassuring.

The red on the floor mirrored the red eyes on the tiles, and the crude drawing appeared to mock and goad her.

Thrusting paranoia battered her from every angle until she held the point of the blade over her heart. She pushed it into her skin until it felt at breaking point. "One big push would do it," she said to herself. She was close to completing the motion, but stopped short of drawing blood as she wanted to take Walker with her.

She was too exhausted to clear up the mess, and so she just dragged herself to bed with congealing blood sticking to her flesh and clothes. She lay on top of her bed, caring not to lift up the quilt, and remained motionless, staring blankly at the ceiling.

"Tomorrow," she said to herself. "It all ends tomorrow."

Chapter Thirty-Nine

Nathan swatted the alarm clock off the bedside table and groaned as he rolled over. The empty dented pillow next to him smelt of citrus fruit, but she'd gone during the night with his usual blessing of taxi fare.

He stretched out his arm and felt the ruffled sheet between his fingers, then reluctantly eased himself out of bed.

Restful sleep evaded him after his bed companion had left. Instead, he was plagued with disturbing images and reflections from the past; especially with haunting visions of the girl he'd seen Walker with that awful night.

The nightmares seemed endless, and he'd been awoken by the alarm, feeling totally worn out and unprepared for the day ahead.

Even though he was awake, the girl's hazy grey eyes continued to trouble him, begging him to free her from her misery. He shook his head to dispel the vivid stare from his mind. He was troubled by there being something freshly familiar about her eyes, something he couldn't quite put his finger on.

As he performed his perfunctory morning rituals, snippets of recent events kept infiltrating his mind. He found that Lily had been troubling him more of late, her pitifully thin body, her inability to mentally cope with stressful situations, and he was sure he'd seen tell-tale marks on her arm. Her arms were normally well hidden except for once when she'd outstretched her arm across his desk, her sleeve rolled up enough for the slash marks to be revealed.

As he was sitting at the kitchen table, buttering some toast, he heard the post as it spat through his letterbox. He rose immediately to check that nothing nefarious had arrived, as had become his habit.

Looking through the envelopes suddenly put him in mind of the incident with the photograph and Lily's peculiar reaction to it. It puzzled him.

Time was rattling on, so he finished his breakfast and darted out of the house, not wishing to be late for work again.

His feet moved briskly along the pavement as he weaved in between other pedestrians drifting along the same route. He remarked how the others appeared carefree, not emotionally laden as he was.

Nathan found himself thinking about Walker on an almost sub-conscious level, as though new seeds had been planted but he hadn't noticed until the first shoots were burgeoning through.

He thought back to when Walker phoned him and asked him whether he ever thought about the patients on Poplar, especially the girl. He then went on to ask him whether he ever wondered whether she was watching him. That comment began to prey on Nathan's psyche. He hadn't thought such an atrocious thing until now. And now he was wondering whether there was more going on in the peripheries of his life than he'd imagined. A shiver travelled up his spine and erected the hairs on the back of his neck.

He shrugged off the negative impulses as he barged past a couple sauntering along holding hands. People in love made him want to vomit. He rounded the corner and almost floored a woman walking a poodle. The woman glared at him as he muttered an apology before speeding off.

He arrived at the clinic to the smell of stimulating coffee, and in the kitchen he found Hugh and Lily discussing ideas for the tiny garden at the back. Nathan saw Lily's transparent fragility edged by the light from the window, and he speculated whether she could possibly be the same girl from Poplar.

He closed his eyes for a few seconds and pictured the gently grey-eyed, honey-haired girl from the past. He opened his eyes again and moved towards Lily, remarking her emerald-green eyes and obviously dyed hair.

"Is something the matter?" she asked, noticing his concentrated stare.

"No, nothing's wrong. I just thought you looked like someone I once met. But your eyes are far too different."

"And you've only just noticed this have you?" interjected Hugh.

"I'd forgotten all about them until this morning. I'm just being silly," he replied, avoiding eye contact with both of them.

Lily shrugged her shoulders and returned to the reception, her heart pounding in her rib cage.

"That was a cheap trick," said Hugh as he replaced the milk in the fridge.

"And you mean what exactly?" replied Nathan as he sat down, expecting a lecture from his friend.

"Comparing her to a past girlfriend. Honestly, Nathan, you can be such an oil slick at times. Have you no shame?"

"I wasn't doing that. If you must know, I wondered whether she was . . ." He paused as saying the words aloud was going to be incredibly painful. "I thought she might be the girl from Poplar Ward."

Hugh almost choked on his coffee, and then looked wide-eyed at Nathan.

"You can't be serious, that's a laughable thought. Not only would that be mightily coincidental, surely you'd have recognised her name on the application form?"

Nathan shook his head, and ran his hand through his hair. "I'm ashamed to say that her name has slipped from my memory, unlike her eyes." He took a swig of coffee, desperately needing a caffeine fix.

"In so many ways, she isn't that girl, but she's such an enigma that I wonder who exactly she is. She's very private about her past."

"There's nothing wrong with that. Anyway, where's all this coming from?"

"Just piecing things together, really. And if you must know, Walker got me thinking."

"Oh God, I might have known he'd be involved somehow. Just forget about it, he's winding you up. Come on, let's get back to work." Hugh left the kitchen and Nathan dutifully followed, although nagging thoughts kept infusing his mind and saturating his soul.

Lily's emotions were divided. On the one hand, she was upset with

Nathan admitting that he'd forgotten her past incarnation, and on the other hand, she was terrified that he'd worked out who she was. "Who I used to be," she muttered to herself. She couldn't work out what was giving her away.

The telephone rang.

"Good morning, Viking Clinic."

"Are you ready for tonight?"

She knew it was him, and despised being checked up on as though she was still the adolescent in his so-called care.

"Of course. Nothing's changed."

"Good. I'm not telling you when I'm arriving, so you won't be nervously clock-watching."

"I'm not nervous."

Walker put the phone down, leaving her with venom in her mouth. Her hatred for him had reached boiling point, but she knew that she had to bide her time until the evening. She also knew that she was, in fact, very nervous.

As she did her paperwork, she noticed how badly she'd chewed her fingernails, a habit she'd taken years to break. She felt like the past was beginning to engulf her.

When lunchtime arrived, she decided that she didn't want to miss her last chance to sit in the public garden. So, she discreetly took her salad from the fridge and quietly left the building.

The sun was breaking through the mounds of billowing clouds, and its warmth stroked her face with a tender touch. As she opened the wrought-iron gate to the garden, she saw, ensconced on a bench, the recently formed couple she'd been watching for a while. A rush of joy swept over her at seeing the union blossoming.

In the same instance as the feeling of elation for their happiness, her heart plummeted into a murky depressive state. She knew she'd never be privy to the raptures of love and companionship as tonight her life ended.

Her life after the age of nineteen had revolved around self-mutilating revenge. Although therapy had clarified her vision, she never mentioned her abuse by the nurse in charge. She wanted to deal with it her way, and now she was unable to escape from the idea of vengeance.

Her salad was untouched when a voice spoke.

"Mind if I join you?"

She looked up to see Hugh standing there holding his familiar sandwich and looking rather forlorn.

"Please do," she replied as she shuffled up the bench and put her handbag at her feet.

They sat silently observing the lavenders bobbing around in the gentle breeze whilst Hugh ate his sandwich. His curiosity had been piqued by Nathan's ramblings, and although he didn't know what the patients on Poplar looked like, he couldn't help glimpsing at her with sideways glances.

"Is there something bothering you?" she asked as she replaced the lid on her untouched box of salad.

"Very perceptive of you." He turned towards her, his shiny brogues shimmering in the sunlight.

"We work closely together, but I'm ashamed to say that I know little about you."

"That's because I'm dull and uninteresting."

"I wouldn't say that. You're quiet and unassuming, but everyone's past is a myriad of significant facts and events."

Lily wasn't blind to the fact that Nathan had probably imparted his thoughts about her, and so he was either digging on behalf of Nathan, or he was just plain curious. Either way, she wasn't prepared to divulge anything that could be interpreted as evidence to her past in the realms of a psychiatric hospital. She decided to play him at his own game.

"What is it you want to know exactly?"

Hugh's neck reddened.

"Nathan seems convinced you look like someone he's met before, and I just wondered if, in fact, you had."

"I think he's met so many women over the years, he feels like he knows every single one he comes into contact with."

Hugh threw his head back and laughed. "You have a point. I don't know why I was taking his thoughts so seriously."

Hugh returned to his half eaten sandwich, enjoying Lily's company more than he felt he should, and she felt content that she'd deflected the conversation away from her past.

"It's not my place to ask, I know, but are you okay?" she asked softly.

Hugh swallowed his mouthful and felt the colour rise in his neck again. "A few troubles at home. Well, with Faith . . ." he broke his conversation as his quavering voice felt too weak to continue. After clearing his throat, he started again. "I mean, it's probably my fault, or Nathan's, but not hers."

"Nathan's fault?" Now it was Lily's turn to move around to face him.

"I think I'm just being silly, but I wonder whether they've been intimate way back. Faith seems to really have an issue with him but she won't tell me why. You must think I'm foolish."

"I'm a little shocked at what you're saying, but I don't see you as being foolish. We both know how Nathan likes female company, shall we say." She blushed as she turned away.

She so wanted to help Hugh as he deserved more from life, but she had so little time left. Perhaps Walker's deed that evening would help him out, she thought. She really hoped that his pain would evaporate soon and that he'd be happy again.

Hugh tapped his watch to announce it was time to return back to work. When they arrived at the gate, he opened it for her, and she was touched by the show of respect that was otherwise absent in her life. He noted the sweet smile she offered him, and he felt a pang of sadness for her. Although he wasn't sure why. Perhaps it was her delicate demeanour that brought out the protector in him.

When the end of clinic arrived, Lily did an extra tidy of the reception area, and then she made sure that she said her goodbye to Hugh. She wanted to reach out and hug him, but she knew that would be a step too far.

Nathan peered into the reception to confirm the evening plans, but Lily had gone. He shrugged his shoulders, shoved his hands into his pockets and ambled back to his room. "I'll see her later," he said aloud.

Lily's appetite was more dulled than ever, so she decided to prepare just a small meal for the evening, a chicken salad with couscous. She saw no point in over-doing it. She thought the forensic pathologist would find their last meal easy to decipher, in a grim sort of way.

She walked around the house like a ghost in limbo, neither feeling pain nor sorrow, just the feeling that she'd been there before.

Walker was right not to tell her his time of arrival so at least the look of surprise on her face would be genuine for Nathan's benefit. However, her nerves were so frayed that she wondered whether she'd be able to carry out her own plan when the time came.

The shower did nothing to wash away the unclean sensation that shrouded her body and mind. She was glad her father had no memory of her as his daughter. She wanted him to be spared the suffering, even though in his role as a parent, he'd caused her much suffering when he and her mother abandoned her in the mental health system.

Her eyes looked alien to her without the green lenses, and she found that part of Maria was gazing back at her through the mirror. A nauseous sensation travelled up her body, and she grappled with the feelings in order not to throw up the bilious content of her stomach.

To enhance the greyness of her eyes, she drew a line along the edge of her upper and lower lashes in smoky grey kohl and finished with a few sweeps of black mascara. She left the rest of her face untouched apart from some clear gloss on her lips. She smoothed down her hair and then walked away from the mirror, no longer wishing to see the image from her past haunting her reality.

The ash-grey silk dress skimmed her bony body as she descended the stairs. The gentle caress of the fabric against her skin made her feel alive to the vibrations of the foreboding atmosphere.

A bottle of wine stood proudly on the kitchen table demanding her attention. She duly opened it and poured a large glass. The liquid felt refreshing in her mouth but acidic to her stomach. Undeterred, she swallowed more mouthfuls to quell her rising panic.

She bent down to the cupboard and pulled out the tatty box. She removed the revolver and checked it still contained the four bullets in the chamber. The metal felt smooth compared to the roughness of the cardboard box, but both textures felt sensual to her fingers. She placed the revolver in her black patent handbag which she then placed out of sight, but not out of reach, behind the sofa.

On the bookshelf, almost hidden out of view, was the camcorder which she'd set up ready for later. She hoped it would make the investigating officer's job easier, and give birth to a sensational story for a newspaper journalist.

It gave her some level of satisfaction to know that the story would be released to the world. She was also pleased that she wouldn't be around for the pitying stares and condescending comments that she would have to endure from society around her. She no longer wanted to play the role of victim.

Her house was its usual sparse tidiness, so there was very little else she needed to do. She put on a classical CD and then she sat down to bite her fingernails with Bach's melodious notes floating in the background.

Chapter Forty

Nathan was of two minds about going to Lily's for the evening. On the one hand, he would have a home-cooked meal that she had prepared, but on the other hand, he wondered whether they'd have nothing in common to talk about.

He knew it would be incredibly rude not to go, and for the sake of harmony at the clinic, he donned jeans and a pale blue polo shirt and then grabbed a bottle of wine to take with him.

He strolled along the pavement holding the bottle like a baby. His mind was filled with scenes from his past, and tormenting inner voices peppered him with his inadequacies towards others. And the girl's eyes now punctured his thoughts whether he was asleep or awake. The stare was getting stronger and more potent.

Every person he passed in the street seemed to have her eyes. Her name was on the edge of his brain, although it had been white-washed over to preserve his sanity.

A conversation with Lily about forgiveness pushed its way to the forefront of his mind. She appeared wistful yet fervent as she talked about the strength required to carry out the sentiment. Who or what did she need to forgive, he wondered?

The street where she lived was tranquil, away from the hubbub of the streets closer to the town centre. It also seemed darker due to the row of trees lining the pavement.

He paused for a second at the gate before opening it. Before he rang the doorbell, he checked his watch and saw that it was ten past eight.

"Not too late," he said aloud, addressing the closed door.

He rang it and waited, half hoping she'd forgotten and had gone out. Seconds later, he saw her distorted shadow approaching through the stained glass, and he prepared a fixed smile on his face.

When the door opened, he almost dropped the bottle of wine as he took a step back, and the fixed smile turned to a gaping hole.

"Bloody hell!" he exclaimed. "Maria Langer."

The name he'd forgotten burst forth from his mouth like water from a ruptured pipe. He stood frozen to the spot as he gazed upon the woman he thought would never survive her youth. An uncharacteristic redness mounted from his chest, up his neck and to his face.

"So you haven't forgotten me," she said quietly.

He couldn't say anything at first except to shake his head slowly. After taking a few deep breaths, and allowing the dew of sweat to evaporate, he drew breath to speak.

"I could never forget. Your eyes wouldn't let me."

She moved away from the front door and beckoned him in. He hesitantly stepped inside, and absentmindedly handed her the bottle before he stood there gawping at her through his hazy eyes.

It was hard for him to comprehend that she was the same person.

"We should sit," she said, ushering him through to the lounge, where moments earlier, she'd visited the bookcase. She offered him a drink and all he wanted was scotch.

Nathan sat warming the spirit with both his hands cupped around the glass. "It's all making sense now," he said in a measured manner. "It was you who sent me the pieces from Poplar, and that's why you were reticent to talk about your past. It's you who has to forgive, isn't it?"

Those last words made him look down at the wooden floorboards, and no matter how much scotch he sipped, his mouth remained dry.

"I've followed your career around the country, from afar. I had to get a solid career of my own to enter your sphere."

"But why not come out publically about the past?"

"Who'd believe me? Anyway, it was more fun playing with your ego and your nerves."

"And what about Walker, did you play with him too?"

"He's always been harder to punish, and harder to fool." She gazed out of the window, feeling her calves tighten every time someone walked past the bay window.

"What do you mean by 'harder to fool'?"

"He had worked out a while back who I was. He thought it was funny that you hadn't."

Nathan's face reddened and the muscles in his jaw twitched. He could picture Walker, in his mind's eye, enjoying watching him squirm and sweat. Walker had increased his fear purposefully, and made the situation suit his own needs, knowing that Lily was in fact the puppeteer on the end of his strings.

"Words seem hopelessly empty right now, but I'm truly sorry for my part in your pain. I should have been stronger."

"Yes, you should have been. I was at his mercy, and you had the power to make him stop. I've hated you ever since for what you didn't do." She took a sip of wine and then whispered. "And I still hate you now."

"I was only a junior doctor, and previously, another young doctor was in my position a few years earlier and had been disciplined and struck off for indecent conduct with a female patient. That was Walker's doing. The doctor was innocent, and he threatened to do the same to me. The doctor killed himself as his future was dead. It was too much to risk, don't you see?"

Knowing Walker as she did, she believed Nathan. That went some way to explain his conduct and attitude in life.

"Did Hugh know back then?"

"No, but I wish I had told him. Perhaps he could have saved me, but perhaps not."

"So who was to save me?" she said as she looked at him with her muted eyes that seared right through his flesh to his remorseful heart. Her eyes looked painfully beautiful to him, though unbearable to look at for more than a few seconds.

"I should have been the one to save you. I was a self-centred, egotistical, amateur playboy, who attracted women with his white coat. Without that white coat, I'd have been nothing. That's what I was afraid of. And I was afraid of Walker."

As he spoke, she reconnected with the junior doctor he once was, which in turn took her back to Maria. Her loathing for who she was resurfaced.

"But you're a respected GP now, so why not expose his grimy past?"

"With what proof? He's well liked around here, the fools." He drifted off momentarily. "Having said that, I've decided that I'm going to the police on Monday, as the guilt is eating me alive." He sat up quickly and lent forward towards her. "We could go together, you're the proof I need. So you see, we could still beat him yet."

Nathan's eyes were alive with hope and excitement, even though he was disappointed to see no reaction from her.

"Surely you'd want to do that with me? They can speak to us separately and see that we have the same story from different vantage points. What can go wrong?"

"Indeed, what can go wrong?" said Walker's voice from behind Nathan.

Nathan froze and then turned his head around to see the vast build of Walker standing there. He looked from Lily to Walker and back again. Why hadn't she moved? Why wasn't she startled more than she was? Questions kept churning around his head, but the answers were not forthcoming.

"Surprised to see me, good Doctor?"

The emphasis on the word "good" was wearing thin to Nathan, but he'd got greater concerns than that to deal with, right there and then.

"What are you doing here?" he said as he stood up and faced Walker, relieved that the sofa stood between them.

"I've come in the nick of time from what I heard of your conversation." Walker grinned like a snarling Alsatian, sending shivers rippling up and down Nathan's spine.

"And in case you were wondering, your poor, precious Lily knew I was coming. More of a bitch now, wouldn't you say?"

Nathan turned his head towards her and saw that she'd remained impassively in the chair, wringing her hands.

"What's going on, Lily? Don't tell me you're siding with him. He abused you."

His last three words hung in the air like ropes on a scaffold, ready for their victims. The atmosphere had a nasty tinge to it. Nathan forced himself to stay strong even though the adrenalin coursing through his veins was urging him to run.

"I'm truly sorry, Lily. I let you down and I let myself down, but this won't solve your emotional pain." He compelled himself to look at her as he spoke, even though it made him want to choke on his own vomit.

"You both had your part to play, but this way, I'm free of you both," she said almost imperceptibly.

Nathan cocked his ear in order to hear her. "In what way?"

"Walker came up with the plan. I had no choice, Nathan. Walker is more powerful than me. You chose your destiny twenty-five years ago when you chose not to report him."

"I know, and I have lived with the pain ever since."

"Really, Nathan? How can you live with such intense feelings for that long? You couldn't even remember my name until today. I just don't believe you." Lily's face was red with emotions.

"Okay," he started. "I had pushed all my memories to the attic of my mind, but when he reappeared on the scene all those emotions came tumbling back." He glared at Walker as his fear had been taken over by anger. He clenched his fists and pulled back his shoulders.

"Don't even think about it," said Walker in his booming voice. "I have a plan, so don't worry, you will get to fight me, but only when I say so. For now, you must do as I say."

Walker moved towards Lily and pulled her up by her arm. He then shoved her into Nathan's unsuspecting arms.

"Please forgive me," he whispered as he looked down at her ragdoll-like body floating in his arms. She gazed into his eyes and remained mute.

"Now, Nathan, I want you to attempt to assault her. I catch you in the act, we fight and, unfortunately, you lose." He towered above the pair as he spoke, a wide grin on his face. He directed his next command to Lily.

"Now don't forget to scratch his face, we need his DNA under your fingernails."

"I won't do it. No one will believe me capable of such an atrocity," said Nathan, shaking his head.

"Who will vouch for you, your string of one night stands and your only friend, the other doctor? Fat lot of good they'll be."

Nathan's head was spinning so fast that he couldn't think rationally. His lifestyle had handed Walker his foul scenario on a plate. His Lothario status would now come into play.

"What are you two waiting for? You look like children with bloody stage fright. Just get on with it," he barked.

Nathan had no idea how to begin, and the thought of hurting the trembling woman there before him was too painful to consider.

"Scratch him, you bitch," bellowed Walker, as he swiped her around the back of her head, making her teeth clatter together with the force. Terrified of further retribution, she reached up and dug her nails into Nathan's right cheek. Her nails stung him, and his natural reflex was to grab her wrist to prevent her nails from travelling further across his face. Following his action, he swiftly released her wrist, horrified at what he'd just done.

They stared at one another, communicating a mixture of fear and anger through their eyes. Lily's loathing of Nathan suddenly took her over as she began beating him on the chest and arms with her bony fists.

"Why did you abandon me?" she cried out. "You could have saved me."

"I'm trying to do that now if you'll let me."

"It's far too late now."

She began swinging her arms around, and her face was contorted with pain and grief.

"I hate you, I hate you," she screamed as her twig-like arms ineffectually pulled and prodded his body. He didn't want to stop her, as he knew she had every right to attack him. But it wasn't enough for Walker.

"Rip her clothes," Walker said, anger leaching out of every pore.

Nathan still could not obey his commands, which Walker could sense, so he stepped forward and ripped the top half of her dress, catching Nathan on the chin with his boulder-like fist at the same time.

In the mêlée, Lily was thrown to the floor, from where she began crawling towards the back of the sofa.

"Stay in here, bitch," said Walker as he continued inflicting wounds on the helpless Nathan.

Lily was inching closer to her handbag as Nathan fell back onto the sofa following a blow from one of Walker's fists. Blood from his mouth and nose sprayed spatter marks across the floor and up the walls. The weight of Nathan's body pushed the sofa back, trapping her handbag underneath in the process. She grappled with it but couldn't manage to free it.

As she remained on the floor, she tried to block out the bone-crunching sounds and muffled wails coming from Nathan. However, they were so intense and continual that she couldn't help but hear his suffering and she was gaining no pleasure from it.

Walker's plan to throw Nathan against the wall seemed to have gone astray, she thought. Angry that she'd chosen such an obtuse place to hide the revolver, she began her own battle of freeing the handbag.

Walker's blows kept raining down on Nathan's weakening body, until he finally rolled off the sofa and hit the floor with a thud. His action allowed Lily access to her bag, and so with the revolver in her hand, she stood up and screamed for Walker to stop.

He didn't appear to hear as he booted Nathan in the chest and head, so she screamed again and brandished the revolver at him. Walker suddenly saw her and stopped still, with a fist in mid-air.

Nathan was still curled up on the floor with both eyes screwed tightly shut, so he was not aware of the new situation in the room. All he knew was that his body was throbbing but the punches had stopped.

Walker suddenly roared with laughter, head thrown back and

shoulders shaking. Nathan opened his eyes to see what the hysterics was all about. His ears were ringing, so he couldn't hear properly, although he could hear Walker's guffaw.

He strained to lift his head and managed to get Lily in his sights.

"Damn it, Lily, what are you doing?" he slurred as blood dribbled from his mouth.

"I was going to let him kill you first, and then I'd kill him, only I can stand your suffering. I thought it would be over quickly, but he just can't help himself." She held the revolver steady with both hands, keeping it aimed at Walker.

"So now I have to move on to killing him," she said as she thrust the barrel of the gun in Walker's direction.

"Don't be so bloody pathetic, woman," said Walker as he took a couple of paces towards her. "You haven't got the nerve." He stepped closer, making Lily take steps backwards until her back was up against the wall.

"Don't come any closer," she said with a faltering voice.

But Walker didn't listen, and continued moving forward with his arm extended to take the revolver from her.

"Don't," she called out.

He was almost touching the revolver as she aimed and fired a single shot. Walker clutched his thigh as he crashed to the floor.

"You stupid bitch," he shouted as he tried dragging himself across the floor towards her.

With the revolver still pointing towards him, she sidled along the wall, humming tunelessly as she moved. He grabbed the arm of the sofa and hauled himself up, staggering towards her as fast as his wounded leg would allow.

Lily began to make squealing noises as his giant frame lumbered towards her, the blood patch on his trouser leg steadily spreading.

Suddenly, Nathan sat up and tried to grab Walker's leg, but Walker kicked out with his uninjured leg, catching Nathan on the jaw. Undeterred, Nathan hooked his hand around Walker's ankle and tugged on it with all his strength, unbalancing him and causing him to fall like a giant oak tree.

Even though both men were injured, Walker remained the stronger and managed to stand again in order to continue attacking a weakened opponent.

Lily mustered up every ounce of strength within her miniscule frame and yelled for Walker to stop. Nathan looked dead to her through her misty eyes.

When it was clear that Walker had no self-restraint, she aimed at him and squeezed the trigger, with her eyes squinting involuntarily.

Walker hit the floor with a dull sound, and landed in a colossal heap onto Nathan's lifeless body. The scene was more bloody and violent than she'd anticipated and she realised at that moment that she wanted Nathan to live.

She inched towards the heap of bodies and gingerly prodded Walker with her foot. He remained motionless. Feeling slightly more confident, she bent down, and with her frail arms she tried to push Walker off Nathan. It took several attempts and eventually she managed to roll him off. He landed with his back on the floor, head lolling from side to side, and a pool of blood collecting underneath his lifeless mass. His glassy eyes stared upwards.

Nathan's eyes were closed but she could see a slight movement in his chest underneath his polo shirt.

"Thank God you're alive," she murmured softly to him as she stroked his red and swollen brow. Taking a cushion from the chair, she gently placed it under his head.

"I'm so sorry, Nathan," she whispered in his ear, hoping that he could hear her.

She stood up and took one last look at the scene before moving to the sofa, where she perched herself on the edge of the seat.

Fat tears rolled down her cheeks as she slowly raised the revolver to her head, pushing it into her temple. She sobbed aloud with shuddering breaths.

At her distressing sounds, Nathan pried his eyes open and saw her sitting in her suicidal position, with every intent to carry it out.

"Lily, no," he called in a cracked voice.

"I've no choice," she said, tears still streaming down her face.

"It's over, Lily, you can start living now."

He heaved himself along the floor, feeling like his leg was broken and ribs were cracked.

Lily sat immobile with the revolver still in position, and the last thing she felt was Nathan's hand on her leg before she pulled the trigger.

Chapter Forty-One
Six months later

"Welcome back," said Hugh, greeting Lily as she stepped through the clinic door.

"Yes, welcome back, indeed," echoed Nathan.

Lily smiled and appreciated the gesture of the vase of fresh flowers on the reception desk and the small fibre-optic Christmas tree in the window.

Everything looked the same, and yet different. A new receptionist, Connie, had been hired to perform the front line duties, so that Lily could concentrate on managing the clinic without dealing with the general public on a daily basis. Her working hours had been reduced until she regained her strength.

She had not wanted to return to the job since the newspapers published the story of Walker, his past and what happened to his victims, one being herself. However, Hugh and Nathan wanted her to stay, so they changed her job description to suit her needs. Connie was new to the area and was seemingly disinterested in local gossip.

Muriel and Rachel had disappeared from the area once the details emerged about Walker, and the family connection tarnished them both.

During her stay in the psychiatric unit, Lily received treatment for her depression, self-harming, and anorexia. She had begun to come to terms with the fact that she would never be free of those conditions, but she had learnt to manage the symptoms, and to deal with the emotional trauma of her past and more recent events.

Nathan looked physically healed, although his torso still bore scars of the inflicted wounds. He had recovered well psychologically after intervention. He felt redeemed by his action of finally saving Lily from Walker. Which ultimately saved him.

The camcorder recording had helped the police and the court to see the events as they happened, and the General Medical Council reprimanded Nathan for his lack of action as a junior doctor, but found him otherwise competent to continue working as a doctor. Nathan was surprised by the overwhelming support of his patients, and he found himself humbled by the experience.

During his period of convalescence, he re-evaluated his attitude to life and decided to make some significant changes, mainly around drinking and sleeping with an excessive amount of women. He had abstained from indulging in one night stands for six months.

Hugh sat in his room deliberating over the events of the past few months. Little had changed with his personal life. Faith had remained as distant as ever, and with her fluctuating moods and sparse communication, he felt a very lonely man. Having resigned himself to an unsatisfactory and solitary existence, he had spent much of his spare time visiting Nathan and Lily in their respective hospitals, in order to feel a connection with people who cared about him.

Due to the inclement weather, Lily, Hugh, and Nathan ended up eating their lunch in the kitchen, whilst Connie had gone Christmas shopping in the town.

Connie was rather fanatical about Christmas, and so the kitchen was festooned with paper chains suspended from the ceiling and another miniature silver tree was perched precariously on the windowsill.

"It's a bit bloody gaudy for me, all of this," moaned Nathan as he waved his arm around the kitchen. Hugh was too busy gazing into the middle distance to respond, and Lily muttered something about him being a Scrooge, which he chose to ignore.

Nathan pressed his lips together to stop himself from passing a snide comment to Hugh, instead choosing to acknowledge that he looked far from happy, let alone festive.

"Do you want to nip to The Crown after work?" he suggested, thinking he might get more out of Hugh away from work.

"I'll think about it," he replied, after finishing his mug of soup and opening a packet of black pepper crisps.

Lily knew that the pair were surreptitiously watching her calorie intake, so she flattened a sandwich between her fingers and nibbled on it for over half an hour, all the while thinking to herself that she would have to go jogging that evening to ease her mental discomfort.

Hugh was not oblivious to Lily's struggle. He believed that he needed to keep a watchful eye over her, as her frail persona would need much time to heal now that she had returned to the real world.

The ordeal of lunch was over for Lily, so she happily retreated to the solitude of her office, away from the commiserate eyes.

After another hour at work, it was time for her to go home. She said a quiet goodbye to Connie and then slipped out of the building into the already darkening day.

She walked at a pace with her head hung low, expecting people to avoid her rather than the other way around. Arriving at her gate, she could feel tightness in her chest and throat, a phenomenon that occurred each time she approached the front door. She forced herself to put the key in the lock and enter the house.

Once inside, her heart pounded in her ears, and to avoid a full blown panic attack she repeated the mantra the psychiatrist had given her.

"The only way forward is not to look back," she said aloud.

After repeating the phrase several times, her heartbeat slowed and her breathing became regular. She walked slowly towards the kitchen, pausing outside the lounge door that closed her off from the room that filled her with dread. She continued to the kitchen and made herself a cup of tea, a habit acquired from her recent stay in hospital.

She could hear the thudding base notes coming from next door, the new neighbours were so much noisier than the elderly lady who lived there previously. Unfortunately, the neighbour had moved away because she couldn't cope with living next door to the "house of death" as it had been dubbed in the local newspaper.

Lily arose and guided herself towards the lounge. In her head she saw the grotesque image of the room daubed in blood spatters and corpses, but the reality was very different.

Whilst she was in hospital, Nathan had paid to have the room cleared, cleaned, redecorated, and completely refurbished. The cleansing process expunged some of his dirty guilt that clung to his soul.

The new style was in keeping with the rest of the house, only the furnishings were of a better quality than she could ever afford.

Nathan and Hugh strolled along the pavement in reflective moods towards The Crown. Hugh had phoned Faith to let her know, only she wasn't at home so he sent her a text. He knew she wouldn't care.

"I think my marriage is over," he said as Nathan brought the drinks to the table.

"God, I'm sorry to hear that. I'm also sorry I've been a bit preoccupied these past few months, I haven't been there for you."

"Don't blame yourself; court was an ordeal for all of us. But don't pretend that you care about my relationship with Faith."

Nathan nodded at the reference to the court, visualising Lily's diminished frame as she sat in the witness stand, barely able to give evidence. He squeezed his eyes shut before turning his attention to his friend.

"I may not be a friend of your wife, but I do care what happens to you. Is there someone else involved?" he asked.

"I've given up looking. If there is, she's totally dedicated to him." He sighed as he picked up his pint to take a few gulps.

The Christmas tree in the corner of the room twinkled with fairy lights and gold baubles, and the log fire roared with flames which licked the stone chimney breast. Small clusters of office colleagues gathered around tables, and all of their festive joy seemed to heighten Hugh's sense of loss and bewilderment.

"She's not even told me what she wants for her Christmas," Hugh said quietly.

Nathan listened as his friend gave an account of the changes in Faith, talking as though he was still at work. And it was that frame of mind that triggered a thought in Nathan's head.

"It sounds to me like she's depressed, and self-medicating with alcohol," he said, nonchalantly, before tossing a handful of nuts into his mouth.

Hugh looked dazed, his eyes fixed on the hypnotic, dancing flames.

"I hadn't seen it like that," he said slowly.

"Well, no, we can often miss things that are too close to home, so to speak."

Hugh gave a wry smile, acknowledging that perhaps his home-life was in more trouble than he had foreseen.

"Do you think it's a good idea to broach the subject with her?"

Nathan raised his eyebrows, wrinkling his forehead.

"I'm not sure I'm the right person to ask. I am here for you as a sounding board, but any action you carry out is under your own free will."

"Were you there when Faith needed you?"

Nathan spat back some of his beer into the glass. "I'm sorry, what's that supposed to mean?"

"When you shared our house and I was away at work for long hours, did . . . did something happen between you and Faith?"

"Good God, no. I mean, in the early days she used to flirt with me but she wasn't my type. As soon as you two got serious, she behaved impeccably."

Hugh slumped back in the chair and let out a long breath. "So you've never slept together?"

"Absolutely not. Whatever gave you that idea?"

"She seems to dislike you immensely and I just thought . . ."

"You just thought that as I'm a whore, I'd have taken advantage of her and that now she's living with a massive guilt complex." Nathan leant forward across the table before continuing. "The women I slept with were always consensual and aware of the transient nature of the exploit. I may be shallow, but I don't abuse my influence over women, especially when they are the wife of a friend."

Nathan finished his pint and waved his empty glass at Hugh. "Your round."

Hugh shuffled up to the bar, a figure of dejection and shame, to be served by a woman wearing tinsel in her hair.

"Do you think she dislikes you because you rejected her? Perhaps I was second best for her?" he said as he returned to the table.

Nathan found his friend's words ludicrous but omitted from saying so, choosing instead to bolster his self-esteem with self-affirming phrases.

"You are definitely the best man for her. She made the right decision."

"I wish I could believe you," replied Hugh. "But I just have to accept that Faith is going to leave me and I'll end up some lonely old bachelor whom everyone pities behind my back." He downed his drink and rose to leave. "I'm sorry, but I need to be alone. I'll see you tomorrow," and with that, he put on his thick tweed coat, wound his scarf around his neck, and left under a cloud of gloom.

A bitter wind blew, and there was dampness in the air. Nathan turned his collar up and headed home with his mind drifting aimlessly as he gazed at the pavement.

Hugh had a slow drive home, peering through the intermittent windscreen wipers as they scraped away the continual drizzle. He occasionally passed another car driving in the opposite direction, and the headlights illuminated the water droplets pebbled on the glass.

A wave of relief gushed over him as he pulled up onto his gravel drive, only to be replaced with despair as he noticed that Faith's car wasn't there. After switching off the engine, he checked his mobile for messages, but he was disappointed.

The house was dark, no welcoming lights left on for him. No appetizing smells deriving from the kitchen, and the wood-burning stove in the lounge was lifeless. The Aga was warm to the touch but as he had no appetite, he poured himself a cognac and sat down at the table with his back to the warmth. He picked up a novel he'd left there that morning and began to read.

Time passed whilst he was engrossed in the book. He kept glancing at the over-sized clock on the wall, and by ten thirty he was feeling very worried. He called her on her mobile only to reach her voice mail. He wondered about informing the police. Fretful and perplexed, he poured another cognac and stared at his mobile, willing it to ring.

Chapter Forty-Two

The drizzle had stopped but the air still had a seasonal nip to it. Even so, Lily was still determined to go for a jog. Regardless of the darkness and lateness, she knew that the physical exertion would help to abolish the repugnant images that germinated in her mind.

As she dressed in layers, she thought about Hugh's sorrow. She hadn't seen Faith for months, and although she'd hoped that Faith would visit her in hospital, it was always just Hugh who came alone.

She thought Faith was blind to her providence at having such a gentle and caring man for a husband, but she was well aware that appearances could deceive. Perhaps he wasn't so thoughtful at home?

She left lights on in every room so she wasn't greeted by shadows on her return.

As she stepped outside, the coldness of the air made the skin on her face feel taut. Nevertheless, after several minutes she became acclimatized and got into a comfortable running rhythm.

Her mind soared with endorphins, but she could not prevent thoughts of Muriel and Rachel from entering her mind. Their disappearance had been a relief, although sometimes she wondered whether they would return to seek vengeance for Walker.

Her feet stomped along the route which took her near Nathan's house. She sometimes wished that Walker had allowed his plan to take place there so she wasn't left with the aftermath in her own place.

When she arrived at his street, she noticed fog swirling under the yellow street light. Only the fog had a distinctive smell of burning, the unpleasant kind and not that of a log fire or barbeque.

On impulse she jogged towards his house, and in the distance she could see a glowing hue, with flames climbing out through the windows casting hot cinders to land on the roof.

Her legs pelted her up the street with an automatic response. As she got closer to the blaze, she could see it was actually Nathan's house that was burning.

She couldn't bang on his front door as she could see smoke seeping through the cracks, so she ran to a neighbour to raise the alarm by screaming and thumping on their door.

Everything happened so fast, the sirens, the blue lights, the shouts, the firemen attacking the door with axes and running hoses into the house.

Lily refused to move too far away from the area as she wanted to check that Nathan was okay. As she watched the scenario unfold in slow motion, she saw a fireman carry out a limp body and go directly to the awaiting ambulance. The blue flashing lights could be seen all the way down the street, reflecting off windows and the underside of the remaining leaves clinging to the branches.

She walked up to one of the policemen and asked if Nathan was okay. All he could tell her was that he was alive.

The smoke had permeated her eyes, so she wasn't sure whether she was spilling tears because of that or whether they were for Nathan.

She raced back home, her mind swirling with fear, apprehension, and sheer desolate sentiments for Nathan. She wasn't sure how she'd feel if he didn't pull through.

Without hesitating, she entered her house, found Hugh's home number and dialled. He answered quicker than she anticipated.

"Faith," he said urgently.

"No, sorry, it's Lily. There's been a fire. They've taken Nathan to the hospital. He's alive, but I don't know how bad his condition is." She shot the phrases out like bullets to prevent him hearing the tremor in her voice.

"I'm coming over, we'll go together." His concern for his wife was suddenly pushed to the recess of his mind.

Lily put the receiver down and found the silence deafening. Panic rose in her throat and she had little strength in her to keep herself calm.

The next twenty minutes dragged, but she hadn't the inclination to do anything to fill the time. When the doorbell rang she realised she was still in the smoke-infested jogging clothes, but it was too late. She opened the door to find that Hugh was still in his work suit. No greetings were said, instead they piled into his car and set off for the hospital.

Hugh's status aided him in obtaining news quickly and he hurried back to the waiting room to inform a dishevelled looking Lily of Nathan's condition.

"He's stable, Lily. He's suffering with minor burns and smoke inhalation."

The relief in Hugh's voice and face broke her resolve and she promptly burst into tears. Without worrying, he put his arm around her shaking body and held her closely into him. He rested his head on top of hers. He really thought Nathan's nightmare was over.

"Do we know how the fire started?" he asked in a low voice.

"No, but I fear Walker's sister may be involved."

He pulled away from her and looked at her tear streaked face.

"We have to tell the police."

She nodded, wishing he'd hold her again, but that moment had gone. She felt a surge of fear about returning to her own house, and as though he read her mind, he insisted that she stay with him and Faith that night. He said Faith wouldn't mind, but Lily wasn't convinced about that.

After collecting an overnight bag, Hugh drove her to his home. As he pulled up onto the drive, his mind was eased by the sight of Faith's car sitting on the drive. Lights were glowing in the house and his shoulders relaxed for the first time that evening.

On entering the house, Hugh called to his wife who came rushing out of the kitchen.

"Where have you been? I've been so . . ." she stopped at the sight of Lily standing there. "What's going on?"

"Long story, Nathan's going to be okay, but his house is a burnt-out shell. It was lucky that Lily saw the blaze and called for help, he could have died." A lump came to his throat as he said those last words.

"Oh my God, you poor things. Come, let me get you a drink of something," she said as she ushered them into the kitchen.

"I said that Lily could stay here for the night, she's a bit shook up."

"Of course," replied Faith with compassion fatigue already settling into her voice that didn't go undetected by Hugh. He hoped Lily had failed to notice the fact.

Faith acted the part, though, by picking up Lily's bag and taking her to the spare room. Hugh watched Lily drag her feet as she followed Faith up the stairs, then he slumped into a chair feeling the weight of weariness upon his shoulders.

He waited for Faith to return so he could ask her where she was that evening. He heard the door to the spare room shut and then the door to the main bedroom. He waited some more, but she didn't return and she hadn't said goodnight.

In the morning, Hugh and Lily sat at the breakfast table, quietly sipping coffee and nibbling on toast. As usual, Hugh hadn't woken Faith as he left the room and neither he nor Lily talked about the previous evening.

As they left the house, Hugh hesitated at the bottom of the stairs, but he didn't blow her a kiss.

Lily enjoyed watching the countryside flow past, as well as discreetly looking at the reflection of Hugh in the window. She thought he had a magnificent profile, with a gently dipping Roman nose and soft flaring nostrils.

She also caught sight of her gaunt face in the reflection, and it displeased her. There wasn't any part of her face that displayed a quality she liked. She'd returned to wearing her green contact lenses as she couldn't abide the dullness of her grey eyes.

Although she didn't relish staying in her own house, she knew instinctively that Faith wouldn't cope with her staying there another night. There was also the matter of escaping Faith's over-exaggerated fussing, which Lily found difficult to marry amidst the air of intrusion she felt.

As Hugh drove along, he sensed a wall surrounding him whenever he tried to connect with Faith. For the rest of the week, he decided to go easy with her, and by that he meant that he wouldn't demand any attention or time from her, and he wouldn't quiz her when she stayed out for longer than he expected.

He had noticed how her moods had become more erratic and he was increasingly concerned for her mental state, always hearing Nathan's prophetic words ringing in his ears.

A week later, Hugh received a call at work from the hospital saying that Nathan was ready to be discharged, and would he be able to collect him.

"Of course. He's staying with me to recuperate."

Hugh arrived at the hospital to find a frail looking Nathan waiting on a plastic chair on the ward. His face and hands were covered in red, shiny patches, and his hair and eyebrows were singed, making the ends look dry and frizzy. He looked like an empty shell and only managed a half smile when his friend walked up to him.

"Are you sure Faith doesn't mind?" he asked in a husky voice.

"It doesn't matter if she does, you need looking after and that's what friends are for."

Nathan stood up slowly as his stiff, swollen joints and tightly stretched skin pained him. Hugh took his bag and then offered Nathan an arm to lean on.

"Any news from the police?" asked Hugh as they hobbled to the car.

"Nothing yet. They're still looking for Muriel as it was definitely arson."

Hugh nodded knowingly as he watched his dear friend through his peripheral vision, seemingly clinging on with what little strength he had left in his arm.

"Do you think it's over now? My punishment, that is," he asked in a hushed tone.

"I do hope so. You've been punished more than enough."

It was Nathan's turn to nod gingerly, every movement of his body causing him excruciating agony.

Hugh eased him into the car and then drove home at a gentle pace, aware that every bump in the road triggered an influx of pain.

Faith wasn't at home when they arrived, although Hugh was too preoccupied to care. He couldn't remember the last time she cared for him.

He guided Nathan to the spare room and tenderly tucked him into the bed without making him wince too much. The sumptuous white pillows supported his aching form.

"I'll keep popping in to check on you, but for now I'll let you sleep. Don't worry about anything, I'm only downstairs."

He walked into the kitchen and put the kettle on the Aga. He could detect a faint musty and grimy smell in the air, prompting him to check the bin, but all it contained was an empty can of air freshener. He then checked the fridge before he gave up looking.

He heard a car crunch up the gravel drive as he sat nursing a cup of tea. He prayed it was his wife. Hearing the key in the door confirmed it was, so he braced himself for whatever mood she would bring with her. Her high heels clipped along the parquet floor, she paused for a moment and then she entered the room.

"Is Nathan here then?" she enquired as she removed her coat.

"He's in the spare room. He's quite weak and shaken up by everything. He needs us, Faith." He hoped she wasn't going to complain.

"I'll take him up a drink and see how he is," she said as she poured some tea from the pot.

Hugh watched her flit around the kitchen and then disappear upstairs. He sat for a few minutes chastising himself for harbouring selfish thoughts. But he couldn't help it. He wondered whether she was up there fussing over Nathan like she used to do for him in the early days.

His imagination conjured up seedy images that seemed so real that he decided to creep upstairs to check on them.

With his heart pounding in his neck, he moved deftly up the stairs, being careful to avoid the creaking steps. He sidled up to the bedroom door that was slightly ajar.

He could hear muffled sounds and he imagined their faces thrust together and roaming hands, so with a deep breath he quietly pushed the door further open and peered around the corner.

He saw Faith hunched over Nathan and a jealous rage imploded inside his chest. They hadn't heard him so he moved closer. It was only then that he saw her holding a pillow firmly across Nathan's face.

"Bloody hell, what are you doing?" he cried out.

Faith turned around, red faced with her eyes screaming fury. Hugh dashed over and pushed her away from the bed. She knocked into the bedside table, tipping over the cup of tea onto the carpet and shrieking out as she slid to the floor.

Hugh removed the pillow, dreading what he was going to find. Nathan looked faintly blue around the mouth, but he was still managing to gasp for breath.

Suddenly, Faith was on her feet pounding Hugh ferociously on the back with her fists.

"You bastard. Why do you all keep saving him? He shouldn't be allowed to live." She was screaming uncontrollably in a high-pitched voice.

"What the hell are you on about, woman?" said Hugh as he turned around and grabbed hold of her wrists. He found her to be freakishly strong as they thrashed about next to Nathan's bed. When he finally managed to pacify her, he stared directly into her eyes, imploring her to explain herself.

She pulled away from him with an air of disgust and betrayal.

"He should have died in the fire but that stupid bitch Maria saved him."

Hugh felt as though he'd been punched in the stomach. He dropped onto the edge of the bed. "You . . ." he started. "You set fire to his house?"

"Yes I did, and I did it for Ian."

"Who the bloody hell is Ian?"

"He's my brother," she replied, suddenly going weak at the knees and slumping to the floor.

"Brother? I didn't know you had a brother."

"Ian was on the ward when Maria, your precious Lily, was. I recognised her but said nothing as I would have had to explain myself." She paused to rub her sore wrists. "Ian was physically abused and humiliated by Walker, and he's never been the same since. I tried to complain but they wouldn't listen, they thought that a paranoid schizophrenic was making it all up."

She glanced across at Nathan with venom in her eyes.

"I wanted to take the complaint further, but Ian was close to killing himself, so I had to concentrate on him instead."

Her hair had been shaken from its bun, which she was now trying to pin back into place.

"Ian has been basically homeless on and off over the years. Occasionally he lives in a hostel, but he can't cope with being inside for long as he feels trapped."

"Is that who you've been spending so much time with?"

"Yes."

"Why couldn't you tell me?"

"I didn't want the whole story to come out, but I suppose it will have to now, won't it?"

Hugh nodded and gazed blankly at the woman who was masquerading as his wife.

"Ian and I wanted vengeance, so he broke into the clinic and Nathan's house to graffiti on the walls, it made him feel better. But it wasn't enough to satisfy his internal rage. It was driving him mad and it hurt me to witness his torment."

Hugh turned towards Nathan to see that he too was now listening to Faith. His eyes were wide, darting from Hugh to Faith and back again. A dry crust of spit formed around his mouth.

"So the foul smell was your brother I smelt in our house and the clinic?" he asked quietly.

"Yes. I thought Ian would be better once Walker was dead, but he wasn't as the past was still alive as long as Nathan was. So I had to finish what we'd started."

"But I still don't understand why you couldn't tell me, were you ashamed of your brother?"

"No, I was hiding the truth about other things, but you might as well know them now."

Hugh checked to see that Nathan was still awake. He was, and he was totally captivated by what Faith was saying.

"I tried to get close to Nathan when he was working on Poplar, but I clearly wasn't his type. I even went to the same pubs as you two, but I never got anywhere. And so I decided to get close to you instead."

Hugh's face became pallid as what he was hearing was sinking in.

"You were my link with Nathan, and as I knew that one day I would exact my revenge on him, I had to ensure that you and I became a solid item."

Hugh brushed his fringe back off his forehead and left his hand there for comfort.

"I have never loved you. Making love was a disgusting chore. It wasn't that I couldn't get pregnant, I was on the pill so I wouldn't. I didn't want a child with you."

Hugh was reeling from the torrent of ugly information and the harsh words that battered his heart.

"But I love you, and I still do even after all you've just said." He spoke softly.

"More fool you, as it's not reciprocated. I will never love you, so get used to it."

Hugh felt the delicate touch of Nathan's hand on his arm. He turned to see his friend utter quietly.

"Do the right thing."

Chapter Forty-Three

The spring bulbs were flowering in clumps dotted around the garden, and the days were beginning to stretch out, adding hope to the air.

Hugh pottered around the kitchen making breakfast. The huge vase of daffodils positioned on the windowsill brought a subtle smile to his face.

He placed a mug of coffee and a croissant on a tray and then headed upstairs. He knocked on the spare room door. Lily was stirring and looked semi delighted and semi shocked to find him standing there.

"Hope you don't mind, but I thought you'd like breakfast in bed."

She smiled and sat up, then smoothed down her hair. "That's very kind of you."

She sipped her black coffee and nibbled on the croissant, mindful that he was watching her.

"The house sale goes through today, right?" he asked.

"That's right, I'm officially homeless from today," she replied, licking some melted butter from the corner of her mouth.

"You're welcome to stay here for as long as it takes for you to find a new place." His face reddened as he ran his hand through his hair.

"That's very generous of you, only I don't want to abuse your kindness. I'm not sure what I want to do yet."

"Oh?" Hugh tilted his head and waited for her to say more.

"I'm not sure that Nathan hasn't got the right idea, getting away from here as far as possible. Too many bad memories," she whispered, as she put most of the squashed croissant back onto the plate. She played with the crumbs with her middle finger, pushing them around the rim.

"The Red Cross is a little ambitious for you, if you don't mind my saying, although perfect for Nathan. I suppose I had hoped that you'd stay around here."

"No good would come of that."

"They've all gone, Lily, all the people who've hurt you. You love this town and you're an excellent manager. I've already lost a good friend out of all of this. I'd hate to lose you, too."

Lily blushed at hearing his words. She wanted to reach out to him but she was scared of the unknown.

"A big part of me will miss you, too," she said, daring to overcome her anxiety. She then summoned the courage to reach out to touch him on the arm. "But you have enough to deal with without having someone like me around. You don't want someone with my background."

"Having a mental illness doesn't make you unlovable or less human," he said picking up his coffee mug to disguise his embarrassment. "Anyway, Faith has filed for divorce from the prison hospital. She wants it done as soon as possible. I'm a free man, Lily."

"Perhaps you should spend some time alone to figure out what it is you want from life." Her voice held a gentleness that touched him.

Hugh looked down at his feet, noticing his well-worn slippers.

"I see what you are saying," he replied quietly.

He looked dejected, and Lily hated hurting him. She wanted to stay but felt that he deserved someone better, although she thought that no one would love him as much as she could.

The town was buzzing with people buying last-minute gifts, turning their collars up to the bitter wind that whistled around their necks.

The Christmas tree in the town square swayed in the breeze, and the star on the top looked precariously balanced.

It was Christmas Eve, and Hugh was in good cheer as he drove home from the clinic. He pulled up onto the gravel drive that was surrounded by strings of lights shimmering in the dark. A large, opulently decorated Christmas tree was illuminated in the bay window.

On entering the house, he was greeted by the smell of mulled wine and baking mince pies.

"I'm home," he called out.

Lily appeared from the kitchen wearing a floral apron and her hair tied back in a loose chignon. A fine dusting of flour lay on her face and hands.

"Hello," she said as she walked into the hallway. "Happy Christmas," she added, blushing softly. She'd made a big effort for the festive season as she felt he deserved it after all that had happened over the past year. She knew his buoyant mood wasn't going to last as she had news for him that he wasn't going to like.

Hugh followed her into the kitchen where she poured them both a glass of warm mulled wine. The steam rose from it like the mist that rises from a lake in the early hours of the morning. Lily thought for a few seconds and then she took a deep breath.

"Hugh, I have something I need to tell you."

He looked at her with the expectant eyes of a puppy.

"We always knew that this situation wasn't permanent and that one day I'd move on." She paused to take a sip of wine, avoiding looking directly at him so as not to see any flickering of pain registering on his face.

"I had hoped that things had moved on since then. I had hoped that your feelings . . ." he coughed then continued, "that your feelings had perhaps progressed towards caring for me."

"Oh, but I do care, and that's why I'm going. I'm riddled with neurosis. I still battle with anorexia on a daily basis, not to mention my fluctuating mental health. I can't give you what you want, what you need."

Hugh reached over the table to try and take her hand, but she whipped it away and placed her hands in her lap.

"Please don't make this any more painful than it is. I'm truly sorry, but this was never meant to be. I've made my peace with my past and now I need to start somewhere new where the fingerprints of my past have never been."

Hugh nodded dolefully and resigned himself to the fact that Lily was right. He only wanted what was best for her, and sadly he'd become intertwined in her past so she needed to leave the crumbs of his life behind her.

He got to his feet and raised his glass. "To the best Christmas ever, and to your future, wherever it may take you. Be happy, dear Lily."

She smiled and raised her glass. There was no need for her to add any words to what he'd already said. The past was burnt and buried, and, at last, she could finally reach out into a world where she'd felt an alien for so long.

The End

Coming from Hemmie Martin November 2013
In the Light of Madness

Acknowledgment

To everyone at Winter Goose Publishing for their continued dedication and support.

About the Author

Hemmie Martin spent most of her professional life as a Community Nurse for people with learning disabilities, a Family Planning Nurse, and a Forensic Nurse working with young offenders. She spent six years living in the south of France, and currently lives in Essex with her husband, two teenage daughters, one house rabbit, and two guinea pigs.

CPSIA information can be obtained at www.ICGtesting.com
Printed in the USA
BVOW021549280513

321808BV00005B/17/P

9 780988 904927